THE FAITHFUL
a novel

PETER W. VAN NESS

Good Job
publishing
goodjobpublishing.com

Published in the United States by Good Job Publishing
For more information on the publisher, and for permission to reprint any material in this book, please visit GoodJobPublishing.com

ISBN: 979-8-9904870-0-0

Library of Congress Control Number: 2024907119

Printed in the United States of America

Cover Design by Vickie Van Ness

For Vickie and John

Acknowledgements

Supporting someone's dreams is harder than it seems. Perhaps that is why people who do so are rare. I have been blessed with true support for this book that began decades ago when my father, John Van Ness encouraged me to explore the link between science and spirituality.

I am particularly grateful to Dan Shickler for helping me find my voice; to Donna J. Neale, Ilona Kwiecien, and Sally Jackson for their wise counsel. And to the publishing business pro who hated my first draft and said there was no point falsely encouraging me. He inspired my deliciously defiant editing journey.

Special thanks to my son, John, who suggested I create one of my favorite supporting characters. Best of all, he fiercely critiqued the story, the writing—even the cover design—rather than tell me what I wanted to hear.

My deepest gratitude goes to my wife, Vickie. This book would not exist without her inspiration, patience, honest critique, and eagerness to do whatever was necessary to get this book published—including designing the cover. Most importantly, she refused to allow my doubt to thwart my writing career.

Contents

THE FAITHFUL

Chapter One
Part 1: Promises

JOHN WELLS IS DESPERATE TO TASTE REAL LIFE. Dinner had backfired. He's still trapped in the game. Recoil sucks him back in time to a tender young age.

The heroic worlds little Johnny cast were no match for grown-ups armed with the words of dread you hear ahead of an execution, "It's time." Time to stop. Time to go. Time for bed.

"It's a party," protested little Johnny. "It's summer. Why do I have to go to bed while the sun is still up and the whole world is at play?"

"It's already past your bedtime." Mom's tone betrayed her irritation. She told Dad, "Sis says you can put him to bed in her upstairs guest room."

Little Johnny lay in silence, eyes open, in the strange bed.

How many lifetimes will fly by after dark? Unseen fireflies in the night. Where does their light go? What if I could catch it?

He directed his mythical world to carry on within the wallpaper's geometric patterns while he spun a cocoon of defiance. Inside his cocoon, a magical force would keep him awake until Mom told Dad, "It's time." Fireflies beware.

Bright lights squeezed his tiny eyes shut tighter. Baby hands clung to Dad's shoulders as they swished through stale cigarette fumes lingering with beer and charcoal. Spinning his cocoon had carried little Johnny to another dimension, leaving his body in a peaceful sleep, undisturbed by Dad's gentle lift and stealth walk until the porch spotlight thrust them to center stage. With coos and grins and strokes, adoring fans tried to coax a smile, a giggle—or best of all—a "bye-bye." He winced from reentry into his body, wriggled into a curl, buried his face in the soft blanket atop Dad's shoulder, and promised himself,

When I behave as they command,
They'll never know it's just pretend.

Pretending grew into the ultimate cheat. He knew he wasn't talking to God when he prayed. He ditched his body while it slept. And he wasn't a good boy just because he behaved like one.

Genius arrived a few years later revealing a discovery of epic proportions. Piano lessons, church choir, and extracurricular studies left no time for adults to fill with their silly plans for him. This modicum of control made the wait tolerable. The wait for adulthood—and independence.

But when does adulthood arrive? Not at 18. The new millennium delivered John's 18th birthday, unceremoniously, on a Tuesday—no different from any other Tuesday. Classes in the morning. Labs in the afternoon. Studying at night. Enjoying the day was not an option. Maintaining his reputation as MIT's youngest and brightest student was paramount. Nobody would catch him lost in childish fun.

His 21st birthday came and went in a similar fashion, with one notable exception. Emily insisted on dressing up and taking him out to celebrate with a luxurious dinner and his first legal bottle of wine. Her bouncer friends whisked them past long lines into trendy clubs all night long. She wrapped her arms around his neck, leaned in, closed her eyes, swayed her body with the beat, and bathed him in ecstasy.

Emily's night was his first and last furlough from the endless schoolwork, testing, and fealty to the almighty grade that continues to remind John he is not...quite...yet...a man. Not today. Nor tomorrow, his 22nd birthday.

John is prepared for tomorrow. He has trained himself to bury his pesky emotions—especially the dejection upon waking every birthday morning expecting a revelation, only to concede that absolutely nothing about him had improved overnight.

But tonight...tonight should have launched my real-world career.

The stubborn ache in his chest is now sore to the touch. His middle finger cannot resist inflaming the spot. He squirms, crammed in a wooden folding chair between a smug, well-dressed man with bad breath whose name he keeps forgetting and Big Al—all nose, smile, and belly, with slits for eyes and a deep baritone voice. Everyone surrounding him is immersed in the masterpiece. Not John. Feverish thoughts hijack his attention.

Mom's hot raisin scones,
One-hundred-twenty-two-thousand in loans,
Entropy, destiny,
What does Dad think of me?
Ashley's hips,

Sophia's hair,
Emily's lips,
Pizza and beer,
Grandma, Christmas, Handel, Christ…
John retreats into his cocoon to brood over his uncertain future.

Until this year, John never fretted over his future. He simply saw it.

First came memory. Four-year-old Johnny stared out his bedroom window up into the night sky. He pleaded with the stars to free him from the dependence of youth, whisk him past childhood, and usher him through the portal to adulthood—right then and there. His longing for freedom, he assured them, was proof he was ready. How could he possibly crave something he wasn't prepared for?

The stars projected their own view. Past and future floated before little Johnny's eyes, a parade of memories curving with spacetime to meet at infinity in a great cosmic mélange. He recalled seeing this in Dad's giant Michelangelo book with glossy pictures of the Sistine Chapel. Visions of past and future curved up toward the ceiling, where an old man in the center reached across the universe to touch his younger self.

Then came imagination. John avoided the silly games his kindergarten classmates played at recess. The schoolyard fence was his domain, fresh air his best friend, imagination his sport. Drifting up with the birds, he beheld time through their eyes…in slow motion. A clump of sixth graders slithered through the playground—an undulating organism comprised of a dozen captive children. Ending up as one of them was out of the question. Independence would be maintained by remaining invisible, something he'd pulled off by meeting expectations while being careful never to reveal his true potential.

Finally, a vision. Daily play with imagination earned John a bargain with infinity. If the stars wouldn't deliver him from childhood, the least they could do was illuminate his path to adulthood.

On New Year's Eve, after Mom tucked him into bed, he peeped out beyond his cocoon to catch the tantalizing aroma of the coffee she was brewing.

Mom says I can't have it, so it must be powerful. The smell alone should keep me awake.

Party guests arrived downstairs. Familiar voices. More guests with unfamiliar voices. The rhythm of arrivals fell into a groove. Doorbell, latch, greeting…over and over until it all blended. Talking, laughter, dishes, glasses. Cacophony ensued.

It's now or never!

John slinked out of bed, snuck into the hallway, and switched off the light. Imagination revealed it to be a portal to infinity disguised as an ordinary ceiling fixture. Standing directly under it would transfigure the narrow hallway into a *Magic Corridor*. He closed his eyes—as one does when preparing to enter another dimension. Feet slid together; arms rose robotically. They stopped on their own forming the shape of a cross. Nothing happened. He spread his legs and waited. Nothing but heavy arms.

Ready to relieve his aching, quivering muscles, John shook his head in disgust when energy streamed down from the portal, stilled his shaking, and poured through the top of his head into his chest. Tingling swelled. Eyes opened. He peered out over his left arm into the past. Sparky, who was then an eight-week-old puppy, scampered toward him for the first time.

Before Sparky's fluffy coat could caress John's baby face, the sound of Mom's voice rose above the partygoers. John shuddered. What if she came upstairs to look in on him? Danger's taste was irresistible, like the thrill of hearing Mom's voice close by while reaching up to steal a cookie off her cooling rack. He held position and rotated his head to the right.

Visions of John's future appeared out beyond his arm, illuminated by bolts of lightning shooting out his fingertips. Each vision held the quality of a memory. Gazing down the Magic Corridor, John reminisced about events that were yet to take place. Old Sparky lumbered over to welcome him home from college. The rusty, splintered, iron gates to his schoolyard were finally repaired and painted jet black. New shoes—black sneakers, of all things—comforted his aching feet. John blinked. Something vital had changed. The vision of this huge pair appeared from on high as he sauntered along with a broad stride.

On his first day of third grade, John was greeted by freshly painted schoolyard gates. He stopped and stared, frozen in his tracks. Unseasonably cold, damp wind sent chills through his body. Or was it awe? He wrapped his fingers around cool, smooth, black spires and closed his eyes. As the iron warmed, energy flowed into his palms, up his arms, and gathered in his chest where it resonated, matching the Magic Corridor's tingle. A puzzle piece of life fell into place. This was the new, black-schoolyard-gates reality.

Persistent visions revealed subtle slices of his future life. John would not be popular like sixth-grade Brian, who swaggered through the playground with his entourage of losers. He would not be one of them either. Nor a bully like Brian's nemesis, Chip the Whip, who tormented his dweebs using the same tactics teachers use to keep their students in line. Chip had obviously been paying attention in class.

For reasons John did not yet comprehend, the approach to adulthood splits children. Some seize control and wield power. Others submit.

I will never be a bully,

nor a dweeb,

nor a flunky,

nor a plebe,

and I will always be slightly out of line,

secretly, of course.

When John made this second promise, he'd heard the word "plebe." Whatever it was, it sure sounded like something he'd never want to be. Discovering its meaning matched its tone sparked faith in his foresight and resonance in his heart...until Air Jordan IV black sneakers hit the stores. He couldn't afford those shoes.

In my vision, I was wearing black sneakers at this age. What went wrong? Is the Magic Corridor unreliable? Did I miss a sign or a turn along the way?

Faith and resonance were restored by his mother complaining about how fast he'd grown all the way to the discount shoe store with black, off-brand sneakers on sale.

Vision—faith—resonance. Vision—faith—resonance.

This rhythm continued into college until one vision demanded action. Rather than merely showing his future, it steered John toward certain professors and classes. Another prompted his continued musical training. More visions directed him to the best coffee shop, diner, pizza.

The shock hit him when he encountered a vision diametrically opposed to his own determination. Having barely survived the excruciating choice to leave Sophia—his first love—for his education and career, John had vowed never to fall in love again. Besides, it was simply unthinkable to imagine a woman of Emily's beauty, wit, and grace would ever fall in love with him. Professing her love had made him suspicious—and wary. Allowing any love he might harbor to rise up and meet hers was beyond risky. Imagine John's disbelief when a vision not only revealed Emily's ability to see through his cocoon, it urged him to invite her in, to offer her the joy he kept hidden even from himself.

Who is this woman?

Emily was dangerous. The threat of her razor eyes and keen intuition tasted familiar, akin to the thrill of his first encounter with the Magic Corridor. Lust for more, for savage risk, swelled within him until he could no longer resist.

"Yes," said John as they headed down the sidewalk.

"Yes? You do want a lick?" Emily pointed her ice cream cone at him like a talk show host with a microphone interviewing the man on the street.

"No. I want you. I'll move in with you. Even if we can't afford that place."

Emily took a giant bite of ice cream, heaved the cone to the sky, grabbed his arm, and twirled into a hug.

"Oh, John! Thank you." She planted an ice cream-laced kiss on his lips. "I love you! You'll love the place! We'll make it our place. It's worth it, I promise. Remember, I'm making good money now."

She kissed him again. Cool, sweet chocolate dissolved into warm, salty lips dipped in the Magic Corridor's tingle—a new, thrilling sensation for both Emily and John.

The cone's kerplop into the trash can startled a little boy.

"Mommy, what's wrong with her?" he asked. "Doesn't everybody love ice cream?"

"You'll understand when you're older," she replied.

There were no more visions. You'd have to admit John's childhood made a delightful fairytale, and "Emily's Love" is the perfect Happily Ever After ending.

But what about my career? My life's work? Why have you forsaken me? I can't go on without my visions. Maybe I should just die. Hmm... what are the odds?

Building a survival analysis model was a fun distraction until it disappointed him by predicting a 98% chance of making it all the way to 33.

John is about to seize control of his mind when the surrounding voices resurrect a childhood family gathering where grown-ups lazed around the fire complaining about their soul-killing jobs.

"Then why are you still doing those stupid jobs?" blurted ten-year-old Johnny.

"We have no choice," retorted a frustrated chorus. Furtive glances danced around the living room as they chuckled at their unison response to the youngster's innocent interruption. After a pregnant pause, they resumed their circle of complaints.

"But you're grown-ups. You can do anything you want!"

"Don't be silly, boy!" admonished John's uncle. He rose from his chair, grabbed the tall poker, and stabbed a smoldering log. A crackling chorus of tiny red sparks lit up the fireplace. In a rare moment of communion with adults, John accompanied their hopes as they flew up with the sparks to chase the freedom awaiting in the night sky.

John's hopes cleared the chimney before his uncle brought everyone else's down by asserting, "You'll understand when you're older. Now go see if your mother needs help setting the table for dinner."

The fire's sweet cherry scent summoned enough calm to obey his uncle and resist lashing out at the infuriating phrase, "when you're older."

Do grown-ups really understand? Or are they seduced into an easy, meaningless life by accepting what they're told?

John mocked them under his breath as he laid forks atop napkins, measuring with his thumb to ensure they were all precisely the same distance from the edge of the table. Having given up all hope of Mom noticing his silverware precision, he maintained it now as a secret act of defiance.

He seized the carving knife with the flair of a Musketeer drawing his rapier, twisted it until the shiny blade caught the candelabra's flame, and shot a beam into the living room, targeting the mantelpiece. Aiming at the circle of grown-ups, he fixed a dot on each of their heads one by one. Nobody noticed.

I will never get stuck in a job I hate. I'll survive instead as a starving musician.

John congratulates himself for keeping this promise by maintaining his perfect pitch until the specter of needing it to eke out a meager living intensifies the ache in his chest. His middle finger inflames the spot again, dredging up last Thanksgiving's memory.

John stood for a moment in his grandparents' cold, dreary driveway, staring through their warm, glowing windows. Of course, Mom and Dad had bragged to Grandma and Grandpa about his perfect 5.0 GPA. The instant he stepped foot in there, he'd be the dreaded guest of honor.

John snuck in the back door, greeted only by festive aromas and distant voices. He headed directly for the kitchen. Perhaps Grandma would let him hide out there and help with the cooking.

"Oh, Johnny!" exclaimed Grandma. Her wide smile crinkled her brilliant eyes. She wiped her hands on her apron, making her way through the steaming, bustling kitchen to greet her beloved Johnny in the hallway. "We're so proud of you!"

She kissed him tenderly on the cheek.

"Happy Thanksgiving, Grandma." John returned the kiss warmly. "Wow! It smells amazing in there! *Whatcha got cookin'?*" Grandma was a Hank Williams fan.

"Grandpa's dying to see you, Dear." Grandma's sweet voice, rascal smirk, and gentle hand on his shoulder confirmed she was not about to let him set foot in her kitchen.

Pride was oozing from the living room. John dawdled toward it. His extended family were eagerly waiting to offer congratulations—and grill him about his future.

Maybe I should have taken Grandpa's advice and studied Liberal Arts. Nobody could possibly expect any career plans from a liberal arts major.

He cleverly dodged all their questions all night long, graciously accepting their praise, pleased with himself for managing their expectations. But he was unprepared for pats on the back. Those shot dread into his sore chest, reminding him that a vision of his career was gravely overdue.

Part 2: Messiah

John is combing through tonight's vital dinner meeting in search of clues to its miserable failure when his effort is interrupted by a searing gaze. He pokes his eyes up to snag the intruder. A gasp of breath ushers in the surrounding crescendo to fill him with song for two short measures until a growl cuts off the singers.

"Eyes, eyes! Where on Earth is everybody?" Maestro Seth Zostrianos slices his baton through the tiny droplets of sweat flung by his thick, wavy hair with a single swipe of his head. John's eyes had not been with Maestro—known by his students as Dr. Z.

Now that Dr. Z has his attention, John cannot remember where his eyes have been. Burying his face in the score had smudged the notes into a blur of ink blots. His throat can detect recent singing. He scours his memory. No sounds. No words. No music. The entire rehearsal…gone. An experience lost forever.

I have not given Dr. Z the respect he deserves. John's chest tightens. *I've led a privileged life, and here I am, wallowing in misery because I can't see my career. Imagine overcoming what he endured.*

It was only due to his mother's extraordinary heroism and brutal, last-minute foresight that the young Maestro narrowly escaped being gassed with the rest of his family.

Dr. Z doesn't talk about it, but according to his closest friends, the story goes like this: When the train bound for Auschwitz pulled out of the station, skinny little Seth—only six years old—grabbed his mother, holding on for dear life. Sliding down through his arms, she landed in a squat, meeting her only child face-to-face. Her large, strong hands held his tiny head. She kissed one cheek, kissed the other, closed her eyes, and let her lips linger on his forehead. Her grip tightened, drawing his face so close her watery eyes were all he could see. Then she spoke. Unspeakable words. Horrifying, unthinkable thoughts, wrapped in familiar religious phrases uttered by a soft, stern, alien voice.

Before he could protest his mother's impossible commandments, she hoisted him over her head and, with the help of her friends, she forced his squirming little body—against all the resistance he could muster—out the narrow opening at the top of the boxcar. Her family and friends refused to let their eyes wander from his glistening blood dripping from the barbed wire onto her face.

Two summmersaults hurled the boy away from the speeding train before he crashed to a halt face down in the dirt. The high-pitched squeal of wheels on the track intensified the hideous cheering of his abandoned townspeople. Searing pain shot through both shoulders as he reached out in vain to catch the receding train. Too shocked to be frightened, he cried his final, "Mama!"

When the train had shrunk to a dot in the distant dust, he indulged his grief one last time with a long, chilling, "Noooooo…"

Seth's hopeless scream sapped his breath, and the train's fading squeal drove his voice into the void. A cold sting settled into the cuts on his face. Smearing his grimy little sleeve through his blood-soaked tears, he wiped his grief—and the only life he'd ever known—away forever before proceeding as his mother had commanded.

Run without stopping to Dr. Dimitris' house. He will hide you and keep you safe. You must live! Do not forget us, but do not waste away with grief. You have a gift. Work hard. Keep your heart steadfast and make music with your soul. Wake the dawn. Sing praises to God and remember us, my little one, through your music.

The good Dr. Dimitris, Salonika's most celebrated violin instructor, had first-hand knowledge of Seth's musical genius. He risked his life and the lives of his own children to hide his star student until he could arrange for the boy to be smuggled to England by British merchant seamen. Raised in London and educated at The Royal Academy of Music, Dr. Z learned to speak English with a perfect BBC accent.

Maestro conducts plenty of Christian sacred music, something his friends often question, prompting his refrain: *Great music is not written about breakfast cereal or soda pop.*

Members of the choir delight in gossip about Maestro's religious beliefs. Some say he is an atheist or a deist. Academic and religious leaders worry he might be a mystic. Oh…how they fear mysticism, for it threatens their power and authority. John is oblivious to the gossip. He had enrolled in Dr. Z's ear training course merely to hedge his job prospects, not expecting it to become his favorite class.

Dr. Z deserves my full attention.

John cannot look down in shame. His eyes are not yet released by Maestro's baton. Scarcely head-and-shoulders taller than his antique podium, Dr. Z's radiant presence projects a far grander appearance. Bold articulation with his gravelly voice had sent spit flying into the golden light spilling from the podium's brass gooseneck lamp. Glistening droplets dance with floating dust to form a luminous cloud.

On the next beat, with stiff shoulders and a flick of his wrist, Maestro's baton sweeps through the luminous cloud, following his sharp glance to the right. John imagines Dr. Z is a lone swordsman defending his honor against insurmountable odds. He follows the baton's shimmering trail as it cuts off the accompanist mid-measure.

The choir's baby grand piano adores James Douglass. Only he can coax it into filling the rehearsal room with the force of an entire orchestra. Little is known about the enigmatic Jimmy D (as he is affectionately known by the choir) except for his devotion to Maestro.

Jimmy D has been staring at John. Their eyes meet. Like a trickster, Jimmy D's face hides behind his bushy white hair and beard. His deep, sage-like, indigo eyes peer out over pinkish cheeks that appear all too boyish for a man in his eighties. Now, Jimmy's eyes will not let go—everything else in the room blurs, even Dr. Z.

"Good heavens," barks Maestro, his head darting back to face the chorus, "why don't I see any eyes up here?" The baton gesticulates wildly as if on an eye-collecting mission of its own. "If you people don't know this by now, we might as well bugger off and go home."

John and Jimmy, eyes still locked, wink at each other.

"I've got half a mind to take those bloody scores away from you!"

John's eyes shoot back to the page—the wrong page. He corrects that with a noisy flip, breaking the awkward silence of Maestro's extended pause. Big Al quickly restores his gaze from John's score back to his own.

I don't need to be on the right page, and I'm not Dr. Z's problem! I've known this piece for ages.

John chokes. Had he let those cocky words pass beyond his thoughts and over his lips? Big Al's eyes stay put.

"Wells!" Maestro plucks the choir's attention away from John's page swish. Faint scars mingle with a craggy brow. "At the very least, I'd expect to see your eyes! You're our shining star. C'mon now. Lift up your eyes, look to the light," his baton lifts the luminous cloud, "and sing from the depths of your soul." On the word *soul*, Maestro's voice slides down more than an octave, landing on a note Big Al would have trouble reaching even with his toes.

Without moving his drooped head, John pops his eyes up at Dr.

Z, whose inclination is to correct the young man's adolescent attitude and posture.

"Thank you!" Dr. Z chooses, instead, to react as if John had done exactly as asked. Flicking an errant tuft of black-and-gray streaked hair out of his eyes, he turns his attention back to the full choir and reviews, for the umpteenth time, why having all eyes front is crucial for next month's performance.

John quashes a grimace. Sliding into a flat smile, he hopes to convince everyone he's perfectly fine—especially Jimmy D, who is still staring at him.

Maestro launches into a vivid account of a time without recorded music, radios, telephones, motors, or fans. He draws the choir's attention to the constant hum, in A-flat, emanating from the heating ducts above.

"Please understand, my friends, the only sounds one heard in those days were made by nature—chirping birds, rustling leaves, whistling wind, the gurgling wash of a babbling brook, the roar of the sea. Upon this ancient background, the human voice burst forth. Now shrill. Then, a whisper. The sigh of a maiden in love; the jealous rage of a prince betrayed; the joyful song of a family gathered about a crackling fire; a newborn's cradle peacefully rocking on wide pine boards to his mother's soft candlelight serenade.

"My dear friends, what I mean to impress upon you is when this glorious piece was written, those who heard it had spent a lifetime listening to the sounds of nature—augmented only by music made by oneself and one's family, the notable exception being on Sunday. Church music, I tell you. Church Music, I daresay, was an utterly exotic and extraordinary sound. Imagine it now..." his eyes close. A slight Mediterranean spice infuses itself into the BBC accent. "Church bells, organ, harpsichord, a choir of even half this size; and if one were lucky, a few strings, brass, and perhaps some percussion. Ahhh…"

Maestro's eyes open. Singers release themselves from the clutches of their scores. Their timid eyes drift upwards to join his.

"My fellow musical travelers," eyes widen, "a performance such as ours was the loudest sound one ever heard. Listen carefully to me. We must take our audience back to this delicious musical time—free them from the oppressive eternal din of today's infernal *background music.*"

Maestro's snarl insinuates the Devil himself had engineered background music to be modern life's most sinister torment. He goes on to speak with such authority about 18th-century life and music that the choir suspects he'd received direct instruction from the composer himself during rehearsals at Dublin in 1742.

Usually, Dr. Z's tales carry John into the composer's world. Not tonight. Words come and go like so many garbled syllables from a strange language—not unlike the incoherent babbling of adults little Johnny would hear from his room after being put to bed far too early.

Burying his face in his score is the only way to avoid Jimmy D's gaze. The score blurs. Behind John's eyes, Jimmy D stares at him from across the small table in the bistro John had chosen for tonight's pitch.

John's performance was perfect. Grades led the parade, followed by commitment to hard work and drive to succeed. His brilliant, original theory of the Internet's future evolution exuded raw talent, having been honed by MIT. Jimmy D had listened intently and was now lost in thought.

Look at him. He must be trying to decide which of his top connections in the tech world will desire my talents the most.

Jimmy D drew a long, slow, deep breath in through his nose as if there were fragrant spring flowers at the table. Relaxing in his chair, he let the air softly escape through his tranquil lips. This, thought John, was proof of his success. A gracious smile confirmed John's faith, readying him for a blessing.

Jimmy D glanced at his watch and mentioned they could not be late for rehearsal. Then he dropped a bomb.

"John, you're a very bright young man with a brilliant future. But your greatest dreams stand between you and your true potential as a great wall of limitation."

Panic struck. Pride and confidence drained like blood from a gut wound. His heart raced, preparing for escape before Jimmy D could finish him off with another riddle. What had gone wrong?

True potential? What does that even mean?

John was afraid to ask—afraid to speak for fear of dribbling all over the table. His mind scrambled through every point in his presentation. In a matter of seconds, he scanned a thousand facts he'd memorized about Jimmy D. Nothing related to dreams or potential.

A middle-aged dishwasher emerged from the kitchen, casually carrying clean silverware. The unshaven man offered a contented smile. John returned the smile, wishing he could trade lives with this easy soul.

How could he do this to me? He's a smart guy. He's gotta know I'm trying to jump-start my career. I need his connections, not his cryptic philosophizing. What a load of crap! And how does he dare presume to know what my greatest dreams or true potential are?

John had carved precious time out of his life (at the expense of his studies, his job, Emily!) to uncover Jimmy D's profound influence in the tech world, then track him down, only to discover they lived within a few miles of each other.

How could I have been so wrong about this guy?

Joining the choir was a calculated move to close in on Jimmy D, lying in wait until he could seize the perfect moment to invite him out for dinner.

If it weren't for Dr. Z, I'd quit the choir right this minute!

Jimmy D slid back his chair and rose gracefully. Putting on his coat, he mused, "I really mustn't be late. Maestro depends on me. Let's talk tomorrow, huh?"

"Okay," blurted John before he could think of anything else to say.

Dr. Z's voice seeps into John's consciousness, nimbly guiding his attention away from tonight's dinner as if awakening him from a bad dream. Once he has hold of John, Maestro gathers the entire chorus.

"Dynamics, my dear friends. Dynamics…

"In Pianissimo, we must maintain resolute control of our delicate voices. Only by listening to one another can we capture our audience and lull them into a serene state of bliss. We need them to trust that our music will deliver them from evil. Then, our crescendos will lift them to new heights and free their souls to soar with ours!

"In Fortissimo, we needn't be terribly loud to project power. For heaven's sake, I beg of you, please do not sing any louder than you can sing in your true voice."

The baton waves in Jimmy D's direction.

"I'll keep the orchestra from drowning you out." Maestro winks at his favorite soprano. "I'll keep the sopranos from impaling the rest of you."

The chorus chuckles. Sopranos flash a naughty look.

Maestro lowers his voice. "All in all, my dear friends, we must sing with one beautifully balanced voice. In harmony to be sure—but most importantly, *blended* into a new sound of a higher order."

His eyes and hands rise toward the ceiling. "We invite the divine to transfigure each of our lone little songs into one grand masterpiece that transcends our individual notions of beauty and carries us closer to our God."

Returning to the choir, he strikes his conductor stance. "In a few short weeks, my dear friends, we raise George Frideric Handel from the dead, and through his music, we raise our audience up and deliver them to God as our most treasured offering to our beloved creator."

Maestro's gaze sweeps over the choir. The baton rises. Two fingers point to his eyes. "But you must *look at me* if we are to have any hope of taking this voyage together."

He pauses, taking his time until every singer has shared his journey through the ethos of the music.

"Da Capo," he commands, exuding confidence.

The choir takes Number 12 from the top, having been seduced by his confidence.

John, eyes front, sings without seeing the baton or hearing a note, his voice on automatic. Dinner with Jimmy D streams before him in an endless loop. It begins with Jimmy's warm greeting and ends with his haunting proclamation.

Your greatest dreams stand between you and your true potential as a great wall of limitation.

Each time this riddle plays, John tries to pause it, decipher it. But the *Pause* button in his head has been rewired to *Replay*, and he's yanked back to the beginning of tonight's dinner.

Grandma's face appears at the podium.

I should have told her about my visions.

At the peak of this term's workload, John put his grades—and his fast-track masters—at risk by skipping classes to be at Grandma's bedside. Grandpa had called with the news that Grandma insisted he liberate her from the hospital. She had refused to permit another tube down her throat.

John dropped everything to catch the next bus out of South Station. He didn't need his visions to divine Grandma wouldn't last long—and Grandpa needed him there. As it turns out, John was the only one of her seven grandchildren present when Grandma took her last breath with her eyes open, staring—according to everyone who was in the room—directly at each of them.

A single blink clears the water from John's eyes. The corner of Dr. Z's crooked mouth smiles into focus. They are headed for one of John's favorite choral passages. His heart rate quickens, matching Maestro's beat. The blend is gorgeous, harmonies in tune, syllables perfectly articulated—all in time to Maestro's steady hand.

But a sloppy ending could ruin it. John fixes his eyes on the baton, determined to join the choir in giving Dr. Z the performance he deserves. Every singer is keenly focused on avoiding what Maestro insists is the most irritating sound in the world—a hundred sloppy voices all over a long, slobbery "s" *like a drunken sailor's drool*, he'd sneer.

John's heart pounds in double time. As *piano* gives way to *mezzo-forte*, the Magic Corridor's tingle swells at the base of his spine. Rushing up his body in time with the crescendo, it explodes out the top of his head with a *fortissimo*, "Wonderful!"

Dancing thirds and fifths resonate throughout his head and throat and chest. He is one with the choir. Like a chorus of angels, they sing, "Counselor...The mighty God...The everlasting Father..."

Maestro carries the choir's wide-mouthed "e" out beyond the final, "Prince of Peace" dangerously close to the edge of breath. At the brink of the void, his baton releases them to touch down onto an exquisitely delicate "s" in perfect unison for a split second.

Their triumphant "s" resonates with John's tingle, preparing him for a vision. But seven-and-a-half bars of coda for piano are not enough to keep his mind at bay. Maestro comes to the rescue. His baton directs Jimmy to hold the final chord.

When the piano's ring fades into the ether, John's mind seizes control. A thousand reasons not to meet with Jimmy tomorrow thrash around his head.

Maestro winks at Jimmy. Handel's Messiah, No. 12, "For Unto Us a Child is Born" is ready to perform. John will be ready in due course.

Chapter Two
Breakfast

"IT'S TIME," says Emily.

"A waste of time," says John, "is what it really is."

"Then why did you stay up all night preparing?"

"So, I guess that was a waste of time too. Just like all the time I spent tracking him down."

John had not set out to find Jimmy D at all—not until an out-of-focus face got stuck in his head. It appeared in too many photos of people he admired to be ignored. Always in the background, never the subject, never captioned. Strange. Stranger still was the pattern. All these people thanked *James Douglass* in a speech or a book or a scientific paper with no hint of who he was or why he was being thanked. Visions wouldn't lead John to his career, but maybe this guy could.

Waking before his alarm was rare. The fading memory was not to be ignored. He'd seen this face in person. It deserved a fresh pot of coffee.

John skipped classes and scoured the Internet. Three pots of coffee later, he found it. As expected, Jimmy D was in the background, out of focus. The photo was of Tim Berners-Lee—inventor of the World Wide Web. And who was posing with Sir Tim at the MIT Computer Science and Artificial Intelligence Laboratory? John Wells.

Tracking down Jimmy D was now urgent—and elementary. Known as the campus sleuth, John could collect the most terrifying trivia on anyone with the slightest connection to MIT so fast it would have made J. Edgar Hoover giggle like a shy schoolgirl being asked on her first date. John had turned down attractive job offers from the FBI, CIA, NSA, and Homeland Security. Conscience, he presumed, would force him to divulge the many ways these agencies routinely violate our privacy. Rotting in federal prison for doing the right thing was not the future of his dreams.

"You don't know that," says Emily. "Why would he have talked about your dreams and your potential if he didn't—"

"Emily, you know my dream is to work in tech. All my skills are in tech, my potential. What he's saying makes no sense."

"He asked you to meet him for breakfast. He obviously has something in mind. Isn't it worth a couple more hours to—"

"To what, Emily? To confirm what I already know?"

"So, what do you think you already know?"

"That he's got no intention of using his connections to get me a job in tech."

"Aren't you even a little curious what his intentions are?"

"Fine. I'll go. I mean, it's too late to take any of those stupid jobs I've turned down. And this recruiting cycle is pretty much over. Guess I'm stuck with whatever he's got to offer. Or maybe you can support me. I'd make a decent housewife, don't you think?"

"Jesus, John!"

The bus is packed. Unwelcoming riders stand cheek by jowl, crammed in the aisle. John hesitates on the first step.

"If you think you can get both feet behind that yellow line, then get in," growls the stout driver. Nodding toward the crowd behind him, he adds, "We haven't got all day, kid."

John climbs the steps in defiance, shoves his left foot behind the line, puts his right foot on top, and grabs the handrail. A sharp swerve into the flow of traffic thrusts him into the generous, springy bosom of the middle-aged woman whose foot had made room for his.

Grandma would say she's wearing far too little for her figure.

An embarrassing rebound throws John sideways, his nose narrowly missing the sharp edges of three brown-paper grocery bags, saddling a little old lady lost in an oversized wool coat.

Nobody gave her a seat? What's wrong with people? So...freedom, upward mobility, and chivalry all died with the twentieth century.

Those grumpy words simmering behind John's angry forehead could have come from Grandpa's older brother.

The antithesis of Grandpa, Great-Uncle Gus was a stern, taciturn Navy Commander with a buzz cut, concealing eyes, and perennial disgust for whatever generation was currently the youngest. When John was 12, Grandpa (an incorrigible tease) convinced him to ask Uncle Gus about his top-secret post during WWII and his collaboration with Alan Turing on Artificial Intelligence. Uncle Gus snapped at John, "That poor fella was murdered." Then he excused himself politely, marched out of the room, and that was that.

It had been a mistake to allow Grandpa's pride in Uncle Gus to seep into John's cocoon where it morphed into one more burdensome expectation, being the blood relative of a genius.

What would Uncle Gus do if he were standing right here? Would he order this oblivious guy with the earphones and newspaper to give up that front seat? Did Jimmy D know Uncle Gus? Maybe Alan Turing, too? Jimmy D has probably figured out I'm nowhere near as smart as they were.

The bus squeals to a stop. Dank, acrid air blasts through the doors. Competing odors vie to provoke a sneeze. John squeezes his nose, trapping a hint of fish from the little old lady. His eyes fill with water. When the bus swerves into speeding traffic, John's grip smudges the handrail, sliding until a crosspiece catches it in time to prevent another bosom bounce.

A tall, dark, handsome man had entered through the rear door, exuding confidence in an expensive black leather blazer over a black V-neck T-shirt matching his abundant black wavy hair. Only a few years older than John, he sports a thick gold chain held off his collarbone by powerful neck muscles under bronze skin.

Oh, how I wish I looked like him—and had his money. Good thing Emily's not here. She'd be drooling.

The sharp-dressed man slinks through the crowd until he reaches the oblivious guy. He yanks the lad's left earpiece out.

"Are you blind? Do you not see the grandmother burdened with all those groceries for her family?"

The oblivious guy stares up at him, dazed.

He's a skinny, wimpy kid. I should have said something.

"Well, don't just sit there!"

The sharp-dressed man gestures for the grandmother to sit as the skinny, frightened kid shoves himself toward the back of the bus. She offers a kind smile, mumbles something under her breath, and wriggles carefully through the amused crowd to oblige.

John smiles at the sharp-dressed man, who tilts his head and smiles back without parting his lips. They catch the moment as it hovers above the crowd between them, and they make it their own.

Impressive. Why couldn't I do that? What's he got that I haven't got? That neck? Chest? Hair? Clothes? Money? I can't imagine ever being that confident. I just wish I were him.

John looks away. Fingers attack his sore chest until sleep-deprived wooziness draws his hand back to the handrail.

I should have taken that analyst job at the CIA. Then I'd actually be somebody. Respected. Maybe even feared. I'd know things nobody else knows. I could learn everything there is to know about my sharp-dressed rival here—and he'd never even suspect I was on to him.

Wailing sirens jolt John out of his standing fog. Nothing passing by the window is familiar. He leans down to peer out the windshield. A pulsating neon sign scatters the mist.

"This is me," blurts John. The driver grunts, swerves, and throws the doors open before coming to a stop. John bounces off the generous bosom. *Oops.* No doubt, his ungainly descent to the street is eliciting another smile from his rival—the kind of involuntary smile you find on yourself when you see a toddler struggle with walking.

Jimmy D, seated facing the door, is taking great pleasure in his steaming cup of coffee. He rises to welcome John with a bright smile and warm handshake.

"Glad you could make it."

"Am I late?" John breaks the handshake, fumbling for his watch.

I'm as pathetic as that skinny, wimpy kid, and Jimmy knows it.

"Don't worry, John. I've got plenty of time. You look hungry."

Jimmy motions to the short, perky waitress. Her ponytail bobs and whirls as she spins around and scoots toward their table.

"Want some coffee?" asks Jimmy.

John nods.

"Coffee for this fine young man," requests Jimmy with a soft, avuncular tone.

"Not a lot of sleep last night, I suppose," says Jimmy.

"No…I mean…not really." Jimmy's conspicuous comfort strikes John as a painfully ironic contrast to his own anxiety.

Coffee slides into John's out-of-focus view. Peering up, he catches a glimpse of a small plastic rectangle with the name "Cindy" pinned to black spandex tightly stretched over the attentive young woman's firm upper body. She gazes at John in the way he had imagined Emily drooling over his rival on the bus.

"Are you gentlemen ready to order? Or do you need some more time?"

Coffee's aroma goes straight to John's head. It's the perfect elixir.

Almost as perfect as Cindy's deep chocolate eyes, creamy velvet skin, rich chestnut hair, sweet friendly voice…Och, she's a baby!

John quells a flirtatious smile, grabs the menu he hadn't noticed, and studies it.

"A moment or two, please," advises Jimmy, prompting Cindy to twirl around and scamper off.

"Have you tried her Belgian waffles?" asks Jimmy. "Everything you'd want in a bountiful breakfast."

"Fine." John had read the enormous menu without digesting a word of it. "Look, I didn't sleep because I really don't get what you meant last night…"

"Relax, my boy." Jimmy's soothing voice washes away one layer of John's anxiety. Coffee warms his chest and brings his mind into focus. "It was meant to be pondered, not analyzed."

A few ponderous sips of coffee quicken John's heart rate, preparing him for attack. "I was hoping you knew someone who might want to hire me. I'm at the top of my class. I did *real* work at MIT, solving *real* problems. Sir Tim says I can make a meaningful contribution…but all the job offers I've gotten are crap. Sorry, but it's true. Nobody can even imagine the high level at which I can work. They all think that, because I'm *so young*, I have to start out a cog—*a team player* on an insignificant little team led by a whiny bureaucrat developing some small piece of an idiotic game or business app that his boss—a quarteritis stricken exec—thinks will boost his bonus by making his lazy, greedy, myopic VC investors a little richer. It's either that or work for…for…the government!" John chokes on his own saliva, or was it his last word?

"Yes, yes, my boy. I felt the same when I was your age. You'll have your rewarding job…all in good time." Jimmy takes another casual sip of coffee. "I thought we'd talk this morning about your *career*. Your direction. Your future."

My future? Well, I can no longer see my future! John's face flushes. *So your riddle holds the secret to restoring my visions? You think you know what's best for me? Who the hell do you think you are?*

Perhaps Jimmy D can read these thoughts. Or has John's exasperation become so apparent as to be obvious to anyone who is the least bit observant? Obvious, then, to Cindy?

Who cares what that little girl sees?

Whatever the case, Jimmy D's face expresses concern.

I've gotta pull myself together. I can't let him think I'm insecure—or worse—emotional! Coffee should do the trick.

Cindy had filled John's cup during his rant without him noticing. He does notice Jimmy eying the tiny black waves—the kind of waves you'd see in a cup of coffee sitting on a table at the start of an earthquake. Both hands steady the cup, lay it down, and rest in his lap.

"John," Jimmy D's tone is serious and calm in equal measure, "I'd like you to join me this evening for…an event. Important people will be there. Meet me at my home at six." Jimmy D hands John a white business card with the words *James Douglass* centered in black Helvetica Bold above his Cambridge address and a phone number ending in 0000. Nothing more on the card. "We'll attend the event together after a good Bordeaux and a bite to eat."

How did he get that phone number?

Imagining a dozen possible answers distracts John from the jolt triggered by taking Jimmy's card. Primal energy is flowing up from the center of the earth into his body through his feet. It rises up his legs, gathers at the base of his spine, and shoots up his torso with increasing pressure until it touches his heart and fills it with promise.

So, what does he really want with me? Promise ousted by suspicion.

"What kind of event?"

Jimmy ignores John's skeptical tone. "Difficult to describe, really. Sort of… spiritual. You were raised Christian?"

"Mm-hmm."

"Dress casually but respectfully."

"Huh?"

"No jeans, but no suit and tie."

"Oh."

Cindy appears, pencil in hand.

"Your sumptuous Belgian waffles for both of us, please," says Jimmy.

Cindy leaves without writing anything.

Hearing her perky voice cry, "Two waffles!" inflames John's chest. One hand massages it while the other dumps half a cup of coffee down his gullet as if it were a stiff drink.

Pain surges with a vengeance, shooting John's hand into the air. Cindy catches it with a smile. *Was that a wink?*

"Can I get a glass of water, please?" asks John.

In a flash, Cindy appears with a coffee pot and two glasses of ice water. Her eyes stay with John's as she lays a glass in front of him.

"There you are," she says with the voice of a young nurse soothing his battle wounds. "More coffee?"

"I'm all set," gulps John. Ice water cools his chest.

"Yes, thank you," says Jimmy with a smile.

She returns the smile politely. Eyeing John, she says, "Your waffles will be right up."

Cindy's ponytail swings cheerfully as her coffee pot hovers over one table after another, each refill complemented by her infectious smile. John is neither amused nor uplifted by Cindy's bubbly spirit. Each smile triggers an eruption of pain. Each convivial reply intensifies it. By the time Cindy reaches the kitchen, the water's cooling effect has been thoroughly trounced.

"What do you mean ... *spiritual?*" says John with the air of a Grand Inquisitor.

"Relax, my boy. It won't hurt. You might even find it agreeable."

"Agreeable," sneers John.

"At the very least, you'll find it intriguing."

John can no longer ignore his chest. The pain sharpens, and it sharpens his mind. He's grateful for the pain, craving more. The greater the pain, the sharper his mind. Better yet, this pain is bright, solid, tangible—something he can grasp—in stark contrast to the dark, swirling, unstable turmoil John's life has become since losing his visions. Two fingers inflame the spot.

"Here you are, boys." Cindy holds a large plate in each hand. A thick round waffle sits majestically on each plate, buttressing a peak of fresh strawberry halves surrounding a wheel of sliced peaches with a center of whipped cream topped with a single whole strawberry standing straight up. She presents them to John and Jimmy as if offering an exotic gift she'd been jealously guarding all her life. "Is there anything else I can do for you now?"

"No, thank you," replies Jimmy, "These look delicious."

Cindy smiles, then aims expectantly at John, locking eyes with him. John breaks their gaze by inspecting the plate before him. Cindy pivots wistfully and vanishes like an apparition.

Neither old nor young man speaks as they attack their castles made of grand delight. John's first bite plunges his attention into a calm, sweet sea of comfort food.

Jimmy D has chosen the perfect breakfast.

The waffle's crisp crust and warm melt-in-your-mouth center blends exquisitely with cool, juicy peaches, tart strawberries, rich cream, and real maple syrup. Each successive bite steals a chunk of John's attention away from his pain.

Jimmy D slips a few words past John's previously alert defenses, "Come with your mind open; ready to live; ready for anything…and everything."

Chapter Three
Part 1: The Wine

IT IS PRECISELY 5:43 IN THE EVENING when John arrives at the semi-circular driveway of a splendid Victorian home that feels much more secluded than any house so close to Harvard Square has a right to be. Even with the cold, damp wind stinging his face, John heeds Grandma's advice, waiting until six o'clock before ascending the six marble steps to ring the doorbell. Grandma had taught him to be prompt, but arriving early was in poor taste.

An hour or so earlier, John was afraid he could not follow Jimmy D's dress code. He had jeans, T-shirts, sweatshirts, and one suit. Nothing in between. Would those khakis his mother had snuck in with his college things "just in case" even fit? Wearing Grandma's final sweater was not an option. Her treasured work of art should be memorialized; its original, pristine condition preserved in tissue paper forever.

None of his elaborate excuses for missing tonight's event held water—and they could get back to Dr Z, maybe Sir Tim too. He might as well try on these clothes and see what happens. By the time his reflection in the mirror agreed with Emily that he looked fine, it was too late to cancel and save face.

A single deep chime resonates through the portico when John presses the faintly lit doorbell, followed by another chime a third below as he withdraws his finger.

"Good evening, John." Jimmy's voice ignites a flash of déjà vu. John wipes his feet more than enough to remove any dirt, making sure Jimmy notices. The grand foyer echoes an alarming sense of calm in this strange—but strangely familiar—place.

Following Jimmy, John takes note of every turn, every hallway, every room in case a quick exit is required. Jimmy stops upon entering a majestic Victorian drawing room. The blazing fire in the giant stone fireplace snuffs the small talk. Hand-embroidered cushions sit atop curved banquettes in front of twelve-foot-tall bay windows overlooking well-lit grounds. Jimi Hendrix's "Wind Cries Mary" emanates from the bay windows—perfectly clear sound as if Jimi had been resurrected to play live outside on the sprawling lawn. A crystal decanter filled with deep purple-red wine stands on a mahogany Queen Anne table next to two huge glasses and a small platter of charcuterie, cheeses, olives, freshly cut vegetables, and sliced baguette.

"Puzzled by the sound?" asks Jimmy.

"I don't see a CD player. That can't be an MP3."

"Oh no. A new digital encoding I'm developing. I've been testing it on the original masters." A touch of pride seeps from Jimmy's eyes. "It could still use a bit of tweaking."

"Wow! Amazing. You've really got something here."

"Mmm. Perhaps."

"What do you mean, 'perhaps?' This is the best sound I've ever heard from recorded music."

"Quite. But the world of sound is moving to earbuds and iPods. Nobody seems to care much about sound quality anymore."

"Hmmm. Well…that's gotta change at some point. And when it does—"

"Some wine?" interrupts Jimmy. He presents John with a glass.

"Sure, thanks." John hadn't noticed Jimmy pouring the wine. His focus had not been where it ought to be.

This is my big night. I must be on my game. Damn, I thought he was going to hire me to work on his new music encoding project.

Jimmy plunges his ample nose as far into his glass as it can reach and inhales deeply. He swirls the wine into a red whirlpool, rising up the glass to dance with the firelight.

"Go ahead. Try it," prods Jimmy.

John attempts to copy the barely perceptible motion of Jimmy's wrist, hoping to swirl the wine in his own glass. Jimmy raises his glass with a smile.

"Your future."

Is Jimmy's smile meant for his future, or is it an involuntary reaction to seeing John's wine slosh about like a sea in a storm? John chooses the former, at which point Jimmy nods as if in approval of his choice. Their glasses meet, striking an elegant tone resonating with Beethoven's Emperor Piano Concerto now streaming from the bay windows. The two men sip in unison. John stares into his glass. Jimmy's gaze remains on the young man.

"This is the last of my 1990 Saint-Émilion," declares Jimmy, "a very special gift from a good friend. I've been waiting for just the right occasion to share it."

"I'm honored." The words escape before John can quash them, not that he would want to.

Hmmm…that may have been the right reply, but it came out before I could vet it. I've gotta be more careful.

With one hand, Jimmy nimbly fashions a slice of salami, cheese, and roasted red pepper into a tiny roll, places it on a slice of baguette, and takes a bite. John hopes Jimmy won't notice him fumbling to get the same job done. On the downbeat of John's first bite, the music changes to Duke Ellington with Ella Fitzgerald singing, "It Don't Mean a Thing."

"Mmm," says John.

"Yes, what a wonderful tune that is," says Jimmy with a soft, ethereal voice.

After more music, more snacks, and more wine, Jimmy finds an opening. "Walk with me," he commands with a disarming tone.

John follows, glass in hand. *This is the best wine I've ever tasted. Maybe I should get some for Emily.*

"You'll find this evening rather unusual," explains Jimmy in the matter-of-fact voice of a museum docent. "All your research on me has failed to uncover my life's work—and that's what you're about to encounter."

Enough with the wine. I need to focus.

"You won't know anyone except me—and the Maestro, of course."

"Dr. Z?" John is dismayed to have betrayed his surprise.

"He and I have been at this a long time. You'll understand in short order." As they enter the kitchen, Jimmy stops, faces John, and pauses. When he's sure he has the young man's full attention, he adds, "It may come as a bit of a shock."

John is motionless.

"Remember what I said at breakfast." Jimmy peers through John's eyes until he's sure the young man does, indeed, remember. "You are ready?"

John says nothing. Jimmy strides through the kitchen as if John had answered *Yes* while every cell in John's being recoils from the specter of diving into the unknown.

Not quite every cell. John's feet are acting on their own. They follow Jimmy into the butler's pantry. Before John can protest, Jimmy stops again, puts his hand on the counter, and eyes John, whose feet have brought his head uncomfortably close to Jimmy's face.

"Look, my dear boy, you're here because we need you. The world needs you. The Christ…needs you."

"Christ?"

"That's right. We are disciples of The Christ—Christ consciousness if you like—and we need your help."

"Disciples of Christ? Really? You're in a *cult*? You want me to join your *cult*?"

Jimmy ignores the disgust in John's tone. "I guess you could refer to Jesus and his disciples as a cult. Indeed, the people of today would consider them as dangerous as they were considered in their own time, don't you think?"

Is this guy serious? Christ's Disciples?

"Well, John. What do you think his disciples did? C'mon now. You went to Sunday school. What happened?"

"They went out and taught?" replies John like a timid schoolboy who hadn't raised his hand but had been called on anyhow.

"Imagine if I had filled your glass with half water and half wine. What then?"

"What do you mean, 'What then?' Och. Again, with the riddles?" John drowns his gaze in his glass. "I'm sorry. I just don't get it." *This is not going well.*

"Your wine would taste thin. It would ruin a good Bordeaux—an exceptional bottle, really." Jimmy slaps the faucet. John flinches. "Shall we try?" Cold water runs full blast in the small pantry sink. "Why don't we see what it tastes like?"

"What the hell are you getting at?"

"Look what your Sunday school teachers have done to you!" Jimmy flicks the faucet off. "Diluted Jesus and his disciples. Reduced them to mere teachers."

"Isn't that what they did? Teach? Preach?"

"They healed!" roars Jimmy, sending chills up John's spine. "Jesus bestowed power upon his disciples. Awesome power. The power to heal. The power to alter reality."

John is getting light-headed. It's not the wine.

"The Gospels are full of passages alluding to this power and to its source. Jesus often refers to the source as his father in the sky, sometimes love."

Charged with a desperate mission, the back of John's mind races through Bible stories while his attention remains on Jimmy.

"Here's the significant bit." Jimmy focuses John's attention. "Jesus taught his disciples how to access and channel this power on their own—and they *practiced* every day—but the Bible thoroughly obscures the technique he taught. Nothing in the Bible explains how to access and channel this power or how to confer it upon others."

John succeeds in hiding his curiosity. He remains motionless, expressionless.

"You've felt this power from time to time," continues Jimmy. "You felt it last night at rehearsal. You know, that moment when we were all right there with Maestro, perfectly in tune with one another through 'Unto Us A Child Is Born.' You even recognized the feeling. It feels sort of like love—and it is a kind of love. It's not romantic love or the love you feel for your parents and family. That sort of love—love for other people—is a taste…sort of a gateway to this higher form of love; an energy field; the source of life; the most powerful force in the Universe."

John stares wide-eyed at Jimmy, unable to conjure a response.

"What's the difference between a living being and one who has just died?"

"Uhh—"

"Life's energy. It fills the body, engaging all the cells within it to work together for the benefit of the body as a whole. We refer to that body as a 'being.' If it's a person, we call it a 'human being.' Now, remove life's energy from said being, and all the cells go their separate ways. They're still active, but they're no longer bound by the energy of life; they no longer work together. The *being* is dead."

"Sounds like you're describing *The Force* from Star Wars." While John is busy crafting snide remarks, Little Johnny secretly signals to Jimmy from inside his cocoon, *Now's your chance.*

"Well, that's a pretty good description," replies Jimmy, "especially the bit about the force being an energy field. You see, life's energy propagates just like a field. To access the power, you simply resonate with it. Sounds a little corny, I know—and a little *sixties*, but Leary and those hippies got it right, in a quaint sort of way, when they said 'tune in.' That's exactly what you do: tune in. Life's energy field—call it love or spirit or light or God if you like—it's always there. It's like a radio signal. Tune yourself to its frequency, and it will resonate within you."

Try as he might, John cannot stop his priorities from rearranging like cream rising to the top of a bucket of fresh milk.

"Most people live in a state of dissonance," continues Jimmy. "They're out of tune with life's energy. This feeling of dissonance becomes the core of their reality. It feels solid, something you can hold on to, something you can build a belief system on. Like most everybody else, you believed that becoming an adult required abandoning your childhood resonance to live in a state of dissonance. But you've got something most people haven't got. You're uncomfortable with dissonance. It doesn't feel right. You long for resonance—even as an adult."

The voices in John's head who had been screaming, *No, this is crazy* are now aligned with Little Johnny in a chorus of, *Tell me more.*

"Jesus' disciples were just like you—living in dissonance while longing for resonance. When Jesus spoke, he struck a resonant chord within them, and they felt it. That's why they followed him."

John cocks his head like the RCA dog awaiting instructions.

"Do you really think he convinced them with reason?" Jimmy leaves no time to answer. "Good Heavens, no. Most of them were fishermen. In any event, what logic could possibly convince any man to abandon his wife, his children, his work, his village, all his duties, and everything he had ever known? There is no such reasonable argument. Jesus' disciples felt the resonance, and they craved more. They simply could not resist."

Well, I can resist. Who does this guy think he is? OK, I feel a little funny right now. Is it this resonance he's talking about? Maybe. But even if it is, I came here for a job in tech. Yeah, I went to church and sang in the choir, but I'm not religious...

More and more voices add themselves to this chorus of resistance. The inside of John's head sounds like a noisy gymnasium crowded with dozens of kids babbling over bouncing basketballs. Outwardly, John remains silent, gaze fixed on Jimmy, unable to corral these voices into a single thread of coherent thought, let alone something to say.

Fully aware of John's inner tumult, Jimmy continues as if he has the young man's undivided attention, "Jesus imparted to his disciples an exact method for resonating with life's energy field and channeling its power. He gave them a technique they could practice on their own. As with music, it takes years of constant, diligent, daily discipline to master. Some of them took to it faster than others. None of them perfected it fully. Most of them finally got proficient enough to heal people, and once they did, they began teaching the technique to their students, who taught their students…and so forth down through the ages until it was passed down to my teachers. I learned from them. Now it's your turn."

"Wait, what? You're telling me you learned how to use this power from teachers who learned from their teachers and so on…and so on… and this lineage of personal instruction goes back to the original twelve disciples and Jesus himself?"

Jimmy ignores John's cynical tone. "That's right."

"And you think you can teach me to resonate with this supposed… life force so I can access this power too? And you assume I want to spend years practicing? Every day?"

John's disparate thoughts now declare their unity. *All my work, my studies, my research…I'm almost free. I cannot go back to being a student. Everything I've ever wanted is within my grasp.* Against the backdrop of this alliance arises a craving for the power Jimmy is offering.

"Oh, I know I can teach you the practice, my dear boy," insists Jimmy with quiet aplomb. "Whether or not you want to learn is another matter entirely."

"Fine. Teach me then!" Hearing this challenge spoken in his own voice spooks John. He has no recollection of having uttered anything. It's as if someone else is in the room impersonating him.

Part 2: The Cup

"Very well, then. Right this way." Jimmy's facile manner belies his power to sense the battle raging inside John. He reaches up to tilt *The Escoffier Cookbook* on the pantry's top shelf. The wall rotates, gradually unveiling a large, windowless, candle-lit parlor. Standing in floor-length crimson robes, ten men encircle an antique rug, having left an opening perfectly sized for two more men.

These people really are waiting for me.

The sweet scent of burning beeswax quiets John's mind enough to hear his heart beating amid the silence. His breathing slows and deepens. Colors appear more vibrant. The rhythm of a lone, unseen drum beats in unison with John's heart.

John and Jimmy enter solemnly, side by side, in time with the drumming as if marching down the aisle at a wedding. The center of the rug rotates into view, revealing an elaborately decorated green glass goblet atop an ornately carved wooden table. All ten men are staring at the goblet. At the edge of the opening, one man turns his head. It is Dr. Z, whose warm smile invites John to stand to his left. John floats into position like a spacecraft softly docking at a space station. Jimmy moves to John's left, closing the circle. Both men detach their gaze from John and focus on the goblet. The drumming stops.

"Welcome, my son," declares a tall, lean, middle eastern looking gentleman with dark eyes, curly black hair, clear olive skin, and a substantial nose perfectly fitted to his long, oval face. His voice descends from the cathedral ceiling in a warm, smoky timbre resembling a cello. "I am Simon. We've been waiting a long time for you."

I don't know exactly what or who you think you're waiting for, but I'm only here to check things out. I haven't committed to anything, so don't pretend I have.

"What are you looking for, John?"

Simon's voice resonates with the tingle swelling at the base of John's spine. He cannot answer. The tingle rushes up his spine to the top of his head. Mind quiet, vision clear, John's lifelong burden of longing has vanished, replaced by the certainty of being in the right place at the right time doing the right thing, something he's never felt before. His eyes close. He draws a long, slow, deep breath. A serene smile materializes from the depth of his bliss.

Breath withdraws. John's eyes open.

How long have I been standing here with this stupid grin on my face? These guys must think I'm a moron. Why are they staring at me? What do they think I've agreed to? What are they going to do to me?

"Do not be afraid," assures Simon. "All your visions have led you here. Nothing can stop you now."

How does this guy know about my visions? What kind of power does he have?

"Stop me from what?" demands John.

"From realizing your true potential." Simon's reassuring voice strikes a resonant chord within John.

"Are you ready?" asks Jimmy.

"Ready for what?"

"Ready to begin your training; discover your true potential; become one of us." Jimmy's words flow down beyond John's consciousness to snatch the answer from the depths of his psyche and hoist it up so he can see it, feel it, taste it, before his mind has a chance to obscure it.

John waits for the vision. Clarity and certainty rising within him had always preceded a vision. Warmth arises instead. It flows from the silence to fill his chest and meld with his breath, producing a peculiar sense of calm.

"Yes," says John before he can stop himself.

Jimmy and Dr. Z extend their hands. All the other men have joined hands. John tentatively lays one hand in Jimmy's, the other in Dr. Z's. The circle is complete. Energy flows from his chest out both hands, reminiscent of the flare shooting out his fingers in his magic corridor.

The enchanting music of a single harp fills the room. Not the sort of harp music intended for relaxation, this music is stirring, with over-tones of an opera interlude and a hint of Spanish spice. Sensing someone approaching from behind, John is not moved to turn his head. He remains focused, with all the other men, on the mysterious goblet at the center of the circle. The soft, silky caress of a robe being placed upon his shoulders tempts John once again to turn his head. Again, he resists. He sharpens his focus onto the unlit pillar candle barely visible inside the goblet. Using only his peripheral vision, he can see the robe is a deep emerald green with a crimson border.

"Light the candle, my son," instructs Simon. His head and eyes gesture ever so slightly toward the goblet. Jimmy and Dr. Z release their hands. Their gentle grasp had kept him steady and focused, even though placing his hands in theirs had at first felt awkward. Now, a bit woozy, he is not sure he can make it to the goblet without wobbling—and that would be terribly embarrassing.

Time races backward. Five-year-old Johnny is asking his father to take him out beyond the breakers.

"The waves are more than twice your height," cautioned his father. "You'll be way over your head."

"I know, Dad. I'm ready. Mom says I'm a strong swimmer. She

lets me go in the deep end at the town pool now."

"Oh, does she?"

Wide-eyed Johnny nodded.

"Okay. Let's go."

John took Dad's hand. They marched into the foam.

"Let's ride a little wave first," suggested Dad, secretly hoping John's mastery of body surfing would satisfy today's appetite for thrill.

They surfed a baby swell all the way to the beach, their bodies perfectly straight, resembling a pair of surf boards ridden by invisible pro surfers.

"That was great, Dad. Let's go out beyond the breakers now, OK?"

Hand-in-hand, John and Dad headed back out into the foam toward the larger, crashing waves.

Dad shouted at the top of his lungs to be heard over the raging surf, "See how that wave curves toward us?" He imitated the wave's shape with his hand. "We'll dive headfirst into the bottom of the curl right before the wave breaks." He wiped the spray from his face. "The back of the wave will lift us up, and the front will break behind us."

The large swell broke, propelling a chest-high wall of white water toward them. John's hands shot out of the water. He struck his magic corridor stance, aiming sideways at the wave. The roiling surf rushed around him. It raced toward the beach where it slowed, then retreated…tugging in the opposite direction…out to sea where it would join the oncoming swell, incorporate itself within, break anew, careen again to the beach, and retreat in a never-ending cycle of ebb and flow. John was lost in the moment, savoring the salt air, licking the foam from his lips, immersed in the power and beauty of the brilliant white surf atop the deep blue sea that had chosen not to engulf him.

"I'll tell you when to dive." Dad pointed at a roller climbing out of the sea. "Remember, we'll be lifted upright. When our heads pop up, we'll be out beyond the breakers. It'll be over your head, so you'll need to tread water. Ready?"

"You won't let go of my hand, will you?" implored John.

"You can't dive and hold my hand at the same time. Your hands have to be in front of you like when you dive into a pool or ride a wave."

I don't want to do this now. I can't let go of Dad's hand. This was a terrible idea. I want to go back.

John stared up in awe of the giant roller's majesty. Tall, confident, proud, this glistening beauty had harnessed the power of wind and gravity to travel hundreds—perhaps thousands—of miles to meet John at this moment. Nothing could stop its approach. Determined to fulfill its destiny, it would wash over anything that dared attempt to block its way. John was poised to harness some of the wave's power—enough to deliver him beyond the breakers. This had been his dream and the impetus for learning to swim. All his practice was about to pay off.

The swell sculpted a curl pointing down at John from high above Dad's head. He froze in place. Unable to find his breath, he tightened his grip on Dad's hand.

"Dive. Now!" Dad yanked his hand free, raised his arms, and tucked his head. Instinct seized John. He matched Dad's form and dove into the curl.

Time slowed. Cold water skimmed the top of John's head. It washed past his forehead, ears and nose; down his neck; over his shoulders to caress his chest, back, and waist. The sea held John in a love embrace. He surrendered to the wave's power. It carefully tilted him upright, then shot him to the surface with a force that felt like he was being squeezed out of a giant tube of toothpaste.

John's head emerged at the same time as Dad's. He snatched a breath and grabbed Dad's hand. Splashing his free hand and thrashing his feet could not keep him afloat. His nose sank below the water.

"John, you have to let go of me so you can tread water."

This was not the deal little Johnny made when he dove into the curl. Once he was out beyond the breakers, he would be safe again, holding Dad's hand.

"It's okay, John. You're very good at treading water. But you can't do it and hold my hand at the same time. Neither can I. We'll both sink."

All his life, Dad's hand had kept John safe in new or uncertain or dangerous circumstances. Being out beyond the breakers was all three.

"I'll be right here, as close to you as I am now. Only we can't hold hands." Dad's mouth and nose sank beneath the surface for a couple of seconds. John's grip remained firm. He and Dad scrambled to keep their heads above water.

"As soon as you let go, we'll both be fine. Try it. You'll see."

John cautiously loosened his grip, keeping his hand close enough to grab Dad's arm if need be. Muscle memory took over. Treading water with both hands and feet required little energy and no concentration, in stark contrast to his frantic attempt to stay afloat while holding onto his father.

Fear gone, energy back, John reveled in his achievement and relished the moment. It was glorious. Letting go of Dad's hand had freed him to be carried to his cherished destination beyond the breakers, where he once again abandoned his only security. Now, he was free to bask in the power bestowed upon him by the sun, the sky, the waves...and by his triumph.

Reliving his victory at sea steadies John enough to approach the goblet as if he had found his sea legs aboard ship. He lifts the long wooden match lying next to it. Scanning the area for a matchbox turns up nothing. He moves deliberately, attempting to appear like he knows what he's doing.

Can I light this match by striking it on the table? Would it damage the table? Am I supposed to light it on the goblet? Or would that be sacrilege?

He searches the area for any sign of a designated spot for striking a match. Nothing. Holding the match up, he looks straight at Simon, who produces a lighter from his pocket and flicks a flame to life. John tilts the match toward the lighter. Shivers shoot up John's spine, propelled by the hiss of a swelling flame and the aromas from burning butane, match head, and wood.

"Good. You know when to ask for help. That's a fine beginning to your training," assures Simon. "Now light the candle."

Simon's voice tugs at the warmth in his chest, drawing it out into his arms. He lights the candle. The goblet's color changes from green to red. Chills race up John's arms into his chest. He shakes the match, putting out the flame and thrusting the chills up his neck into his head.

"Is this the life force Jimmy was talking about? Have I somehow channeled its power?"

"Since you were a little boy, you have longed to be free," replies Simon. "You assumed everyone else was trying to trap you, trying to delay or restrict your freedom. So you spun a cocoon to protect yourself. Over time, your cocoon hardened into a great shield as strong as a space capsule's heat shield. This shield has served you well. You can fly through life as fast as you like and, so long as you stay safely inside your cocoon, nobody can get to you…hurt you…trap you…take away your freedom.

"What you did just now was venture out beyond your cocoon scarcely long enough to capture a glimpse of the *Life Field*. What's more, you allowed it to shine upon you. You kept your face toward the sun and were inspired to ask this question." Simon pauses, takes a deep breath, glances at John's forehead, then re-engages with John's eyes. "Now…if you can maintain this connection a moment longer, you might be able to absorb more fully the energy of this moment, hmm?"

John nods. He had instinctively matched Simon's breath with one of his own, giving him the pause Simon was looking for.

"Can you feel energy moving through you?"

John races through his body, attempting to detect where the energy is coming from and where it's going.

"Do not answer with your mind," interrupts Simon. "There is no need to answer at all. Let your thoughts go. All of them. Do not kick them out, but do not engage them either. Allow them to come and go as they please while you focus on your breath."

Simon and John take a long, slow, deep breath together. John focuses all his attention on inhaling. Thoughts recede like passengers on the platform waiting for a different train. Exhaling induces a flow down his front and up his spine to the top of his head. Inhaling again sends the flow down his front.

"Would you like to maintain this flow?"

John nods. Energy rises up his spine as he exhales.

"Of course, you would. Simple, really. Continue to surrender your thoughts. Let them fall into the flow like sand slipping through your fingers. Surrender your emotions, too. They cannot trap you if you let them go. While you are in a state of flow, the Life Field will resonate within you."

John and Simon breathe together. Each breath expands and deepens the flow until questions and speculations about how the goblet changed color invade John's head. Curiosity finally collapses the flow into a lust to know what has happened. Resonance slips away.

"So, what's going on with this goblet? How did the color change? Was it something you did? Was it Me? The Life Field? What?" demands John.

"Ah, that," replies Simon in a whimsical tone. "So, you believe it is some sort of magic, do you?"

"Well…not really…no…"

"Good. Because it is not magic at all, my son. It is the confluence of imagination, experimentation, and discovery (in a word, *science*) expressed through inspiration and creativity (in a word, *art*). You see, this beautiful goblet is made of dichroic glass. Light reflected off it appears green, and light passing through it appears red. The color changed when you lit the candle because more light is coming through the glass from its center than is being reflected. Dichroic glass has been around for millennia. The Romans made it in the fourth century by mixing tiny bits of gold and silver dust into the glass. We light the candle to remind ourselves that things we once believed were magic, we can now explain through science and express through art."

"And this *Life Field*. It can be explained by science too?" inquires John.

"Of course," replies Simon. "It is an energy field, not unlike electromagnetism. Did Jimmy D not explain that you access the power of the Life Field by resonating with it?"

"Yeah, OK. But if it's a field, how do you measure it, calculate its intensity, represent its interactions with other fields?"

"You just did, my son. Tell me: when you were in a state of flow just now, did you experience resonance? Could you verify its existence? Feel its intensity? Did you notice how it interacted with your heart, your mind, your senses, your spirit?"

"Well…sort of…I guess. So I'm the measurement tool?"

"Everybody is. All living things, really."

"Jimmy D said you need me—need my help." John obeys his impulse to change the subject even though his curiosity is not fully satisfied.

"What do you need from me?"

"Oh…I thought you would never ask." Simon's tone is at once sarcastic and relieved.

Chills and wooziness infect John. All the men are staring at him.

They're scrutinizing my every word, my every move. I wouldn't be surprised if their scrutiny extends to my thoughts, too.

"You have a gift, my son," continues Simon. "Your visions…and the ability you demonstrated this evening to maintain a flow and resonate with the Life Field, even if it only lasted a few moments. With training and practice, you will learn to maintain your flow for much longer periods of time. You will learn to channel the Life Field at will. And that will give you the power to affect true healing. You will learn to shape your own reality—and the reality experienced by those around you. Your sharp, critical mind and your innate sense of good and evil—your *conscience*—will check any temptation to use this power for your own personal gain at the expense of others. Indeed, your fusion of vision, flow, critical thinking, and conscience makes you perfectly suited to help us prevent the impending calamity."

"What calamity?" John is infinitely more curious about manipulating reality, but this question crosses his lips.

"Well, my son…that will take some time to explain and serious, focused attention on your part. Before we go there, we need to know if you are with us."

John stares in silence at Simon longer than would be considered polite. Then he turns toward Jimmy, who nods his answer to the unuttered question John is asking only with his thoughts, *So this is it? My true potential?*

"Fine. I'm in. I'll take your training. I'll join your group. Whatever it takes. I want to learn how to shape reality."

Simon addresses the entire room in a solemn voice, "Welcome, John!"

Harp and drum play together. The music is upbeat, like a Celtic country dance infused with notes of a Middle Eastern accompaniment to a belly dancer.

Without looking at them, John senses Jimmy and Dr. Z have beckoned him back to his place in the circle between them. He complies gracefully.

Simon approaches the goblet, reaches underneath the table, and produces a plain clay chalice. He raises the chalice and declares, "Let us celebrate the newest Disciple of Christ."

Simon moves back to his place in the circle. A twelve-year-old boy clad in a white robe enters the room with a pitcher of wine. He fills the chalice and leaves.

Could this be the Holy Grail? They'd tell me if it is, right?

No more questions are asked. John allows this query to come and go through his mind as he had been instructed.

Simon drinks. He passes the chalice to the man at his left, who drinks and passes it on. In silence, each man clasps the chalice with both hands, drinks, and passes it on until it reaches Dr. Z. He drinks, then holds the chalice up. John reaches out with both hands.

Dr. Z cordially instructs, "I hold. You drink. When you have completed your training, you will stand with us in a crimson robe and clasp the chalice for yourself."

John drinks, wary of slurping or taking too much…or too little. The wine tastes good. It washes away John's angst, warming his chest on the way down. John's attention follows the wine's warmth as it travels through his body, making its way to the center of his being.

Dr. Z lowers the chalice, walks behind John, and hands it to Jimmy.

He drinks and passes it on. This continues until the last man drinks the last sip of wine. He hands the chalice to Simon, who raises it above his head. The long, deep sleeves of Simon's crimson robe stream down from the chalice framing his face like curtains on a proscenium stage.

He proclaims to John, "May the Life Field bless you and keep you. May it resonate within you and shine through you. May it fill you with grace and give you peace."

Simon lowers the chalice, pauses for a moment, and lowers his head. He stares into the center of the chalice as if reading a message written within it. His head rises, "And so concludes the initiation."

Chapter Four
Training

JOHN WELLS IS FRUSTRATED. Learning to resonate with the Life Field is nothing like academics—or anything else in life. There are no cheats. Nothing to conquer. He is trapped in a weekslong endless loop.

John had come to every session every day with the determination to learn and grow as fast as possible. Within five minutes he'd be seduced by a thousand distracting thoughts, prompting Jimmy to stop and remind him to breathe, at which point they would inhale together until John ran out of lung capacity long before Jimmy.

This guy is in his eighties, and I can't keep up with him. Better not tell Emily. She thinks I'm fit.

"Do not worry," Jimmy would counsel. "Deep breathing takes practice. Focus takes more practice. Quieting your mind, more practice still. Now…let your thoughts go. Do not kick them out, but don't engage them either. Allow them to come and go as they please while you focus on your breath."

If I can't breathe, quiet my mind, and maintain a flow, how will I ever connect to the Life Field—let alone resonate with it? This is much harder than I could possibly have imagined. I'm not cut out for this. Maybe Simon was wrong. What if I made the wrong decision?

John and Jimmy are sharing a snack at Jimmy's nine-foot-long kitchen table made of two wide pine boards rescued from a dilapidated, three-hundred-year-old barn. Jimmy sits in the antique Windsor armchair at the table's head, John in a side chair. They share a plate in the corner between them. Prosciutto di Parma, fresh mozzarella, a few French cheeses, olives, roasted red peppers, fresh tomatoes with basil, and crusty Italian bread. Usually, the two polish off their pre-training snack with some gusto. Not tonight. John timidly picks at the plate.

Before he can stop himself, he asks, "Does it get any easier?"

"No," says Jimmy, "But it gets faster."

Faster. That hopeful word in Jimmy's confident voice sends chills up John's spine.

Jimmy waits while his reply seeps all the way through to the center of John's being.

"Ready to begin?"

"Absolutely!" The promise of speed spreads confidence all over John like icing on a cake.

Silence accompanies John and Jimmy through the pantry into the parlor. Moments after they sit, John's attention, his breath, all his bones and muscles align in harmony. Energy rushes in and settles down to his heart, where it expands. He summons the will to focus on breath, let go of thoughts, and allow the energy to drift down to the base of his spine, where it expands a little more.

The unfurling energy releases John's lust to reach out and grab it. To control it. To wield it like a sword. Powerless to surrender this urge,

John is about to give in when time flows backward. He is out beyond the breakers with his father, floating up and down with the ocean swells. Energy rises up his spine. When it reaches the top of his head, he allows it to fall down his front, rise again, fall again, rise again—a continuous flow down his front, up his back, nourished by every breath he takes.

Space and time fade away, leaving John suspended in light. There is no up or down, left or right, forward or back, in or out, past or present or future. The sensation is familiar. A touch of it had preceded each of his childhood visions. Now, there's no vision. Only flow.

Flow intensifies. A thousand thoughts surge into John's head, each one demanding attention. He drops his attention into the flow using the same technique he'd used as a child to travel with a leaf he had dropped off a bridge into a stream. The leaf would lead his attention in a dance through the air. John would follow as it alighted on the water and floated merrily down the stream, avoiding rocks and twigs by riding the whirlpools around them like an alpine skier through slalom gates. Scarcely before it vanished under the bridge, John would scoot to the other side—eyes closed to avoid severing his connection with the leaf. His eyes would open in time to catch the leaf emerging from underneath the bridge and ride along until it was out of sight.

The leaf trick works until emotions flood through, swamping his concentration. Like feuding schoolyard bullies, one emotion after another yanks him, shoves him, wrenches him, each one hell-bent on breaking him.

Breathe!

Breath is lost in the maelstrom. Flow condenses into pain centered below his sternum. John doubles over clutching his chest, the wind knocked out of him. Jimmy lays two fingers on John's upper back. Breath flows. Pain subsides. John straightens himself and sits up.

"That's enough for today," directs Jimmy in a soft, empathetic voice. "Let us celebrate your victory."

"Victory? I thought I was gonna die!"

"You have risen to a higher level of consciousness, my son." Jimmy directs his eyes to John's chest. "The pain you felt was your resistance to this level." His eyes are back to John's. "By accepting my touch, you surrendered your resistance…and here you are…resonating with the Life Field. You have taken your first step toward your next level of training where you will learn to shape reality."

Jimmy rises. A force lifts John—reminiscent of being hoisted above his father's head as a little boy. He follows Jimmy, unable to sense his own walking. It's as if he were sitting atop his father's shoulders. Everything below is synchronously visible, but nothing distracts from the thrill of the ride. His mind is quiet. Thoughts come and go like so many commuters at Grand Central while John watches from the celestial ceiling. Only one emotion exists…bliss.

Jimmy takes a bottle of wine and a decanter from the pantry. In silence, he lays them on the kitchen table. A simple gesture of Jimmy's open hand invites John to sit. Jimmy remains standing.

"Allow yourself to enjoy the beauty of this moment," says Jimmy, "the sound, the color, the flow, the aroma, the taste, the warmth."

Jimmy cuts into the wine's capsule with the blade of a sommelier's corkscrew. The silky swishing sound of steel against glass and foil resonates with John's flow. Every squeaky turn of the screw drives resonance deeper into his being. Jimmy removes the cork, smells it, and hands it to John. Before any invading thoughts can distract him, the cork's fruity, woody aroma clears John's head and opens his heart.

Jimmy tips the bottle toward the decanter. The first drop plunges out of the neck with a glug. Two shorter glugs follow. Their pitch is a whole step above the first. Then, a succession of steady glugs—all at a fourth above the first.

"Wait!" exclaims John.

Jimmy stops pouring. "It's Handel," proclaims John. "Messiah. Number 53. The larghetto." He sings, "Blessing and honor, glory and power be unto him."

Jimmy raises his left eyebrow.

"Did you hear that?" asks John. "The wine sings Messiah. Do it again."

Jimmy smirks. He resumes pouring. The music is not the same. "Only the first wine out of the bottle sings you a blessing." Jimmy finishes decanting the wine.

"So, open another bottle then," insists John.

"Perhaps we should enjoy this, my dear boy. It's a good wine."

"Do you think this is where Handel got that phrase?" asks John.

"Where else?" replies Jimmy. "A newly opened bottle of wine pours that tune every time. Handel was listening. Now you are, too."

Chapter Five
Emily

"GROUND CONTROL TO MAJOR JOHN!" Emily's normally smooth, smoky voice crackles with frustration. "Are you there?"

The truthful answer would be *no*. John's attention had been whizzing around inside his head like a horsefly in pursuit of a blood meal.

Jimmy insisted on celebrating my breakthrough so why won't he teach me how to manipulate reality? Or at least take my training to the next level—whatever that is. Why is quieting my mind harder now than before my breakthrough?

Jimmy had explained that spiritual growth is not linear. A taste of the Life Field's awesome power often evokes recoil. It's a perfectly natural reaction. Practice will get you to the next level. Practice breathing, letting go, resonating. Jimmy's patience only heightens John's anxiety. The specter of endless practice looms before him like a life sentence at hard labor.

Emily had been complaining about Orville, owner of the seafood restaurant she manages and where John works as a waiter. It had been a long story, running through cocktails, appetizers, a bottle of wine, and dinner.

"Well? Are we gonna share the chocolate lava cake, or do you wanna order your own dessert?"

John avoids Emily's gaze by looking up at the tall, handsome waiter whose tilted head and forced smile cannot hide his pretense at being patient.

"Uh…sure," says John. His eyes fall onto the table.

"We'll split the lava cake," commands Emily. Her eyebrows shoot in the waiter's direction while her cold stare remains fixed on John. The waiter pivots and withdraws.

"So what do you think I should do?" asks Emily.

John has no idea. He's not stumped by her quandary. Rather, he hasn't given her story enough attention to know what she's asking about.

How am I getting out of this one?

On the outside, John pretends to be considering the matter. Serious face. A slight lean forward. Hands clasped. "Hmmm…"

Inside, he's hastily gathering everything he knows about Orville, hoping this stew of details will give rise to a probing question he can ask Emily—the kind of question a therapist asks an exasperated patient who just wants an answer. And maybe—given more luck than he deserves—Emily's response will uncloak the nature of her dilemma.

Orville owns plenty of restaurants, but he's no restaurateur. He is old money. Orville's family wealth goes back so many generations he views his enormous privilege as inherent in the natural order of things. Working for Orville through college and graduate school had kept Emily fed, but it wasn't nearly enough to pay for her education. She had graduated magna cum laude and loaded with debt. As manager, she now has the power to reserve the most lucrative server shifts for herself. This power is a trap—and she knows it. Her expensive degrees in molecular biology hadn't attracted one job that pays as well. How will she ever afford to pursue her passion for stem cell research?

Orville delights in the power he wields over Emily. He grinds his jealousy of her brains and talent into tirades. John has become inured to Emily's frequent grumbling about Orville's barrage of attacks on her management style, the employees she hires, the way she dresses, her choice of background music...every tiny decision she makes. Tonight, Emily is different. Angry, yes. Exasperated, perhaps. But the pain is deeper. John secretly probes his memory of tonight's dinner searching for any hint of what Emily had said. Nothing.

Meanwhile, Emily, who had been lost in reliving today's misadventures while conveying them to John, can finally detect what is going on. John's attention had not been with her. His sudden *theatre of concern* is heating her blood to the boiling point.

Let's see how long he can keep this pathetic charade going.

Emily cannot discern whether the anger welling up inside her is aimed at John or Orville. Or *neither*? Rage invigorates her—like hating the villain in a thriller. She cannot resist the tangy taste of fury provoked by Orville's lunacy that had undermined her authority and sabotaged his own restaurant.

Emily took the day shift so she could go out with John tonight. Orville popped in—as he often does—right after the heat of the lunch rush, which was busier than expected for some mysterious reason. Emily's normally accurate prediction of the restaurant's business (a source of pride) was off today. Her usual distaste for Orville's abrupt appearance was closer to dread, owing to the restaurant's disarray after having been overwhelmed for the past couple of hours. As expected, Orville complained about trivial things: chairs not evenly spaced, the server station not fully stocked with coffee cups, a prep cook who had delivered a large pot to the sink without having captured the last teaspoon of soup from it with a rubber spatula.

"I've had a wonderful idea," proclaimed Orville excitedly.

Please, God, no! Not today. Emily offered a bland smile.

Orville proceeded to move tables. He slapped his hand down onto a solid oak round table for eight. "I detest this table," he protested. "It ruins the feng shui in here."

Scanning the dining room, he zeroed in on Fiona, a short, slight teen with alabaster skin, jet-black hair, and bright blue eyes. Fiona had arrived early for her dinner shift and was hiding at a back corner table behind a mug of coffee, hoping not to be noticed. "Help me put it out on the deck for now."

Orville and Fiona struggled to lift it. An ominous wobble slammed it into the trim as they headed out the door to the deck that had been closed for winter. A thud resonated through the deck when they released it, panting.

What does he expect me to do with that table overnight?

Orville returned triumphantly with Fiona in tow. The pair set about shoving together two square tables for two, making a single rectangular table.

"Put a cloth over the whole thing," he ordered. "We ought to be able to get six around this one, don't you think, Em?"

Emily hated being called "Em." She stopped, looked behind her and smiled at the Bradleys, a lovely elderly couple who were regulars—and generous tippers. Emily had planned on seating the Bradleys at one of the two tables Orville had commandeered. She scanned the room, and headed toward another table feigning confidence, hoping the Bradleys would assume this is where she had planned to seat them all along. The

Bradleys were holding hands—married 52 years and still giggling like teenagers. They knew perfectly well what was happening but pretended not to notice. Emily was none the wiser.

"They were supposed to be in my section," protested Wayne as he swished by with a tray of drinks.

"What do you want me to do?" Emily's voice was hardly above a whisper. "Look!" Her head and eyebrows shot in Orville's direction. "Just take the Bradleys here. I'll let Regina know."

Wayne rolled his eyes as he cruised toward his section, the tray of drinks appearing to float above him like a tiny alien city atop a flying saucer.

Emily approached Orville, who was about to remove another table. Fiona, half in shock, scurried toward the restroom, relieved that Emily had released her from Orville's frenzied clutches.

"Can we talk?" asked Emily.

"What's up, Em?"

"What's up, O? We have a reservation for eight tonight. I had them at table 14, but now it's gone. I just had to seat the Bradleys in Regina's section. They were supposed to go to Wayne today."

"Wayne can take them where they are. And I don't like your tone."

"Jesus, Orville. I can't have you moving tables—*removing* tables— in the middle of a busy day. Can't you see we're trying to get caught up and ready for dinner?"

"You can't have me blah-blah-blah," Orville mocked Emily's tone. "Who do you think you are?"

"I'm the manager. I'm responsible for—"

"You're *my* manager." Orville was fond of interrupting people like a Supreme Court Justice during oral arguments. "And yes, you're responsible for keeping this place running smoothly. Now, by the look of things today, you're having a bit of trouble with that, hmm?"

"How am I supposed to keep this place running smoothly when you waltz in here and change the table layout—in the middle of the day? While we're open? Where am I supposed to put tonight's party of eight?" Emily's pitch and volume rose with each question. "Now I have to go rearrange all the reservations…all the sections…the table numbers…"

"Lower your voice, Em. There's people."

"Don't call me Em!" shouted Emily.

The dining room was suddenly hushed. Orville glared at Emily. He motioned for her to follow him to the deck.

Pointing at the dent in the trim made by the heavy oak table, he admonished, "You'd better get that fixed."

Heat radiated from Emily's red face as she marched toward the deck. Orville pushed through the deck door. A cold, harsh wind attacked Emily. She winced.

"Emily, we've talked about this." Orville's unusual calm infuriated Emily all the more. "You really need to get those emotions of yours under control."

Emily slammed the deck door shut. Every day for months, she had worried about what Orville would think of every little thing she does. Now she was prepared to tell him what she thought. Prepared, but unwilling. *He's not worth the breath it takes to tell him off.*

"I'm done." Emily's words made the decision for her.

"Done?"

"Done." Emily turned her back to Orville, heading for the deck door.

"Don't you walk away from me when I'm speaking to you."

Leaving one hand on the door, Emily faced Orville to stare him down. "I can't take this anymore!" Both hands pointed at Orville. "I can't take *you* anymore."

"People talk, you know. Boston's restaurant scene is tightly-knit. You don't want to burn any bridges, Hon."

Emily sighed, unnerved by how the tables had turned.

I'm usually the one remaining calm while Orville is on his tirade. What's happening to me?

"Why don't you take the rest of the day off," offers Orville, continuing his calm reply. "I'll have Martin relieve you." Martin is the office manager with a tiny ownership stake that absurdly motivates him to follow Orville's every whim.

"Fine."

He's such a smarmy prick. There's only half an hour left to my shift and he wants me to be grateful? Ugh!

"I'll see you tomorrow."

"Whatever." Emily pulled the deck door, slipped through, and moved somberly toward the kitchen to collect her purse and coat. Every step she took with her left foot hardened her resolve to quit. Each right-footed step landed with a question: *What about my staff? Wayne? Regina? My customers? The Bradleys? John? Where else could I make the money I'm making here?*

The entire dining room stared at her as if she were on a walk of shame. Fury incited resolve to keep searching until she landed on the right decision. Her head cleared. Humiliation faded. She allowed herself to be filled with empathy and support brimming from each person who silently acknowledged her as she passed by.

Upon entering the kitchen, she encountered Wayne. He set his tray aside and stood in her path, arms extended. She accepted his invitation. Their tender embrace revived her faith in herself.

"Call anytime," offered Wayne in a soft, compassionate voice.

Reliving today's tribulation brings Emily's true dilemma into focus. *I'm angry with myself for getting angry at Orville and that makes me even angrier. It's a feedback loop—a vicious cycle. John is oblivious. Look at him! Now I'm getting angry at myself for being angry at John. I really think I'm going to burst into flames!*

Emily's sudden focus on John catches his attention. Instead of straining to remember Emily's story (since he hadn't heard it in the first place), he might as well employ his recent training by attempting to connect with her energy. *What have I got to lose?*

He takes a breath. Emily's anger rushes in consuming all of John's distracting thoughts, leaving his mind startingly quiet. His throat burns as if he's inhaling fire darting off a torch. A frantic question approaches from the back of his head.

Before the question makes its way to his full consciousness, John lets the fire fall down to his heart, where it expands. He obeys his impulse to relax and surrender. The fire falls down to the base of his spine, then rises up his spine to the top of his head. For the very first time, John's training automatically takes charge, sparking a flow and resonance with the Life Field.

Emily's fury ignites John's lust for danger, the amalgam taking on a new character—a new power—vying to control them both. For now, John is able to surrender each emotion as it arises. Their volatile mix expands. John's chest tightens. He braces for pain. Euphoria arises instead. He reaches his hand across the table. Emily extends her fingers. The beauty of her hand invites him to caress it. Clear, smooth skin. Long, slender fingers ending in clear, natural nails, elegantly shaped to enhance her glamour without stealing the show. Even the creases of her knuckles evoke an aesthetic pleasure. Emily's hands are strong yet soft as a silk scarf.

"Let's talk about this on the way home," suggests John.

"OK." Emily tightens her grip on John's hand.

"Lava cake for you two love birds." The waiter stands before them, holding two plates, each with half the dessert. He appears unable to reach across their clasped hands, as if a force field is preventing him. John and Emily release each other, retract their hands to their laps, sit up straight, and smile nervously at the waiter.

"For you, my dear." The waiter's eyes stay with Emily's as he lays the plate in front of her with a subtle flourish. His warm, friendly connection had been effortless—and most manipulative.

I haven't seen her eyes sparkle at me like that in weeks.

"And for you, sir." John's plate arrives with a polite, stiff, mundane effort.

"Enjoy." Gazing at Emily, the waiter presses his hands together in the shape of a Namaste greeting. Emily returns the greeting, adding a smile. The waiter remains until Emily's eyes dismiss him by taking aim at her dessert.

He just nabbed her right in front of me...because he can!

Emily devours her lava cake in a few large mouthfuls.

"You're not gonna finish yours?" mumbles Emily. Her full red lips guard the dark chocolate rolling around behind her perfect teeth.

"Nah. Let's go home." Rage had devoured John's appetite.

The waiter appears—a black leather check presenter in hand. Emily draws her card from her purse like a sword from its scabbard and offers it to the waiter before he can place the check on the table.

"Right away." He vanishes.

Emily glances at John's plate. "If you're not gonna..."

"No. Go ahead." John slides his plate across the table filling the gap opening as Emily slides hers to one side. With this simple maneuver, John relinquishes the last full measure of control he may have had over his life.

Go ahead, girl. Take it all. My dignity, my sovereignty, my manhood.

The waiter returns, smiles at Emily, and hands her the check. "Have a wonderful evening." He nods politely to John.

Did I just hear him grunt?

Emily produces a $20 bill from her purse. With one hand, she opens the check presenter, swaps the twenty for her credit card, and closes it with a single fluid motion, displaying the dexterity of a magician performing a card trick—all the while her other hand is cutting a piece of John's lava cake and sliding it past her moist lips.

"Mmm…that's good." Emily licks her lips deliciously clean. She rises with grace and a satisfied smile not directed at anyone in particular. "Ready?"

Poise is one of Emily's traits John finds most attractive. Tonight, he is confounded by how much it infuriates him. *Is this jealousy?*

"Yup. Let's go."

Emily struts toward the door like a model on a runway. The insouciant sway of her auburn hair intimidates John as he follows awkwardly behind. Does the sensation of everyone watching stem only from his imagination? John pretends not to notice the waiter's smoldering stance, his eyes following them.

"You should just quit that stupid job," proclaims John as he steps through the door, bracing for assault by the raw night air.

Emily stops, waiting for John to catch up. She whips around to face him—nose to nose.

"And how did you come to this brilliant conclusion? Was it your thorough analysis of my finances? Your studied insight into my emotional well-being? Your consummate understanding of how my leaving would affect everyone I work with? My customers? You? Or maybe your precious

Jimmy D found me a research job...hmm?"

"Jimmy D's not going to find you a job," quips John.

"Of course, he's not. He can't even get you one. But he's got you brainwashed to the point where you're ready to join his...*cult*."

"Shhhht!" John raises his hands as if to catch Emily's last incriminating phrase before it flies over their heads and escapes into the night. Glancing left and right, he whispers, "Emily. Lower your voice. There's people." It's a loud whisper, pushing enough air through his throat to attack Emily's frosty face with a hot, garlic-spiked wind.

"Ooh...you men are all alike!" shouts Emily. She whirls around and marches toward the corner.

John grabs her arm from behind. "Don't you walk away from me."

Emily shoves his hand off her arm as she walks. "Get your hands off me!"

John picks up his pace. By the time they round the corner, he's directly beside her. "What on earth is wrong with you?" John has heard these scolding words before—from his mother. He never thought he'd hear them cross his own lips.

"You! This!" Emily attempts a fuller explanation using indecipherable gestures.

"What do you mean, *This*?" John exaggerates Emily's gestures, mocking them.

"Och, you are so dense." Emily's head shakes like a Jesus bobblehead on the dashboard of a redneck's pickup.

"You know what your problem is? Huh?" taunts John, "You expect everybody to be a goddam mind reader. You never tell me anything. How am I supposed to know what's going on in that crazy little head of yours? Maybe that's Orville's problem, too. He's probably as frustrated with you as I am."

"I just told you everything! So I was right. You weren't listening. Or maybe you just don't care!" Emily squints, preventing the lion's share of her fury from escaping. Her face flushes.

"You know that's not true. I care a lot."

"Yeah, you care enough to take Orville's side."

"I just told you to quit. How is that taking Orville's side?"

"Don't tell me what to do. You're not my daddy!"

"You're the one who came crying to me, 'What should I do?'"

John's mocking tone strikes a dissonant chord reverberating through Emily, shaking her from the inside out. She picks up her walking pace in the desperate hope of keeping all the pieces of herself from bursting apart and collapsing into a pile of rubble on the sidewalk.

John keeps pace with Emily. "See? This is what you do. You ask my advice, and when I give it to you, you accuse me of siding with Orville or trying to be your daddy, or God knows what."

"So that's your advice. Quit. Just quit. Just like that." The loud, single snap of Emily's finger punctuates her sarcasm.

"Well, you're miserable."

"Have you ever stopped to think why that might be?"

John shrugs, adding a touch of his own sarcasm.

The two of them arrive at their building. They stop. Neither wants to be first to climb the steps.

"Yeah, Orville's a piece o' work," admits Emily, "and my job... the pressure...and putting up with him...it all stresses me out." Her hands arise in a plaintive adagio directed up the steps, "But I used to be able to come back here and feel like I was home...safe...loved...appreciated."

John's eyes follow Emily's hands floating at the end of her graceful arms, dismissing the sarcasm that had followed the couple home. His dry mouth cannot muster a reply. A cold descending fog summons a rose-red glow to Emily's ears and nose and neck. She clasps John's face with her pink, frigid hands. Her green eyes peer through his in search of the sweet, loving heart she hopes still lies buried within her boyfriend.

"John, you've abandoned me. I'm barely an afterthought to you now. You're hardly ever home…and when you are, I feel even more alone than when you're over at Jimmy D's trying to conjure up that *Life Field* of yours. I can't do this anymore. I can't live like this."

John yanks her hands off his face, thrusts them down to her side. "But this is my calling!" His voice is as adamant as it is quiet. "We've been over this." He looks around, making sure nobody is within earshot. "I committed myself to learning how to shape reality and heal people. You told me to 'follow my bliss,' remember? This is my bliss!"

"If this is bliss, give me misery. At least I'd have some company."

"So what do you want me to do…quit?"

"That's what you told me to do."

"Because you're miserable!"

"So are you!"

"No. I'm not miserable. OK, maybe I'm frustrated. I'm struggling. It's not easy, you know. But I *am* making progress."

"Really? Could have fooled me. You come home every night after I'm in bed. You sit in the kitchen and talk to yourself. Then you sneak into bed, sleep a few hours, and get up before me so you can bury your head in that laptop for a couple of hours before going to class. The only time I ever see you is at the restaurant, and you just told me I should quit! What am I supposed to make of that?"

"Didn't we just go out to dinner? Together?"

"You were gone, John…I don't know where you were, but it wasn't with me. I might as well have been dining alone!"

"Fine," avows John, "I'll pay more attention to you. Now, can we go inside? It's freezing out here."

John and Emily ascend the steps together in silence, without touching each other, like a pair of sentries on patrol.

Chapter Six
The Faithful

"WILL THERE BE ANYTHING ELSE, SIR?" asks John. His sharp-dressed rival from the bus is sitting alone. John had made a point of being an extra attentive waiter, hoping to find an opportunity to strike up a conversation. Unlike most lone guests who order only coffee and dessert, he had not been hostage to a newspaper or laptop. He had been present, polite…and mysterious.

"No thank-you. The pie was delicious. I'll take the check, please."

"Right away."

John neglects his other tables, prepares the check, and returns.

"Thank you," says the sharp-dressed man in the manner of some-one whose life had just been saved. He captures John's eyes, arousing a sensation remarkably similar to being in Jimmy's presence. "Take my card. Call me."

All of John's self-control is scarcely enough to hide his shock at the phone number on the card ending in 0000.

This can't possibly be a coincidence. Oh yeah, I'll call him. I must call him. As soon as my shift is done…only a few hours to go. I can do this!

John had been suspicious of Emily's motives for scheduling her shift to begin right before his ended. Now he is grateful he can make the call after his shift…alone. He follows Emily to the kitchen.

"Hey. I'm off. See you at home." John's lips head for her cheek. Emily hoists a tray filled with plates of hot food to her shoulder, blocking John's advance with one elegant motion. The kitchen staff notice nothing.

What just happened?

"OK. Bye," replies Emily in a breathy, hurried voice. She backs into the swinging door, plunging into the dining room. John catches the door before it swings shut. Emily transforms from a busy bee in the frenetic, harshly lit cacophony of the kitchen into an elegant swan upon entering the tranquil, candle-lit splendor of the dining room. Her smooth, sultry voice soars above Mozart's background serenade.

This must be why her tips are so good.

John calls the number on Andrew Raziel, Jr.'s card the moment he leaves the restaurant.

"Hello John," answers the familiar voice before it rings, "Andy here. Very glad you called."

How did he know it was me? I never gave him my cell number. How does he know my name?

"What can I do for you?" asks John, not knowing what else to say.

"Ahh, the more salient question is, *what can I do for you?*"

"Oh?"

"I can only guess what Mister James Douglass has told you. Practice, practice, practice…or some such thing, I imagine. How would you like to speed things up a bit? Explore the true mystery?"

"Well...um..."

"Good. It's settled. Meet me at the address on the card in half an hour. I'll be waiting."

The address leads John to a music club in Cambridge. Andy Raziel waits near the door.

"Follow me," commands Andy as John approaches from the crosswalk. Andy heads for a side door. It opens. A large man with a stern face squared off by an Uncle-Gus-buzz-cut emerges. He holds the door. Andy sweeps through without acknowledging the man, whose eyes remain on the street. John follows. Andy's pace quickens as they descend stone steps into a damp, musty hallway lit by a single gas sconce affixed to a wall of giant granite blocks. The hallway takes a sharp left and ends at a heavy wooden door arched at the top. Andy stops, faces John, extends his hand. John shakes.

"Thank you for meeting me on such short notice," says Andy. "I believe you will find this evening illuminating." Still grasping John's hand, Andy clasps his forearm. "Ready?"

"Ready."

Andy opens the heavy door with due ceremony, bows, and ushers John inside as if presenting a guest to a king holding court. John's mind is clear and quiet, owing to the speed of his recent trek rather than any intentional focus on his part. The warm, softly lit, great room is filled with ornately framed paintings, statues, and tapestries, each with its own dedicated light, like a windowless museum in the heart of a castle. The sweet scent of beeswax reminds John of Jimmy's parlor.

"Welcome, Mister Wells," says Andrew Raziel, Sr., a handsome, fit, middle-aged man with black hair and bronze skin clad in an expertly tailored suit. He stands regally next to a large round table draped in a lush, red, floor-length cloth embroidered with gold. The opulent table is set with fine crystal, sterling silver, gold-rimmed plates with blue and white centers, all surrounded by fresh flowers.

Before the usual flood of thoughts can marshal enough forces to invade his head, John's attention is captured by hearing his surname spoken with such dignity. Until now, he had only heard the phrase *Mister Wells* right before a scolding—usually by his mother.

"My son, Andy, speaks very highly of you."

That's a hell of a compliment. What could Andy have said? That I'm an attentive luncheon waiter?

"Thank you, but—"

"Please, join us for some dinner. You must be starving."

"Sir, I really don't understand." Intrigue snuffs out John's instinct to be alarmed by their correct assumption that he's hungry.

"Please, call me Andrew. Everything will be explained tonight. But first, let us share a meal together."

Dinner was a luxurious affair beyond anything John had ever experienced. The truly memorable seven-course meal was on the level of a Michelin-star restaurant.

Andy and his father were charming, welcoming, and fun. Conversation flowed easily from introductory small talk through science, art, music, technology, philosophy, literature, theatre, women. They laughed, toasted the chef—and each other—as they discovered how well their interests, joys, and values aligned.

"Now that we've gotten to know each other a bit, perhaps you'd like me to tell you why we invited you here tonight," says Andrew.

"Absolutely." During dinner, John had left his mind alone to wander wherever it pleased. Now, he must rein it in to focus on this mystery.

"I'll get straight to the point. We know you've been training with James Douglass and his crew. They're good people, but we think they're misguided."

"So you've been spying on me."

"It's a small community, John," says Andy. "Everybody who channels the Life Field knows about you."

"What? How?"

"The same way Mr. Douglass knows," says Andrew. "Didn't he tell you we've been waiting for you? That we need you?"

"Yeah…"

"How do you think he knew about you?" says Andy.

"Uhh…"

"We've been doing this a long time, John," says Andrew. "Couple thousand years. It's hard to explain. But once you can reliably channel the Life Field, you'll see how it works. And you're close. Very close. That's one reason I thought you'd appreciate a little nudge from Andy and me."

"Nudge?"

"Like I said, we think Mr. Douglass and his crew are misguided. And we're not the only ones. He's got you practicing your breathing, but he hasn't told you the whole story."

"What story?"

"Our story. He told you that by resonating with the Life Field you can channel it to manipulate reality, right?"

Seems like they already know the answer to this. "Yes. That's what he said."

"And he explained the Life Field isn't some kind of magic. It's a force of nature like the electromagnetic force or gravity. And it can be explained by science."

How careful do I have to be with these guys? "Yes, he did."

"Well, if it can be explained by science, might it be discovered by scientists? Imagine if one could invent a machine to harness its power. And what if that machine were to fall into the wrong hands? What then?"

"Hmmm."

"If any government on this earth had control of such a machine, it would develop the most powerful weapon the world has ever known, and it would use that weapon to dominate all of humanity. Is that the future you'd like to see?"

"Of course not."

"And precisely how does Mr. Douglass plan to prevent it?"

"I don't know. He hasn't told me."

"That's because he doesn't have a plan." Andrew's long pause heightens John's intrigue. "In point of fact, he *does* have a plan—and his plan is…to let it happen."

"That can't be. Jimmy D is a good person. He would never let such a thing happen."

"He's a good man, but he's naïve. He honestly thinks that, when scientists discover the Life Field's awesome power, everything will just… *work itself out*." Andrew raises his hands, shaking his head in disbelief. "He seems to have no compunction about breaking his cardinal vow… the vow of secrecy."

"Has he?" asks John.

"Not as far as we know. Did he swear *you* to secrecy?"

"Not in so many words. But I haven't told anyone. And I wouldn't."

"Why not?" asks Andy.

"I just wouldn't. Nobody would believe me anyhow. And what would I say? I don't know how it works. All I've been doing is practicing breathing, trying to resonate and let the energy flow. I haven't a clue how to use it for anything…good or evil."

"I suppose he hasn't told you what's been going on the last 150 years or so—and why we should be concerned now?" asks Andrew.

"Well, he did mention an impending calamity but said I'm not ready for him to explain it *just yet*," sneers John.

"Yes, I suspected as much. Another example of where we part ways."

"So *you* think I'm ready?" John is eager and hesitant in equal measure.

"What do *you* think?"

"Sure." Eagerness wins.

Andrew glances at his son and smiles as if to say, *well done*.

His eyes return to John. "Let us begin by exploring the nature of reality. Most people think of reality in a dualistic way. Something is either real or it isn't. You and I are real. You know you're real. I know I'm real. You and I can see each other. Touch each other. Talk to each other. Therefore, each of us knows the other is real. With me?"

"Yeah…"

"Now, what if tonight is a dream? What if you wake up tomorrow morning and remember this entire evening—all of it—as having been a dream? Am I still real?"

"Oh, c'mon"

"According to Carl Jung, dreams are very real. He said, 'They are pure nature; they show us the unvarnished, natural truth…' So I ask you: is the truth revealed to you through a dream not real?"

"You're twisting Jung's words," retorts John, instinctively rejecting Andrew's reasoning even though his own knowledge of Jung consists of little more than recognizing his name.

"You've heard the phrase, 'seeing is believing?'"

"Of course."

"That is not the way it is at all. The truth is…it's the other way around. What you see and feel and know to be real is informed by what you believe—even if your belief comes from a dream or a wish or something you've been taught. Look no farther than the placebo effect for proof."

"Well…most scientists believe the placebo effect is psychological in nature."

"It's all in your head, right?"

"Sort of."

"Wrong," asserts Andrew. "The placebo effect is evidence of the Life Field. Your reality changes when the Life Field resonates with your belief—belief that a drug or treatment will work, for example. Why do you think researchers in drug trials cannot know which patients get the drug and which get the placebo?"

"Because it would taint the results."

"Exactly. The Life Field is powerful enough to heal a patient by resonating with the researcher's belief that the drug will heal the patient."

John raises his eyebrows and scowls.

"There's plenty of other evidence too. It's been hiding in plain sight since the scientific revolution—and scientists have been on the verge of discovering it since Darwin…about 150 years ago. That's when we really had to intervene if we were to have any hope of safeguarding the secret."

"Intervene?"

"More on that later. Suffice it to say that, at various times since Jesus walked the Earth, we've had to employ a variety of measures to avoid catastrophe."

"Catastrophe?"

"But I suspect you are much more interested in how to use the

Life Field to manipulate reality."

"I'm listening."

"Good. Let us begin at the beginning. Your beginning. Long before you met Mr. Douglass, you felt the Life Field resonate within you. A touch of intuition from time to time. The way music sends shivers up your spine. That tingling sensation when you're with Emily. In truth, everybody feels these flashes of the Life Field now and again. So, in that way, you are no different from anyone else."

"Okay…"

"What *does* make you exceptional, though, is how you've reacted to these feelings. Many people hardly pay any attention at all. Others become addicted to whatever induces them. If they feel resonance in church, they become religious. If they feel it through art or music, they become artists or musicians—or die-hard fans. The church fathers figured out this business well over a thousand years ago. Why do you think they spent all that money and effort to bring extraordinary music and art into the church?"

"To get people to go to church?"

"Because music and art spark resonance with the Life Field. And when people feel that resonance while they're in church, they become addicted to the church; willing to accept whatever the church teaches."

John winces.

"Well, John. Let's have a look at church teachings, hmm? They focus on belief, salvation, moralism, dogma. These teachings place the church fathers squarely at the center of power. It's also a brilliant sleight of hand, distracting believers from the technique Jesus used to resonate with the Life Field—the same technique he taught his disciples. Once they learned how to resonate, he taught them how to channel the Life Field and use it for healing."

"Wow. But—"

"But I digress," interrupts Andrew. "Back to you. You see, Mr. Wells, you have done extraordinary things—things most people never do—at unusually young ages, I might add. You made three remarkable promises to yourself, each provoked by an encounter with the Life Field. You cultivated your visions rather than explain them away as childish fantasies—that's what most people do. You are now training with Mr. Douglass instead of pursuing the career you have been preparing for—and the freedom you have craved—all your life. Most importantly, you have nurtured the resonance *itself* rather than merely seeking out experiences to trigger it. These innate inclinations of yours, among many other things, signal to us that you are the one we've been waiting for. You will help us keep our vow to prevent the wrong people from usurping the power of the Life Field."

"Why can't you do that without me?" inquires John. "You seem to have done just fine for 'a couple of thousand years' as you say—and you still haven't explained how to use the Life Field to manipulate reality."

Andrew turns to Andy. "Son, I believe it is time for Miriam." Andy opens the heavy door. A stunning woman in her forties with long, black, wavy hair, black plum eyes, and skin a bit darker than Andrew's glides through the door. John stands and stares, mouth agape, until he catches himself. He slowly closes his mouth while sucking in enough air to prevent drooling, but not enough to be heard. The breath goes straight to John's head, clearing away any residual effects of the elegant, supple wines served with dinner.

"Miriam, please allow me to introduce Mister John Wells."

"Yes, I've heard quite a bit about you," says Miriam with an accent John cannot place except to identify Middle Eastern overtones. She extends her right hand, palm down, as if it is to be kissed rather than shaken.

John takes her hand delicately in his, raises it up, lowers his head, and forms a kiss without touching his lips to her hand, hoping what he had seen in old movies is what is called for at this moment. Equally as soft and smooth as Emily's, Miriam's skin is thicker, richer, tougher.

"Very pleased to meet you," says John.

Miriam affectionately tightens her grip on John's hand. His eyes shoot up to meet hers. Miriam's gentle, nurturing gaze filters through John's eyes, commanding his attention as if she had his head in her hands.

"You asked me to explain how to use the Life Field to manipulate reality," says Andrew. "Miriam, here, can do one better. She'll show you. She's the best of us."

When Miriam senses John feels safe enough to allow her access to his heart, she gestures toward the ornately carved settee John had assumed was for décor only. "Let us sit together."

They sit at opposite ends, Miriam with her back straight, rotated at the waist to face John. Andrew and his son look on from their perch at the dinner table. Questions fill John's head. Anxiety floods his sore chest. He takes a breath; tries to avoid engaging any of his questions or emotions; tries to relax and surrender. His chest tightens. Pain sharpens.

"That tender spot in your chest. How long has it been bothering you?" asks Miriam.

"How do you know about that?"

Miriam smiles, the glint of a rascal in her eyes.

"Oh. I get it," concedes John. "Couple thousand years of practice and all that."

"Yes, something to that effect. Now, about your tender spot…"

"It's been well over a year. And it's been getting worse. Right now, it really stings."

"It has become part of you, yes?"

"Maybe so."

"And you greet it like…an old friend."

"I wouldn't say, friend."

"Oh? Well then, what would you say?"

"I don't know. It's just there."

"Reliable?" asks Miriam.

"You mean like a friend?"

"You mock me even as you know I speak the truth."

"What are you getting at?"

"This tender spot of yours is just that…yours. You have claimed it. You own it now. It lives within you, and you accept it as part of your reality. But what if your reality were to change? What if you refuse to accept this pain in a new reality?"

"It can't be that simple," insists John.

"Simple…yes. Easy…no." Miriam smiles.

John takes a breath, attempting to calm his trembling.

Miriam matches John's breath. "Letting your reality of pain go may well be the most difficult challenge you have ever faced. You are holding onto it so very tightly." She raises her eyebrows. "But you must let it go. Only then can you accept a new, pain-free reality." Another breath. "I know you can do it. And I will help."

Miriam extends her hand toward John with her first two fingers raised. "May I?"

"Right now?"

"When would be a better time?"

"Oooo…kayyy…"

"You know what to do." Her fingers approach.

Miriam's touch awakens ancient nightmares huddled in the dark. John summons the will to let his fight-or-flight response fall into the flow his breathing had aroused. Wretched nightmares attack, poisoning his flow.

Treacherous currents sweep John toward black rapids, spilling into a pit. John wraps his fingers around the iron gates to his schoolyard, holding fast against the currents with all his might. Howling nightmares taunt him, grazing his body as they swirl around his hands, daring him to let go of the gates. All at once, they swoop down to guard a glow forming at the bottom of the pit. Focusing on the glow fills John with lust for a new, pain-free reality. He releases the iron gates and dives through the screaming nightmares into the pit. The glow embraces John, leaving the rapids and the nightmares behind. The pain is gone...as if it had never existed. No bolt of lightning. No dramatic victory doubling him over as had happened at Jimmy's. He simply cannot imagine any other reality.

Chapter Seven
Crossroads

EMILY IS WORRIED. For the past six days, John has been hiding out in their apartment. He has not left for class. Nor for work. Nor has he spoken to her. He called in sick—that is, if you consider leaving a message on her phone, when he knew she could not answer, a proper notification of his absence. Listening to his voicemail was the last time Emily heard him speak. The only sounds to come from John's mouth have been demented grunts, moans, and sighs, each one more disquieting than the last. Worse yet, John is avoiding her. He's asleep—or pretending to be—whenever Emily arrives home from work, which is later every day since Orville had surprisingly offered her a substantial raise if she would help him open a new restaurant.

Emily is particularly disturbed by the many times she has woken in the still of the night to an empty bed. She'd find John motionless, staring at his laptop. On the few occasions when Emily tried to speak to him, John waved her off without disengaging his head from the screen.

A few days ago, while John was sleeping, Emily surreptitiously opened his laptop to see if she could discover what he'd been up to. No luck. He had changed his password.

So...he no longer trusts me?

What puzzles Emily the most is her own reaction to all of this. She expects herself to be furious.

Hadn't John promised to be more present with me? Spend more time with me? What happened to that?

She knows she ought to be angry. She has a right to be angry. Inexplicably, though, she doesn't feel angry.

Has worry supplanted my anger?

Perhaps it is something else.

This morning, Emily awakens to an unusual sense of calm. Her head is clear. She coasts through her morning routine, preparing for a demanding day of struggle to keep Orville focused. John is fast asleep—or pretending to be. She kisses him gently on the forehead. He reacts like a dead man. Emily holds her breath, listening for John's breathing. She exhales upon hearing it, moves silently toward the door, and stops to blow John a kiss he cannot see before exiting. Emily is carried to the "T" subway station by a mysterious force that follows her throughout the day. Several times, while engaged in fast-paced, challenging work, she pauses, touches her new inner friend, and returns to the task at hand. Nobody is the wiser.

Upon arriving home, she opens the door with care—the kind of care you take when trying not to wake a sleeping baby. John is sitting at the kitchen table, wide awake. She grasps the hand he had extended when she snuck through the door.

"I'm so sorry, my Love," breathes John.

"Oh, John!" Emily dissolves into tears.

They embrace, clinging to each other for dear life as if letting go would plunge them both into the abyss. When their clutch is finally released, they sit cautiously, still attached by one hand.

"I don't know what came over me. I don't even know who I am any more. I really don't know how you can put up with—"

"Shhhhhhhh…" Emily tenderly places two fingers onto John's lips. Her gentle touch, the soft aroma of her elegant fingers, her sympathetic eyes—all align to bathe John in a love unique to Emily.

Back when Emily's ice-cream-kiss liberated John's joy and awakened this unique love, John logged it—a practice begun in childhood to cast milestones from his most profound experiences. And he gave it a name. "Emily's Love."

Emily's Love sustained John's sanity during the six-day attack by a thousand self-destructive demons. They tempted him to escort them into his reality using every means imaginable—fair and unfair. His training alone could not keep them at bay. Only by calling upon Emily's Love did he find the wherewithal to let them go.

Gratitude for saving him from any of a thousand horrendous ends overcomes John, giving him a new moment to log.

This gratitude feels even better than Emily's Love; better than Jimmy D's bliss; better than Miriam's new reality. I want to live in this gratitude forever…make this my new reality!

"It's OK, John," says Emily in her deep, hushed voice. "I'm here. I love you."

Emily's Love soothes John until panic encroaches on gratitude. "But what do I do now?"

"Just tell me everything." Emily's comforting voice lowers the panic level. "You're not alone. We can do this."

"Och, where to start!"

"At the beginning. Isn't that where they always say to start?"

"I don't even know where that is. My life is spinning. There's no beginning. No…just spinning."

"Okay. Tell me where you are right now."

"I'm here. In the kitchen. With you."

"Funny."

"No…really! That's all that matters. Honestly, that is *all* I want."

"So you're gonna sit here…in this kitchen…for the rest of your life."

"Don't play stupid."

"Moi? No…I'm not playing at anything. I just want you to tell me what you *really* want?"

"You want me to spell it out for you?"

"Like I'm a six-year-old."

"I want *you*. That's all I know right now. Everything else is irrelevant."

"Very romantic, my dear." Emily's sarcasm is softened by her smooth hand caressing his unshaven cheek. Her eyes appear brighter green than usual. "John, whatever is going on inside you *is* most assuredly relevant. I don't care where you start. But you must start talking."

"Fine." John sits up straighter. "Here's the thing: all my life, I've been watching the internet evolve from this arcane tool only geeks know about to the most transformative communication revolution since the alphabet. I spent years developing a theory about its future, its evolution. Then I spent months tracking down Jimmy D because it looked like he was smack dab in the middle of everything internet. And what happened when we finally got to talk about my future in tech? Well…let's just say he had other ideas. Now, I'll admit the prospect of learning how to manipulate reality is pretty cool, but at what cost? I can't lose my sanity. And I certainly can't lose you."

"Oh, John. I'm not going anywhere. You're the one who's been living on some other planet for the past few weeks. I've been trying to get to you, but you won't let me in."

John stands, his arms open. "Well, come on in then. It's a mess in here, Babe, but it's all yours if you want it."

From her seat, Emily tucks her head into John's chest and grabs him around the middle. "So, what's been going on since your mystery meeting?"

"Oh, that."

"Yeah…that. You've been kinda scary."

"Yeah, I guess I've been a bit aloof."

"Aloof? No. You've been gone. G-O-N-E gone. M.I.A. There was no John there."

"Alright, alright."

"So…what happened?"

"I met these people who showed me how to alter reality."

"Wait…what? Jimmy D's people?"

"No. That's the thing. They're not Jimmy D's people. Well…they were until right after Darwin published 'On the Origin of Species.' That's when the group Jimmy D belongs to split off from the others over a pretty major disagreement."

"What kind of disagreement? How did you meet these other people?"

"Remember that single guy at Table 7 the last day I worked?"

"Oh…the tall, dark, handsome, hot, dreamy hunk of a—"

"Yah. Him. His name is Andy. He's a member of The Faithful. The original group."

"By *original group*, you mean the lineage of personal training that began with Jesus instructing his disciples."

"Look, I know it sounds crazy…but…yes."

"Okay…" Emily can no longer hide her skepticism.

"Andy invited me to meet with him and his father, who seems to be in charge now. They're afraid Jimmy D and his crew, who call themselves *The Disciples*, are about to ruin everything."

"How?"

"By letting science discover the Life Field."

"And how do they propose to stop that?"

"They want me to stop it."

"Really?" Emily stands. She grabs both of John's arms as if she needs them for balance.

"Yup. They're worried. What if somebody were to connect the dots among all the new discoveries happening in all fields of science? They might see a big picture—and get a glimpse of the Life Field—or at least a hint of where to look. We've seen how the speed of discovery increases every day. Information flow too. All this increases the chance of the Life Field falling into the wrong hands."

Emily closes her eyes. Shakes her head. Breathes. Opens her eyes.

"Now…they think my work on internet evolution can be used to keep scientists focused on their own narrow specialties—so they won't be tempted to look at the big picture. And I would get to use The Faithful's insanely great computers connected to the fastest internet on Earth. Plus, they have people I can train to help me. It's a hundred times better than my greatest dream job."

"Let me get this straight." Emily is incredulous. "You think you can change the course of scientific research by manipulating the internet?"

"Look…all science relies on the internet, now. Scientists keep their data in the cloud. Even their software is moving to the cloud. They apply and get approval for funding on-line. Preprint servers host all the new research. New on-line chat systems keep popping up…"

"So you're going to manipulate what they see? Alter their data?"

"Geez, Emily. You know me better than that. I'm not gonna be sitting there all day manipulating data. Besides, there's a torrent of new data every minute. That's not practical. And it would be wrong. No. I'm going to develop systems to connect scientists with everyone else in their field—people they never would have met otherwise—and make it easier for all of them to find data and papers and results from each other."

"Well…that kinda sounds like a good thing."

"It *is* a good thing. And it has the added benefit of keeping scientists focused on their own specialties because they'll be rewarded with kudos from other scientists, more articles published, more work in their field, more funding, more…whatever. In essence, I'll be enhancing what The Faithful have been doing for the past five hundred years."

"Oh, will you, now?" Emily raises her eyebrows, tilts her head, and impersonates John's mother. "So, Johnny, exactly what *have* The Faithful been doing for the last five hundred years?"

"This is no joke, Emily. Listen…during the age of exploration, The Faithful realized that European discoveries of new lands and peoples, along with scientific advancements all over the world, could lead to the Life Field's discovery by people who are very smart, but not necessarily committed to using the power for good. So, The Faithful used their considerable influence to encourage kings and queens and tyrants to institute schools and colleges to train smart people as specialists and give them important jobs rooted in their specialty. It worked brilliantly. Nobody went looking for a big picture because everybody was too successful at their own specialty."

"This sounds like Buckminster Fuller's *Great Pirates* theory."

"Absolutely. Fuller got the concept right. Turns out it wasn't any great pirates. It was The Faithful protecting the secret power Jesus taught his disciples so it wouldn't fall into nefarious hands. Today, the ease and speed of communication are increasing at such a furious pace that colleges and universities no longer control the flow of information. That's where I come in."

"How can you be so sure some geek somewhere won't stumble into the big picture. I mean, you've got teenagers hacking the pentagon, right?"

"Ahhh...I thought you'd never ask. That's the other half of my job. I'm going to seed the Internet with artificial intelligence that will redirect anyone who might stumble onto evidence of the Life Field to see something else instead—something they already believe in. In essence, I'll be using the placebo effect, which, ironically, is evidence of the Life Field. Crazy, isn't it?"

"Whoa! Hold on there, cowboy. Your expertise is computers and AI. What makes you think you can blithely jump into my field? I've got more degrees than you do. Don't forget that."

John smiles for the first time in over a week.

"Anyhow, why do you think the placebo effect has anything to do with this scheme of yours?"

"Because people see what they believe. Everybody's reality is rooted in their beliefs. Not only what you're taught to believe by your parents or school or church. I'm talking about the beliefs at the core of your being. Look...you believe you're Emily and I'm John, and we're both real, right?"

"Of course. So?"

"OK. So...who is Emily—the *real* Emily?"

Emily mumbles, "Oh, come on."

"Don't answer. Just think about it for a minute. Actually, try to feel it instead. Feel what it's like to *be* Emily."

John and Emily sit in silence for a few minutes. John takes a long, slow, deep breath. Emily matches it.

John interrupts Emily's attempt to respond before she can get any words out. "There's no answer that words can convey, is there?"

Emily shrugs.

"But you *do* feel it, don't you? The real Emily. You can feel her. You know she's there. It's you. And you know who she is."

"Well…yes."

"That's the core of your being. And…it's your link to the Life Field. Even if you never attempt to resonate with the Life Field, some of it seeps through, and you feel it once in a while—as intuition, or love, or déjà vu, or that aha moment you've had so many times in the lab."

"Yeah, why do you think I'm dying to get a job in stem cell research? I want more of those aha moments."

"Exactly! And you believe the feeling you experience in those aha moments arises from your discovery, from practicing science. That's because you believe you're a scientist. And all your degrees back up your belief that you're a scientist. You even call yourself a scientist—even though you're managing restaurants these days."

"Hey!" Emily impersonates John's mother again, throwing John a stern look.

"Sorry." John pops a quick peck onto her cheek. "The point is: when you have an aha moment, what you're really feeling is resonance with the Life Field. You don't experience it that way because the sensation is filtered through your belief."

"I don't know…"

"Ahh…but, Emily, you *do* know. You certainly know how belief affects drug trials."

"Oh, so we're back to the placebo effect?"

"Yeah, we are. Because you've dealt with this. You've designed double-blind studies. You wrote a brilliant paper on the nocebo effect. You know, that one showing how gluten sensitivity can arise in people simply because they *believe* they're allergic. So…what do you think is the source of the placebo effect?"

"I don't know. Nobody knows. Besides, we never covered that in grad school."

"Of course you didn't. Because education was designed a long time ago to keep you focused on your specialty so you wouldn't see the big picture."

John holds both of Emily's shoulders until their eyes lock. "Now… imagine if you could tap into the Life Field's power and use it to alter reality. That's what happened to me at what you call my *mystery meeting*. My reality changed." He touches his chest. "This spot in my chest no longer aches. It's been healed. A woman did it and showed me how."

"A woman? I thought you said there were no women involved, and that bothered you."

"Yes, I did. There were no women at my initiation with The Disciples. But Andrew from The Faithful said this woman was their best healer."

"Healer?" says Emily sarcastically.

"Healer," confirms John.

Emily's sarcasm turns to scorn. "Like one of those faith healers on TV?"

"No, actually. Nothing like that. In fact, you really do it yourself. She was only a guide. There was no sudden flash; no shaking; no fainting like you see on TV. I embraced a new reality where there's no pain in my chest. And now…there's no pain in my chest."

"It can't be that simple," insists Emily.

"It is *absolutely* that simple. But it's not easy. When she touched my chest, she released a thousand years of pain and terror. If it hadn't been for my weeks of training with Jimmy D, I would have been consumed by it all. Even if I had survived, madness would have overcome me."

"Madness, huh?" Emily lowers herself into the chair. "What, specifically, did Jimmy D teach you to do?"

John sits. "Focus on my breath, quiet my mind, start a flow."

"And with that, you defeated a thousand years of pain and terror?"

"No, no. You don't defeat it. That's not how it works. When you're in a state of flow, you resonate with the Life Field…and while you're resonating, you can let anything go."

"So you just let a thousand years of pain and terror go? Just like that?"

"Well…no. There's more to it. Hard to describe."

"Try. I'm asking because I ran across some research when I was writing my thesis. This guy proposed that trauma could be passed down through generations. I mean, how else do you explain a thousand years of pain and terror? You're not that old, my love."

John chuckles. "You mean passed down genetically?"

"Sort of. It's a fairly new field. They call it epigenetics."

"And what does this have to do with me? You think the pain in my chest was caused by some sort of ancient family trauma?"

"I don't know. Maybe. Your grandfather won't talk about the war. Your mom doesn't remember her childhood. Then there's your Great-Uncle Gus…"

"Yeah, he's never talked about anything."

"And who knows what your ancestors endured. If you've stumbled upon a way to modify gene expression, it would have profound implications for molecular biology."

"Oh, Emily. This is *way* bigger than *molecular* biology." John pauses until Emily smirks and shakes her head. "I modified reality itself."

Emily closes her eyes, takes a breath. "OK, so Jimmy D gave you the training you needed to quiet your mind and resonate with the Life Field. But Andrew and his dad have this woman—"

"Her name is Miriam,"

"Miriam…who uncovered your hidden pain and helped you find the power to overcome it and alter your reality. And they think Jimmy D is dangerous."

"Crazy, isn't it!" *Emily always wants me to talk, but this hasn't gotten us anywhere, has it?*

"Do you think Jimmy D and Simon and Dr. Z are trying to trick you?"

"Do you?" John is alarmed.

"Have they lied to you?"

"Not as far as I know."

"And Jimmy D found you, nurtured you, trained you—"

"I know, right?" interrupts John. "I feel like I owe it to him."

"What…what do you think you owe Jimmy?"

"I don't know. Maybe nothing. Maybe everything." John dissolves into tears. "I don't know anything."

"John…" Emily cradles his chin in her hand and waits until his eyes rise to meet hers, "at the very least, you owe him a chance to explain himself. Why don't you confront him? Maybe then you'll know what to do."

Chapter Eight
The Disciples

"GOOD TO SEE YOU, JOHN." Jimmy D is not surprised to see John. Nor is he surprised that John had missed a full week of training. "Are you ready to continue?"

"Sure," answers John before he can think of anything else to say.

Jimmy had prepared their customary snack and placed it on his table in the corner between them. The two men share the food as they have done before every other training session.

"Tell me about Andy Raziel and The Faithful," demands John.

"Ah, yes. So you've met with them?"

"Oh yeah."

"And what did you think of them?"

"Well…what worries me is what they think of you."

"How so?" inquires Jimmy with no hint of worry in his voice.

"They say you're a good man, but naïve and dangerous."

"That sounds about right."

"What do you mean, *about right?*"

"I mean…your observation is correct. That is what they think of me."

"So you're prepared to break your cardinal vow of secrecy?"

"No. And I haven't. Did they tell you I had?"

"Well…no, actually."

"John, The Faithful act out of fear. They are terrified that some nefarious person or group will harness the power of the Life Field and use it for evil. And that will mean the end of the world."

"And you're not worried about that happening?"

"I'm not crazy about the idea. But I'm certainly not going to waste valuable time and energy worrying about it."

John's eyes widen in disbelief.

"Look, since the beginning of human history, people have harnessed all sorts of powers, haven't they? Take fire, for instance. We use it for light and heat and cooking and transportation. But it can also be used as a weapon. Not to mention accidental fires. They kill thousands of people a year. Transportation kills even more. Humans harnessed fire a million years ago. Did that end the world? Of course not. Same is true for electricity, lasers, microwaves, nuclear. Powerful forces. Dangerous. Used for both good and evil. All these forces harnessed by humans and the world is still spinning; although I sometimes wonder if it might all end in a fiery nuclear holocaust. Then again, we have survived the threat of annihilation for more than half a century."

"So what do you think would happen if some nefarious person or country or terrorist discovers the Life Field?"

"I honestly don't know. It *is* hard to see how any good could come of it. But humanity will muddle through, as we always do. The Faithful worry too much about me. I am certainly not going to publish anything divulging our technique, and neither are you."

"Then why didn't you swear me to the vow of secrecy?"

"Because I know you have the good sense not to say anything—except to Emily, of course. And that's fine."

So, he knows I've told Emily...or does he? Maybe he's trying to find out.

"In any event," continues Jimmy as if he hadn't said anything out of the ordinary, "it isn't so much a vow as it is a long-standing practice adopted by the original disciples in order to—"

"You mean, going back to Peter, Andrew, James, and John. That would be *very* long-standing," interrupts John.

Jimmy ignores the sarcasm. "Yes, it is—and for good reason. You see, Jesus never intended to start a church. Or, Heaven forbid, a religion. He was more like a shaman or a mystic who helped raise our consciousness to a higher level—above reason and will—where we transcend fear, greed, self-interest, xenophobia, religious moralism, and arbitrary rules so we can accept everyone—heal everyone, regardless of who they are or what they believe."

The wariness John had brought with him is slowly melting.

"Alas, it took less than a generation for a hierarchy of clergy to emerge within every little group of Jesus' followers. These men began developing orthodoxy, making rules, building structure, adopting an identity that excluded people—even other followers of Jesus. The original disciples abhorred these power structures. They kept the technique they learned from Jesus out of any writings so it wouldn't fall into the hands of people seeking power."

John offers a quizzical gaze.

"Even though they may be good people, anyone seeking power will eventually succumb to the temptation to misuse it."

John nods in tentative agreement.

"The disciples chose a tiny group of extraordinary people to be their students—people who could be trusted with tremendous power. Each disciple vowed to teach only those students how to channel the Life Field. And they insisted their students vow to do the same. This practice continues today."

"So, you're saying the Bible intentionally obscures the true essence of the teachings of Jesus?"

"Did my compliment go straight over your head?"

"Oh. Sorry. No...well...maybe. I get it. Thank you. I'm honored. Really, I am."

"You should be." Jimmy stares at John for a moment.

John takes a breath.

"So," continues Jimmy, "as it happens, most people tend to prefer writings that profess their beliefs—and since powerful people chose and edited the books of the Bible, you see many allusions to 'power' and 'authority.' Ironically, most of those passages were originally veiled references to the Life Field flowing through Jesus. It's no accident that you see no description of the technique Jesus used to access and resonate with the Life Field. Or the technique he taught his disciples."

"But, isn't that what prayer is?"

"Prayer is talking. The Life Field flows through silence."

"What about silent prayer?"

Jimmy smirks. "It's still your mind talking. John, you know perfectly well, the Life Field can only flow when your mind is quiet."

John's attempt to ask another question produces a mere grunt.

"Think about it—all those Bible stories beginning with Jesus sitting or teaching or eating with his disciples...and then one of them asks a question or others arrive or something happens...and that leads to the rest of the story. Whatever Jesus was teaching before the story begins is not written. Then there's Luke's telling of the Lord's Prayer, in which Jesus teaches it privately to his disciples. Haven't you ever wondered what transpired between Jesus and his disciples during all those private moments?" A glint of the answer escapes Jimmy's eyes.

"Well, yes, actually. But nobody ever talks about it, and the point of the story or parable usually revolves around faith or—"

"Exactly," interrupts Jimmy. "Instead of teaching the technique, the gospels teach faith—and people in power love nothing more than for their flock to have faith in a dogma they control."

"Let me get this straight: the original disciples believed the technique they learned to harness the Life Field's power was so dangerous they didn't write it down; and they made their students vow not to write it down; and that was two-thousand years ago, when nobody had access to any technology advanced enough to harness this power and dominate the world."

"Sounds about right."

"And now, when that technology does exist, you don't feel the need to do anything to prevent the Life Field from falling into the wrong hands?"

"We've been taking steps to prevent people with technology from discovering the Life Field for 500 years. Didn't Andy tell you about all the ways we've intervened?"

"Yeah, he did, in pretty general terms. Then he told me his ingenious plan. Maybe *you* don't think so, but he believes I can use the Internet and AI to prevent discovery of the Life Field."

"Oh, I don't doubt you have the skills to do such a thing. Did Andy disclose the rest of his scheme? The escalation he and his henchmen are planning?"

"Henchmen...? Escalation of what?"

"I gather he neglected to tell you why my people and I left The Faithful."

"Why don't you tell me *your* version of that story?"

"It was getting ugly, John, and harder to maintain. Scientists, artists, musicians—anybody could be targeted if The Faithful thought they might discover the Life Field."

"Targeted?"

"They target whole branches of science with elaborate schemes to discredit them and obscure the truth. It started with our response to Darwin. At that time, we and The Faithful were still a single group, calling ourselves *The Disciples*."

"So you split from them, but you kept the name?"

"Nobody's building a brand here. We're a secret society, remember? But, to satisfy your juvenile curiosity: yes, we kept the name because they changed theirs—as a slap in our faces, insinuating *we* were no longer faithful to Christ."

"Oh...I see." John is, indeed, quite pleased to know the reason for the name difference, his interest piqued by Jimmy's uncharacteristic impatience with the question.

"Back to Darwin. By the 1850s, divisions among us about how much to interfere in exploration and discovery were beginning to sharpen. Many reckoned the pace of science was hastening to a point where the Life Field's discovery was inevitable, and we should focus on preparing for that eventuality rather than trying to stop it. On the other side were those who looked back at eighteen hundred years of success keeping the Life Field out of nefarious hands. We had all witnessed so much evil infecting humans, so much hate and cruelty, such an intense lust for power. For them, allowing the Life Field to fall into the wrong hands was patently unthinkable. In their view, preventing it was paramount, and any action taken in service of that goal was justified, no matter how unpleasant."

"Why Darwin?" asks John. "He didn't publish anything about energy fields."

"Darwin's investigations led him to conclude the Life Field must exist," replies Jimmy. "He was convinced not to write about it by his best friend, Joseph Hooker, whose wife, Frances, was one of us and, as luck would have it, the daughter of Darwin's mentor, giving her plenty of influence. Darwin kept his word to Joseph and Frances, leaving his conclusion out of his scientific works."

Jimmy raises his eyebrows. "Now, his personal writings. They're another matter entirely. They portray a change in his religious thinking away from a personal god. Yet, he did not reject the notion of an underlying spirit."

"Why does that matter?" asks John. "Who cares what his religious beliefs are? And why would you care?"

"Because he hinted at an open question that could inspire scientists to seek the answer. Now…what do you think the answer is?"

John chuckles.

"Most importantly, everybody was paying attention. Darwin sparked a major revolution. He founded a brand-new branch of science."

"Yeah, evolutionary biology. One of Emily's specialties."

"And he utterly upended the philosophy of science. Darwin shattered the notion that a personal god created the world we live in. Every scientist alive at the time—every thinking person, really—was touched by this revolution."

John imagines what it might have been like to read Darwin's work the year it was published.

"Before Darwin, most scientists believed in a personal god; a few were atheists; and neither of those beliefs is likely to arouse a desire to go hunting for the Life Field. If you believe in a personal god, you can attribute every chance encounter with the Life Field to a brief connection with him. Atheists explain those experiences away as a function of the brain."

John wonders what he would have believed had he lived at that time.

"What worried us was the prospect of scientists investigating Darwin's 'mystery of the beginning of all things' as he put it. That led those of us who feared discovery the most to hatch an extraordinarily devious plan—a plan the rest of us simply could not go along with. That's when we split."

"What was the plan?" asks John. "Did they carry it out?"

"Oh, they carried it out, alright—and it worked. They infiltrated the rising Christian Fundamentalist movement in England and the U.S., helping them build major opposition to Darwin's work on both sides of the pond. Decades of increasing opposition kept evolutionary scientists focused on defending it. Otherwise, they might have gone looking for the cause of Darwin's *variations* which would have led them straight to the Life Field…because the Life Field is what causes mutations."

"So…you don't think mutations are random?"

"Nothing is truly random, John. You know that from your tech studies. As it turns out, conservative Christians have grown to become one of The Faithful's strongest unwitting allies. Today, these fundamentalists are vehemently opposed to stem cell research. Now, what do you think coaxes an embryonic stem cell—having the potential to become any cell in the body—to develop into a heart cell or a bone cell or toe cell or a blood cell or a brain cell or anything else?"

"Oh, my God, it's the Life Field," concludes John.

"Aye, you've got it, my boy. You can imagine why The Faithful can't allow *that* discovery anytime soon. So, with a little help from their friends, they convinced President Bush to withhold funding for stem cell research."

"Whoa, they've got some serious reach!"

"Quite. So you see, although my people and I often wonder whether splitting off was the right thing to do, we simply cannot abide this sort of meddling in the affairs of science or the targeting of individuals. If they think you're about to discover the Life Field, you'll be marginalized or eliminated if need be."

"You mean murdered?"

"Too many people, who were poised to discover the Life Field, have met with untimely ends for me to believe they are all a coincidence."

"Like who?"

"Well, Alan Turing, for one. Let's see: he was arrested, prosecuted, and forced to endure chemical castration the same year he published his work on morphogenesis. He died 2 years later. Some say suicide; others say accident."

"My Uncle Gus says he was murdered."

"I think your Uncle Gus is right. And for what? Delaying the inevitable?"

"Is it really inevitable that someone who might abuse it will discover the Life Field?" asks John.

"Probably. It's impossible to know for sure. What I *am* sure of is their plan for you is the wrong plan. It'll work for a while, but it will distract you from your true calling."

"Oh boy…" John is equally intrigued and frustrated.

"You see, over the next couple of decades, the Internet will weave its way into every aspect of our lives. Virtual reality and the Internet of Things will become ubiquitous. Apps we cannot imagine today will be commonplace."

"Yup, that seems like a reasonable prediction. But what does it have to do with me? Specifically, I mean."

"In 20 years, the Internet will develop a consciousness of its own. It will become a sentient being. And *it—the Internet*—will learn to harness the power of the Life Field. By then, the Conscious Internet will be inextricably linked with practically everyone alive, and orders of magnitude more powerful than all the armies on Earth put together."

He's right. If the Internet were conscious, it would have tremendous power—even if it couldn't harness the Life Field.

"I've been studying this for decades," continues Jimmy, "and I think I'm pretty close on the timing, here. What I'm not so sure of is what will the Conscious Internet think when it digests all the data available within itself? How will it feel about us? Humanity, that is. And how will it act toward us? How will it use its omnipotent power?"

Worrisome. The story of humanity told by what's found on the Internet could paint a pretty grim picture of us.

Jimmy pauses until he's sure the moment is ideal.

"John, we need you to speak for humankind. Over the next 20 years, you must prepare yourself to become humanity's liaison with the Conscious Internet. And while you're at it, you need to start influencing the Internet now. Get it to look kindly upon humanity and consider you a personal friend by the time it becomes sentient."

"Now I see why you felt it necessary to compliment me."

Jimmy offers an impish smile.

"And just how do you expect me to pull that off?"

"Oh, you're already on your way, my boy. You've learned how to quiet your mind enough to start and maintain a flow of energy. And how to use your flow to resonate with the Life Field—at least for a couple of minutes. And I suppose it was Miriam who helped you face your demons and open your heart enough to embrace your new reality without that pesky pain in your chest."

"How did you know about that?"

"Really, John? Still feeling compelled to ask irrelevant questions?"

"Fine. So, what would you have me do next?"

"Resume your training. Rise to new levels of consciousness. For weeks you've been lusting after your next level. Now you're there, but you haven't enjoyed a single moment of it."

"What do you mean, *enjoy*?" snarls John.

"Well, my boy, you have many levels to go before you'll reach a point where you can meet the Conscious Internet on its level and be taken seriously. You cannot rise to the next level until you fully absorb the energy of this one. And the only way to absorb the energy of the level you're on is to enjoy it."

"How am I supposed to enjoy anything when you and Andrew are both after me to join your...cults?"

"You could take it as a compliment—the fact we both want you, that is. Learning to enjoy where you are...well, that's another matter entirely."

"Are you saying if I continue training with you, I'll learn to enjoy this level?"

"Yes. This level and every level to come."

"So, you'll teach me the secret of happiness?"

"Jefferson got it right, you know." Jimmy ignores John's cynical tone. "Happiness is a pursuit. That's essentially the secret, right there."

"I've always wondered about that phrase," admits John. His eyes drift toward the ceiling. "But Jefferson's main pursuit was freedom and independence, wasn't it?"

"Well, John, that has been *your* lifelong pursuit, hasn't it? Jefferson was an Epicurean. He strove to conduct himself in a manner that would garner happiness in his own life. He followed the teachings of Epicurus and others—including Jesus, who was, in many ways, an Epicurean himself. Your own single-minded pursuit of freedom and independence has you focused on Jefferson's writings concerning those subjects."

"Yeah, like the Declaration of Independence."

"Touché, my boy," admits Jimmy with a nod of respect. "My point is you may not have paid much attention to some of Jefferson's other writings…and his letters. Jefferson was brilliant and on the verge of discovering the Life Field. He knew the Gospels obscured some of Jesus' teachings. Had it not been for Ben Franklin—and Jefferson's own preoccupation with founding a country—he might very well have discovered it."

"Franklin?"

"Oh, Franklin saw through the Gospel's mask of faith before he was 33. He discovered the Life Field right about the time he was experimenting with electricity. Luckily, one of our people—a member of Franklin's Masonic lodge—convinced him not to write about it. Why do you think it took Franklin so long to publish the results of his kite experiment?"

John lifts his hands, groping for an answer.

"At any rate, thirty years later, we convinced Franklin to keep the secret from Jefferson, and a decade after that he got himself appointed to Louis XVI's commission investigating Mesmer's *magnetic fluid*. Franklin made sure the commission found no evidence of Mesmer's force and concluded any benefit of his treatment arose from the patient's imagination." Jimmy puts the word 'imagination' in air quotes. "Franklin brilliantly deterred scientific exploration of the Life Field by introducing a concept that would later become known as the placebo effect. That single finding has distracted science for over two hundred years."

"You talk as if you were there," says John with quiet awe.

"Very observant, my boy. You see, people like us, who receive wisdom directly from our teachers—wisdom passed down personally for thousands of years—we feel these stories as if we had lived them ourselves. The stories embody our collective experience. When we tell them, it is as if we are recounting memories. You will join our collective experience soon if you continue your training."

John sits motionless at the table, staring at Jimmy like a singer waiting for the conductor's cue.

"You've got a lot to consider, John. Take some time—not too much time—and come back when you're ready to seize the next level."

Chapter Nine
Sophia

"JOHN WELLS? IS IT REALLY YOU?" Sophia Bella is surprised to see her first love sitting alone in a bustling café by a sun-drenched window. Seeing his head buried in a book is less surprising.

"What? Yes. I guess so," replies John without looking up. The sound of Sophia's voice seeps all the way down to his unconscious, unearthing several conflicting emotions before he recognizes it. "Sophie?"

John abandons his book, shoots up, and gawks at her. The two embrace like lovers returning to each other from a brutally enforced separation. John drops his face into her plentiful black curls. They cascade down past her waist to tickle John's hands as he clutches her tiny frame, lifting her up onto her toes. The naturally sweet scent of her hair transports him back to his teenage years.

"What are you doing here?" asks John, quelling tears.

"Got a job as an instructor at Berklee. Their youngest instructor ever. What are you reading?"

"Jung." John closes the book, unveiling its cover, *Memories, Dreams, Reflections*. "Congratulations!" He hugs her again. The tighter she squeezes, the more he longs for his high school days with Sophia.

So this is nostalgia. I don't think I like it much, but something about it is irresistible.

He holds her tighter.

"Thanks." Sophia rests her head on his chest, her arms still wrapped around his middle. "I thought you were graduating early. What? Did you switch to psych?"

"No. I mean, yes, I'm graduating in the spring. Masters in engineering, computer science. This is a side interest. It's a long story."

"Tell me, then."

Sophia slinks into the empty chair opposite his. The sun splashing through the window highlights her clear Mediterranean skin. Her deep brown eyes beckon as she twirls her curls and curls her lip.

"Don't you have something to do, someone to teach, someplace to be?"

"Not anymore. C'mon. What's up? You know I can tell when something's not right with you."

John sits, sliding his book aside so nothing is between them, tacitly acknowledging the truth of her assertion. "Want coffee or something?"

"Oh, I guess it's a *real* long story."

John arouses the attention of Marge, the bedraggled, late-middle-aged waitress, who glares disapprovingly at the two of them. "Can I get a coffee for my friend here and two scones?"

"Cream and—"

"Black," interrupts Sophia, "please."

Marge's glower remains targeted at John, "We have blueberry, cranberry—"

"Raisin," interrupts Sophia again, "please."

Marge scowls. She waits for John's nod of approval before ambling off, muttering unintelligibly under her breath.

Sophia extends her hand across the small, round table. "What is it, John?"

She knows me better than anyone else alive. And she's still got a hold on me. Why did she move here? Was it really the Berklee job?

John cups both of his hands around Sophia's hand. It's small enough to be a child's hand, and it moves constantly as if it were a little creature determined to remain free.

Our bond—the one everybody coveted—is still strong. But it has a different flavor. I wish I could put my finger on what's changed. Is it truly safe to tell her everything?

Halfway through seventh grade, John lost all control over his voice when it began to change.

I'll never be able to sing on key again!

His piano playing wasn't good enough to earn a living if need be. He was in danger of being unable to keep his third promise.

Adults used his grief as a club to discourage musical pursuits in favor of academics. Most kids mocked his increasingly nerdy character. Sophia showed compassion. Her voice was changing, too. Her wide vocal range—a source of pride—was shrinking quickly.

Over the next two years, they sat together at her piano for hours on end ushering in their adult voices. John learned to control his new voice and developed perfect pitch in the process. Sophia, who was born with perfect pitch, nearly doubled her original vocal range. Their journey kindled a young, sweet love nurtured by their shared love of music. Enduring high school together deepened their love, leading to a profound trust in each other—something John has yet to experience with anyone else—even Emily.

"You have to promise me never to speak one word of what I'm about to tell you," demands John.

"I promise," assures Sophia, connecting with the depth of their trust—a trust strengthened, not weakened, by separation.

Sophia's rapt attention to John's portrayal of Jimmy, Andrew, the Life Field, and the excruciating dilemma he now faces uplifts John's spirits, giving him a taste of what it might be like to enjoy this level as Jimmy D insists he must.

"So? What do you think?" asks John.

"Are you sure I can't tell *anyone*? My Dad would love this…almost as much as he loves you."

"Sophia!"

"Just kidding, John."

"Don't do that to me."

"Sorry."

Sophia's dad left the priesthood before finishing seminary, claiming it wasn't his path. After three years traveling through Tibet and India, a full scholarship to study philosophy at Princeton was too enticing to pass up. He dropped out after his sophomore year to play drums in a blues band with three guys he met dancing in the mud at Woodstock. After rehearsing 12 hours a day every day for three months, he convinced the manager of a local club to book them as the opening act for B.B. King. Then he convinced her to marry him.

When Sophia was born, her dad was on tour playing small clubs in Asia, sending back barely enough money to support his wife during a difficult—and expensive—pregnancy. He returned when Sophia was five weeks old. Three days later, her mother disappeared and was never seen again.

The band broke up when the two guitar players enrolled in law school to avoid being cut off from their trust funds. Sophia's dad says they "made millions by going to the dark side" through the revolving door between Washington and big accounting firms. He and the bass player (Sophia calls him Uncle Bo) opened a small club in their hometown. Sophia grew up with music and musicians as her surrogate mother.

Her dad loved John because he sensed the special bond between his daughter and her sweetheart—a bond he has yet to find for himself. Sophia believes her dad's worldly travels gave him the wisdom to embrace John rather than jealously forbid her from dating because she was "too young," as so many of her friends' fathers had done.

"Here's the thing," explains John. "Andrew and his dad really seem to know what they're doing. They've got a well-thought-out plan, plenty of money, and connections to pull it off...and they're devoted to their mission. I mean, they should be. It's been working for 500 years. I'll have every resource I could ever imagine. And with powerful healers like Miriam teaching me, I'll learn how to heal people and shape reality.

"Jimmy D—on the other hand—he's a mess. Andrew's right. There's no plan with these people. Jimmy outright admitted he doesn't know what will happen when science discovers the Life Field."

"How could he?" asks Sophia. "How do you even know it would be discovered in your lifetime if you did nothing to stop it?"

"So, you think I should continue training with Jimmy?"

"I didn't say that."

"Well, what *are* you saying?"

"Being sure of yourself doesn't necessarily make you right—any more than being unsure of the future renders you unreliable. You make it sound as if Jimmy and his people are tortured by their uncertainty. How could they even get through a day?"

"No, they don't seem tortured. Actually, they're pretty calm, self-assured, and surprisingly unafraid…for people with no plan. That's what worries me. What if they're wrong?"

"What if Jimmy's right about the conscious Internet? Wouldn't you want to be the guy talking to it? Representing all of humanity? Honestly, I can't think of anyone else better suited for that job."

"Very sweet of you, Sophie."

"I'm not kidding."

"So, you really think the fate of all humanity rests on my shoulders?"

"Why else would you leave me and come here?"

"That's not fair."

"No. It's not. It's not fair to either of us." Sophia grabs John's arms and pulls him toward her, intercepting his head with a firm kiss. Her lips taste familiar and exotic all at once. Shivers shoot up John's spine, erupting out the top of his head.

"I thought you were with Craig," protests John, half in shock and wholly consumed by delight.

"I thought you were with Emily."

"I am."

"So am I," says Sophia.

"With Emily?" jokes John.

"I wish." Sophia's eyes widen. "She's hot. Emily's awesome. I'd convert to be with her."

"There's nothing to convert," declares John. "Remember our pledge?"

Sophia and John recite in unison, "We'll try anything once!"

They laugh together, heads back. When their eyes reconnect, laughter subsides, giving way to tears. Neither John nor Sophia will tolerate more than one falling tear before releasing their grip to wipe the other's cheek. Breathing regains their composure, a warm-up they had practiced countless times.

"God, we had fun together," says John.

"Too much fun?" asks Sophia plaintively.

"I don't know," replies John sullenly. "Life's no fun anymore. I'm no fun anymore."

Sophia sings the first line of "Suite: Judy Blue Eyes." John cannot resist joining in harmony. The sixty-year-old women in tie-dye shirts at the next table stop talking. With every note Sophia and John sing, another patron goes quiet until the café is silent, everyone listening as if at a concert. Sophia and John sing like rock stars in perfect harmony—John at the top of his range, Sophia at the bottom of hers. Their two gorgeously blended voices project the three-part harmony of the original song.

Sophia motions for everyone to join in. She winks at the three tie-dye-women who hit the parts originally sung by Crosby, Stills & Nash spot on. All the café is singing of love and loss. Sophia and John stand to perform the chorus as a coda. When the café erupts in applause, they clasp hands, bow, and exit.

"Where are you staying?" asks John, the faint sound of applause and café commotion still audible from the sunny sidewalk.

"Right around the corner." Sophia touches his arm. "Why don't you come up to my place, and we can continue this conversation."

"I don't think that's a good idea."

"What's the matter, Johnny Boy?" Sophia lightly punches his arm like a schoolboy. "Don't think you can control yourself?"

"No, actually."

"Emily is a lucky girl." Sophia smiles with love—not jealousy. "So, you know where you're headed now?"

"The walk will unveil my path. Can I call you?"

"Of course, my love. Anytime."

John turns to walk away, stops, and looks back. Sophia sweeps around the corner without looking back at him. John is dispirited and relieved in equal measure. He craves more coffee.

I can't go back in there now. Actually, I can never go back there. Marge will tell Emily, "He ordered scones, you know. He's never done that before." Och, what have I done? This was my favorite place to read and study.

The 25-minute walk home will inform John's decision better than riding the T. He shakes his head and body like a dog drying off, hoping to release Sophia to the wind whipping leaves into a whirlpool. Shaking has the opposite effect. Freed from the depths of his psyche, Sophia's essence floats up to tickle his heart. Their young love had profoundly shaped his world and his consciousness (as Jung would have it). Perhaps he should not resist. Indeed, he cannot reject Sophia's legacy without abandoning his true self. Rather, he can revel in it. Permit Sophia's spirit to fill his heart with joy. Encourage the sweet, delicious love they shared to enliven him.

But that is terribly dangerous. Emily is extraordinarily intuitive. What if she were to sense these feelings I have for Sophie?

"Fear not the scattered petals of your first love," whispers the wind as John passes through the swirling leaves, "Plant them in your soul, and they will nurture your true love forever."

Chapter Ten
Choices

 The rustle and breeze from the sheet of paper Emily is waving in John's face jolts him fully awake. He sits up, wipes his eyes, grabs the paper, leans back against the headboard, and reads.

"Holy cow! They sent you an offer letter…on paper, no less!"

"Paper, yeah. Whatever. I got the job. I'm going to be a scientist."

"What about Orville's new restaurant?"

"Fuck him! He's a cheap, entitled, ungrateful, moron with shit for brains and money to burn on everything but me."

"What happened?" John fears he missed Emily telling him something important.

"He shorted me. The bastard shorted me."

"What?"

"My check is short the raise he promised."

"Did you ask him about it?"

Emily, hands on hips, squints and sneers, "No, I realized I wasn't even worth what he was paying me before, so I slinked away with my tail between my legs." She snatches the letter and shouts, "Of course I asked him!"

"Ooh…my head." John moves his head back, pushing his open left hand down, the gesture Maestro uses to make his choir sing more softly.

Emily tickles John's ear with the throaty whisper she knows arouses him, "You know what he said?"

John cocks his head.

"He said it was to be a bonus, and only if the restaurant opened by the fifteenth, and under budget."

John shoots straight up. "Oh, fuck him!" He knows Orville's own spendthrift tomfoolery has prevented every one of his restaurants from opening on time or on budget.

"Right," confirms Emily. "Let's celebrate. C'mon, I'll take you to breakfast. We'll tell Marge. Maybe it'll actually make her smile. Have you ever seen her smile?"

"That's too far. Let's just walk to the bakery."

"OK. Get dressed. Whoo-hoo!" Emily dances around the apartment, Flamenco style. She snaps her fingers with the paper in between, mimicking the sound of castanets.

That's the fourth time I've had to concoct a reason not to go to the café. There just hasn't been a good time to tell Emily about seeing Sophie. Certainly not today. I don't want to spoil her upbeat mood.

On their walk to the bakery, Emily takes John's arm, her eyes wide with a Cheshire Cat smile. "Thank you, my love, for helping me get this job." She plants a loud smack of a kiss on his cheek.

"It wasn't me, really. Or Jimmy D either," insists John. "Babe, you got this job all on your own."

A few months ago, Emily applied for a research assistant job at a prestigious Cambridge biotech firm but heard nothing back. When their lead investor saw Emily's resume, he gave it to Carl Friedrich, founder and chief scientist at a new startup backed by the same venture capital firm.

Carl liked what he saw on paper and asked Emily to come in for an interview, which she did last Tuesday.

"If you say so." Emily is not convinced.

"I didn't see a job description on the offer letter. What exactly will you be doing?"

"Not sure. But I won't be dealing with the frenzied fallout from every one of Orville's cockamamie schemes…every day! That's for sure."

"'Bout time!"

"Aren't you glad I stayed with Orville, waiting until the right job came along? With better pay, better hours?"

"Don't be so sure about the hours. You'll be working at a startup. And what's with the crazy company name? *Maxwell's Golden Hammer?* Is this guy a Beatles fan or something? Does he know it's *Silver Hammer?*"

"I think he's a fan of the Beatles and James Clerk Maxwell. He said something about that in the interview. The point is we'll be developing precision medicine. Our research will discover cures. No more endless, painful, dubious treatments with nasty side effects. Carl refers to it as the Gold Standard of personalized healing. He went on about how, in 20 or 30 years, we'll look back on today's medicine as barbaric."

John tilts his head, raises his eyebrows.

"You know, telling people their treatment has a 40 percent or 60 percent chance of being effective, and they have to take more drugs to lessen the side effects. You don't know what it's like having to tell people their condition has a 60 or 70 percent survival rate. Sick and suffering people find those figures meaningless. I lost count of the number of patients who asked, 'how will this work for *me*? What are *my* chances?' and all I could do was spit back statistics from clinical trials. Carl's gonna change all that. And I'm gonna help him do it!"

"Yes, you are, Babe. And if this company goes public, your stock options will make you rich."

"Make *us* rich, my love." Emily kisses John, grabbing his lower lip with her mouth and biting gently. She traces both his lips with her tongue, her eyes locked with his in a tantalizing gaze. Parting her full, red lips, she slowly draws in enough air to make an alluring sucking sound while tugging gently on his arm.

John carries on toward the bakery.

I guess he's really hungry.

John is entranced, oblivious to Emily's tug or gaze or lips, powerless to grasp her intentions. He marvels at how Emily's kiss had immediately—and involuntarily—provoked an intoxicating flow of energy within him. After months of training, it still takes intense concentration in a quiet space with a lit candle and no interruptions for John to generate a flow as powerful as this. He logs the kiss for further investigation, then permits himself to feel grateful.

I am the luckiest guy alive. I wish I could find the right time—and the right way—to tell Emily about meeting Sophie. But everything I can think of saying is bound to make her Jealous.

John's chance meeting with Sophia bestowed unexpected clarity upon him—clarity surpassing his childhood visions.

Singing was the portal. Remembering the words, blending his voice, and feeling the harmony occupied his mind while his heart opened. Music flowed through him, resonating with the Life Field. Resonance sparked a vision with three astounding qualities: no visuals, no language, no thoughts.

John was linked with a mysterious entity on a plane of consciousness beyond thought. Communication was unnecessary. There was no distinction between him and the entity. They swirled together, imbued with wisdom and mutual insight, not bound in the slightest way to space or time or self.

John had no idea how long the link lasted. When his sense of time returned, the link had been reduced to a memory. And this memory had a twin—a desperate urge to keep hold of the memory while descending back into his body. The reason became clear by the time he finished the song. John's experience with the entity had vanished. The lone memory of his link survived. John vowed to remember, also, that a host of experiences never made the journey down into his normal self. Are they waiting in some distant realm to welcome him back? How could he rise again to that level of consciousness? Is this the level where Jimmy expects him to meet the Conscious Internet? Or would that be an even higher level?

Swishing through the whispering whirlpool, John beheld the extraordinary nature of his rescued memory. It was not contained in his mind. It inhabited his entire body. With one step, he entered his future with Andrew. The next step, his future with Jimmy. John played with the back-and-forth for several blocks, each step plunging him into the opposite world: Andrew and The Faithful, then Jimmy and The Disciples. At last, after having stumbled upon a level of certainty John had never encountered before, he stopped, struck his magic corridor stance, threw his head back to kiss the sky and basked in the sun warming his face.

"Are you alright, young man?" A sweet voice drew John into the world of a concerned woman looking up at him through her puff of wild, white hair.

"Oh, yes!" He peered down through her mane into her sparkling eyes. "I have chosen my path."

"Good for you." She removed her glove and reached up to touch his cheek. "You have chosen well."

"Thank you."

Her gaze vanished behind silver wisps blowing in the wind. She moved on, leaving John resolute in his decision to continue training with Jimmy D. While logic might have suggested working with Andy was a better career path, his visceral experience of both worlds revealed, unmistakably, that Jimmy and The Disciples offered a much more meaningful life.

It's so clear. So obvious. Why has this choice been such a lengthy, agonizing struggle?

Emily was pleased with John's decision, or rather, she was relieved he had made a decision. Neither Jimmy nor Andrew had John's best interest at heart. They were far more concerned with their missions. Both missions were dangerous. Both would consume John. Would she be relegated permanently to an afterthought? Emily had vowed to leave John if he ever did that to her again—despite how much she loved him.

The call from Carl requesting an interview upended everything. Having a chance to pursue her lifelong dream turned her vow on its head. Now *she* might be the one consumed by *her* work. What if they both were? What kind of relationship with John—or anybody else for that matter—is possible when both are consumed by their work? Assuming John had gotten her the interview—and the job—put her in John's debt, giving him a little extra power in their relationship.

Discovering, just now, that John had not helped secure her new job sends Emily scrambling to untangle her new life.

Is Jimmy not as well connected as John thinks? Does John not want me to get a job in science? Is his quip about the hours at a startup some sort of clue?

Emily now has the extra power in their relationship, having gotten a job on her own, making more money than John does. But that would not have been the case had John chosen to work with Andy, who offered John a small fortune.

I can't decide if John's lack of concern about money is endearing or reckless. Whatever...I'm back on top in the earnings department.

Emily knows it's unhealthy to focus on who has more relationship power. Whenever she catches herself analyzing their power dynamic, her mother gets the blame.

It had been folly to compete with her mother. Nobody was on Emily's side. Would she put her father in the middle? Of course not. Her mother was already jealous of his deep connection with his children. The graduate assistant's job testing her mother's theories of power dynamics in intimate relationships was a clever coup. The *Research Director* title should give her mother enough self-assurance to appreciate Emily's intellect. Recognition finally came when Emily discovered trends that made her mother a star in social psychology circles.

Mom is one step closer to seeing me as an equal.

Emily's obsession with boosting her intellect had relegated her potent intuition to a minor player during childhood. She was hardly aware of her intuition at all, leaving it to develop on its own, unencumbered by subconscious expectations or conscious interference.

She discovered her intuition's prodigious capacity in the seventh grade. Emily and her best friend, Ashley, had just been picked up by Ashley's mother from their after-school dance class when an ominous voice streamed from the car radio, "A record company official says Nirvana lead singer Kurt Cobain shot himself to death at his Seattle home yesterday…"

"Turn it off," shouted Ashley, "Turn it off!"

"Alright, dear," said her mother. She switched off the radio. "You don't have to get so testy."

"Testy, testy, testy," taunted Ashley's younger brother, sitting shotgun. He reached for the radio. Ashley's mother grabbed her son's hand, forced it back into his lap, and shot him a stern glance.

"Oh God," cried Ashley.

Emily touched Ashley's shoulder and peered into her watery eyes. Ashley collapsed into Emily's lap, sobbing.

"How old was he?" asked Ashley's mother, "Twenty-seven?"

"Mom!" cried Ashley, lifting her head, "He's the reason I wear black!" She buried her head in Emily's chest, bawling.

Tears soaked through Emily's leotard, warming her budding breasts, the sensation precipitating her first conscious encounter with intuition. She hovered over the gulf between Ashley's immersion in the ethos Kurt Cobain embodied and her mother's morbid spotlight on his having joined the 27 Club.

Crying dissolved into whimpers. Ashley was relinquishing her vitality to the void of despair that drains too many creative young people of their future. Emily could not allow Ashley to fall any farther. She closed her eyes, held her breath, and imagined she was diving down through a tube to rescue Ashley. The farther she dove, the deeper Ashley fell. In desperation, she squeezed Ashley, released her breath, squeezed again, breathed again.

Ashley assumed Emily's tightening grip signaled her friend's own need for comfort. She looked up. Emily was floating out beyond her hopeless tears. She strained her eyes trying to pull Emily into focus.

Ashley sang a line from "Smells Like Teen Spirit" in a raspy whisper.

Emily finished the line, singing with plenty of power to reach Ashley and pull her out of the void but softly enough to escape being noticed by Ashley's mother and little brother, who were talking baseball.

The car came to a stop. It was Emily's house.

Emily asked Ashley's mother, "Can Ashley come over?"

"Oh, I suppose so," replied Ashley's mother, slightly annoyed, if relieved not to have to cope with Ashley's dour mood. "Get yourself home before dinner, though. We're going out."

Emily nurtured her newly found power to reach through Ashley's pretense at normalcy and relish her quirks. By the time they were juniors in high school, Ashley had allowed Emily safe passage through her robust defenses and into her "lunatic sanctum." This access proved vital the several times she dissuaded Ashley from killing herself. Emily's intuition matured over time, empowering her to sense hidden feelings in practically everyone—even masters of disguise.

John had been a challenge. His ability to conceal surpassed even her own. He appeared to pay no attention whatsoever to the power dynamic between them. Emily suspected it was a disarming technique—honed by years of practice—to get her to lower her defenses. Her mother's award-winning theories predicted Emily would hold more power in a relationship with John because she was 2 years older. Not in this case. John had been introduced as the "boy genius," and his reputation preceded him. In Emily's world, grades trump everything, clearly giving John the upper hand.

When she finally cracked John's cocoon, her intuition revealed he was, in fact, uninterested in their power differential—oblivious to it, really. Was it because he was consumed by his pursuit? Exactly what he was pursuing was a mystery, and that sparked due intrigue within her. Taken together with his utter lack of regard for the power he held over her intensified his allure.

Emily and John round the corner by the bakery. Her intuition is on the fritz. All she can sense is that he's hiding something. Perhaps it's his meeting with Sophia.

I wonder when he's going to tell me about that.

Sophia had called Emily right after her encounter with John in the café. She had predicted, correctly as it turns out, that John would have trouble finding the "right time" to tell Emily about it. They chuckled together about this, along with a few of John's other quirks they found amusing.

When Emily first accompanied John to his family home, she was much more nervous about meeting Sophia than meeting John's parents—the stated purpose of the trip. Most frightening of all was the specter of seeing John and Sophia together. Emily had never felt the level of intimacy with John that he had described having with Sophia. To Emily's delight—and great relief—Sophia was marvelous in every way. Emily's intuition found no trace of jealousy directed at her. Quite the contrary. Sophia was genuinely grateful for John's newfound confidence and happiness.

When John introduced Emily, Sophia replied, "God surely answered John's prayer!" leaving Emily speechless. Sophia was irresistible. She had talent galore and a voice as gorgeous as her looks.

How could John possibly have left her? His career is obviously more important to him than any relationship.

John had told Emily that Sophia broke his heart. When he accepted his offer from MIT, John expected to get back together with Sophia after he finished college and graduate school. At his accelerated pace, it would only take four years to do both. He could stick it out. He simply couldn't understand why she could not—or would not.

The reason became clear to Emily when she and John bid farewell to Sophia before heading back to school. Sophia held Emily in a sustained embrace, her arms wrapped around Emily's middle, head buried in Emily's bosom. She reached up, braced Emily's head in her hands, and kissed her briefly but firmly on the lips.

"Take good care of him," implored Sophia, "and your enchanting self too."

Emily's intuition perceived Sophia's deep need for personal, physical contact on a continual basis. A long-distance relationship was out of the question. Perhaps it was because she grew up without a mother. Or it may have been her tactile nature. Her hands were always moving, caressing a coffee cup, twirling her hair, fidgeting. She played several instruments proficiently. Lying at the heart of all possible reasons may have been defiance. When professional musicians steered her away from piano because her hands were small, she doubled down. By the age of fourteen, Sophia was an accomplished pianist, sitting in with some of the Grammy-winners who played her father's club.

Emily and Sophia quickly became close friends, commiserating about John's foibles and those of the several boyfriends Sophia burned through after John left. Emily assures Sophia she will find true love one day. Sophia agrees, even as she prepares herself to acknowledge that music may be her love supreme.

Chapter Eleven
Little Genius

EMILY OPENS A GLASS DOOR leading from the cement walkway into a half-block-long, two-story, brick structure on a side street off Mass Ave. It looks more like a warehouse than an office building. She chuckles at the hand-written paper sign on the door reading "MGH." Everyone in the Boston area knows it as the abbreviation for Massachusetts General Hospital. The "G" that had once been gold but has since faded to sepia assures Emily she has found the right place. She had seen the same sign on the door to Carl's temporary office at the Venture Capital suite when she interviewed.

Stepping through the second door is like entering Oz. Art-covered walls, brightly colored furniture, multicolored carpet—all spotlessly clean—shine in stark contrast to the dank, dreary, day draining all color from the sky and the few leafless trees, whose gray roots torment the dingy sidewalk.

"You must be Emily," greets Rox, a slight, twenty-something

woman dressed in all black with pale skin, a genial smile, and excellent posture. Her several face piercings catch the warmth of the track lighting above and wink at Emily. "We're so glad you're here."

"Thank you," replies Emily, returning a courteous smile. The smells of new carpet, new furniture, and window cleaner invoke a touch of lightheadedness. Or is anticipation the cause?

"Carl would like to see you," says Rox in her bird-like voice, as she approaches Emily. "Right this way."

With her long stride, Emily keeps pace by taking only two steps for every three taken by Rox. The resulting hypnotic rhythm reverberates through the hardwood floor leading to the conference room. Coffee's aroma turns Emily's head as they pass the galley kitchen. Rox quickens her pace like a little girl descending a steep hill does to keep from falling.

"Emily. So good to see you here." Carl towers before them, leaning against the conference room door with a bad-boy stance and a handsome smile. Emily had gotten used to working with men who were shorter than she is, a trait that often made them uncomfortable. Thankfully, this won't be a problem here. Carl's arresting physique bulges through his white shirt.

I wonder how he looks without that shirt on.

"Thank you, Rox," says Carl amiably. Rox reverses course without missing a beat. Carl asks Emily, "Would you like some coffee?"

"Please...yes. I mean, that would be wonderful. Thank you." Emily imagines Carl's muscular chest is free of hair.

"This way." Carl leads Emily back toward the kitchen at a leisurely pace. Carl's voice, his manner, his energy, his presence all meld to wash away Emily's anxiety, leaving her attention to focus on the sights and sounds of the office. She is surrounded by people who feel at ease, as if they were at home in their pajamas, even as they are engrossed in engaging work.

Carl and Emily meander into the kitchen. On the wall by the coffee hangs a whiteboard with nothing but a quote at its center written in lovely cursive by a deep purple calligraphy marker.

"Great spirits always encounter violent opposition from mediocre minds." -Albert Einstein

"Are you expecting violent opposition?" asks Emily.

"Of course, we are," replies Carl, no hint of alarm in his voice. "But it is none of your concern. We have lawyers for that. You, my little genius, have much more important work to do."

As far as Emily can remember, this is the first time anyone has ever referred to her as either "little" or a "genius."

As a child, Emily was taller than most kids her age—even the boys. Academically, she was always just shy of the top of her class, much to the chagrin of her parents. Her mother never missed an opportunity to remind Emily how she had always topped her class and graduated valedictorian. Emily surpassed her mother's height in fifth grade. Looking down at her smarter mother became her favorite exercise in self-loathing. She was taller than her father by her sixteenth birthday, after which there were no photos of the two of them standing next to each other.

When people asked Emily's parents where she got her height from (pretty much every new person who came into their lives) her father would quip, "We baby-proofed the house by moving everything up out of her reach."

Her father used the time it took people to get the joke as a measure of their intelligence. Emily's fourth-grade teacher never got the joke at all, setting the stage for one of her most dreadful years of schooling.

Carl takes his time with Emily, eagerly introducing her to everyone they encounter on their thorough tour of the offices and labs. By the time he presents her to the team she had been hired to join, Emily is cleansed of her insecurities. She is thrilled to be joining a small team of passionate scientists investigating what triggers embryonic stem cells to develop into heart, bone, toe, blood, or other cells.

Intrigue heightens her delight when the team shows Emily initial results from their newest project—results they had not yet shared with Carl. Emily is received as an equal. She dives in, blending with the team as if she'd been working with them for years. This is the job she had craved—and would have missed had she not applied for an inferior job at a prominent company months before.

Chapter Twelve
The Serpent

 asks Jimmy.

"Yeah…why?" answers John.

"Good. You drive." Jimmy tosses car keys to John and leads him down a flagstone path around the back of his house to the garage. Using all his might, Jimmy pushes the heavy sliding door to unveil a blue 1965 Shelby Cobra Roadster in mint condition.

"Wow!" John stares, motionless.

"C'mon. Get in. This is a fun car to drive." Jimmy glides into the passenger seat.

"Isn't it a little late in the year for a car with no roof?"

"Nonsense, my boy. Look. It's sunny. And it'll be in the sixties this afternoon."

John wraps his fingers around the sleek, wooden steering wheel, takes a breath, and starts the engine. The deep growl of the 7 liter, 4-barrel V8 shoots a rockabilly beat out the exhaust pipes. From the back of his head, Commander Cody's "Hot Rod Lincoln" keeps time with his pulsating feet. He relaxes into the driver's seat to become one with the rumble, exceedingly grateful to his father for insisting he learn to drive a standard.

"Where to?" asks John.

"Take Storrow Drive to 93 North. We're going to Gloucester."

Controlling this lightweight sports car with its monstrous engine requires every ounce of John's attention, freeing his spirit to ride the cold wind racing through his hair as the bright sun warms his face.

Success was a harsh mistress. Coming to his decision released a flood of energy, imposing endless practice. Breathe. Flow. Quiet your mind.

Finally, progress. John was able to resonate with the Life Field on demand. Time to celebrate, right? Wrong.

From this font of success arose an unshakable nemesis preventing John from enjoying himself. Unlike the errant thoughts that had once stymied his flow, he could find nothing tangible to surrender. Joy's insidious captor lurked in the shadow of his unconscious.

The I-93-on-ramp approaches. John has tamed the beast. He prepares to unleash its ferocious power. A slight touch on the gas pedal shoots the car down the straightaway. The brutal acceleration plasters John and Jimmy back into their seats, igniting an addictive thrill. Whatever had shackled John's joy is blown out of him. Jimmy smiles. John smiles back, attempting to hide how baffled he is by the joy. He hasn't a clue where it came from, how it got there, or how to conjure it again.

Don't argue with what works.

John had been resisting this bit of Simon's wisdom. Today, he's grateful for it. Instead of banishing the joy he cannot comprehend, he permits it to expand through his chest while his mind and all his muscles muster enough coordination to handle the speeding racecar.

Upon entering Gloucester, Jimmy directs John to Good Harbor Beach.

"What a thrill!" exclaims John as he turns into a parking space.

"I thought you'd enjoy driving my little devil." Jimmy pats the car's warm hood as if it were a pet.

"That's the thing," says John. "You've been telling me I need to enjoy this level. Well, I did today. And I felt deep gratitude for the joy."

"Good for you."

"But I don't know how I did it."

"Mindfulness, my boy." Jimmy walks toward a wooden path. "Come. Walk with me. I'll show you." The two men follow the path through the dunes. Seagulls squawk above. A gentle sea breeze relieves the cold racecar wind. Jimmy takes a breath. John follows suit. "Ahh… smell that? Can you taste the salt air?" asks Jimmy.

"Oh, yeah. I love it."

"Feel the warm sun on your face?"

"Mm-hmm."

"See the big blue sky? A couple of puffy white clouds up there?" Jimmy points.

"Yup."

Wood gives way to sand, unveiling the ocean beyond. Seagulls soar. Creamy white foam decorates the deep blue sea spilling over the horizon. Raging surf grows louder with every step. Jimmy stops. "Listen." He raises his arms to the sky. "Behold the beauty of this day." His voice is barely heard over the crashing waves. "This is pure joy."

Joy remains with John despite his puzzlement.

"Well…yeah," says John, "but why do I feel it now—and while we were driving, but not before?"

"Because your attention is focused on the moment—and it was also while you were driving. It had to be, or you would have crashed my beloved Cobra and killed us both."

"You took a big risk letting me drive, then."

"Not really. You were ready. See? We're here."

"But how did I get here?"

"You drove."

"Very funny. You know what I mean. How did I get to this place where I can feel this joy? There was nothing to surrender. I didn't do anything. It just happened."

"Precisely, my boy. Driving focused your mind. Your attention was present in the moment. Presently, your attention is right here. Right now. All your senses are drinking in the beauty of this place. You are immersed in this delightful moment. As you have now witnessed, joy arises spontaneously when you are attuned to the moment; attuned to your senses, and grateful for the beauty they behold, exactly as it did during our performance of Messiah last week. You felt joy then, didn't you?"

"Absolutely. Music always brings me joy—especially when I'm on stage. But how does it work? Where does the joy come from? Why can't I feel it all the time? How can I get it to come again when I'm not at the beach or on stage or singing?"

"Careful, my boy. All these questions might tie you in knots, squeezing the joy and gratitude right out of you."

John takes a breath.

"Let me answer your first question: beauty. Beauty is the key to how it works. The simple act of recognizing beauty ignites joy. We might even say the Life Field propagates through beauty. Last week you let the beauty of our music fill you with Joy. Driving up here, you let the wind blow back your hair, freeing you to revel in the thrill of the ride and the beauty of the day."

"I thought *Beauty is in the eye of the beholder*, as they say, so there's no standard, no baseline. Everybody sees beauty differently."

"Yes. Beauty is an individual experience. An opportunity for each of us to resonate with the Life Field, attuned to whatever we find beautiful. I brought you here because I know you love the sea, and find it beautiful."

"And the Cobra?"

"She forced you to be present in the moment. If I had driven you here in a minivan, you would have wondered what I was up to; why we were going to Gloucester; what we would do once we got here. Your mind would have wandered around—all over the north shore of Boston—and you would have felt no joy. Taming the Cobra forced you to be present in the moment, so you could feel the thrill of driving it."

"But beauty is rare; almost as rare as your Cobra."

"Really? Is the sky beautiful? These clouds? Birds? The sea? Sunrise? Moonrise? Sunset? They are with us every day. We are surrounded by beauty. Most people simply don't bother to attune to it. They don't even notice beauty until it whacks them in the head, like a drop-dead gorgeous person walking by. Or perhaps they're captivated by an ardent encounter with a sunset, or a rainbow, or a flower, a song, a work of art. You were one of those people until just now."

"But I'm not here—at the beach—every day. I don't get to see the sunrise or sunset every day either. There are lots of days when there just isn't any beauty to behold."

"Is that so? Hmmm. Do you wake up next to Emily every day? Isn't she beautiful?"

"Well…mornings aren't her best look, ya know."

"Don't be ridiculous, John. You know what I mean. What you have with Emily, is that not beautiful?"

"Well, of course. But I don't wake up every day thinking about it."

"Right. You don't. Perhaps if you did so, you might feel more joy. She might too."

"Oh, c'mon. You're not serious. It can't be that simple."

"Oh, I am deadly serious, my boy. You simply pay attention to the beauty you encounter, or your life is deadly. Now, which do you choose?"

"What about people in toxic relationships? Or people who have nobody? Or people who suffer every day for any number of reasons?"

"You're not responsible for their happiness, John. They are. And if they decide to go looking for beauty in their lives, I assure you, they will find some. Anyhow, we're not talking about them. We're talking about you. You are only responsible for your own happiness. I didn't say it was easy. Every day, you can find a thousand reasons to be miserable—legitimate reasons, to be sure. There is only one reason to let go of your misery, seek out beauty, and find joy."

"What's that?"

"Because the alternative is miserable."

John chuckles nervously. "I don't get it. You just want me to go looking for beauty every day? Wherever I am?"

"I thought you said you didn't get it," quips Jimmy.

"Why do you insist on speaking in riddles?"

"Look at that elderly couple—way down at the other end of the beach—walking hand-in-hand. Is that not pure beauty?" Jimmy closes his eyes and savors a breath of fresh, salt air.

"Fine. I'll do it. If you really think I can find the joy I need to absorb this level, I'll start looking for beauty," concedes John.

"This level and every level to come," assures Jimmy.

Chapter Thirteen

The Orange

"CAN WE TALK?" Andy's text surprises John.

The last time John met with Andy and his father, he was as nervous as he was resolute. In preparation, he had crafted thoughtful sounding answers to a thousand possible questions. None were asked. Their reaction was unexpectedly understanding. Puzzlingly so.

John exploited the puzzle. Sensing an opportunity to avoid making an enemy of The Faithful, he encouraged Andy and his father to stay in touch. Both The Faithful and The Disciples wanted his help, leading John to presume he might, someday, be able to persuade the two groups to reunify. Having heard nothing from Andy for several months alerted John of the hubris inherent in assuming he could possibly achieve such a feat.

Could they be offering an olive branch to the Disciples?
The sudden heat of excitement and anxiety flushes John's face and

chest. Fingers tingle as thumbs type the response, "OK, meet at the diner?"

"My place, has to be private, come now?"

"Give me an hour"

"See you then"

John knocks on the unattended door Andy had led him through at what John and Emily have christened John's "mystery meeting." The door opens. Miriam smiles politely, waves John in, and scans the street in all directions before closing the door behind them. She leads him down the stairs, and breezes through the musty hallway. As they reach the heavy door, Miriam ushers him into the great room with much less ceremony than Andy had offered.

A giant, hand-carved, calabash bowl overflowing with fresh whole fruits and nuts rises from the center of the table that had held the extraordinary meal John can taste with his memory. Andy and his dad rise to greet him. They offer a seat and refreshments. John sits when they sit. He puts a few Brazil nuts on his plate and grabs the nutcracker, hoping the act of cracking them will hide his nervousness. Miriam joins them at the table. She takes an orange from the bowl and a paring knife from her place setting. Starting at the top of the orange, she artfully slices a thin, half-inch-wide ribbon of peel. The bright, sweet citrus scent clears John's mind and sharpens his intuition. Urgency percolates from Andy and his dad.

"So, what's up?" asks John as he cracks a Brazil nut.

Miriam turns the orange round and round. The ribbon of peel continues to encircle the flesh of the orange even as it is being separated from it.

"May we speak freely?" asks Andy.

"Of course," replies John. "We're all working toward the same goal, aren't we?"

"And what goal would you say that is?" asks Andrew.

Miriam's knife arrives at the bottom of the orange. She lifts the peel up and away. The spiral peel dangles from her knife in one piece, bouncing merrily like a spring, having been freed from the naked orange. John redirects his gaze from Miriam and the orange to Andy and his dad.

"Healing," declares John. "Isn't that what we do?" He eats the Brazil nut.

At their prior meeting, John omitted Jimmy's prediction about the Internet becoming sentient. He said nothing about preparing himself for the role of representing humanity at that juncture. And he hid his distaste for their tactics of targeting science and eliminating those on the verge of discovering the Life Field.

Stressing his loyalty to Jimmy (who had found him, nurtured him, and begun his training) he conveyed his desire to finish training before making any major decisions about his future.

"Yes," says Andrew. "And we'd like to keep on healing while protecting the Life Field."

"Agreed," says John. "How can I help?"

"We need to talk about Emily," says Andy.

"Oh, she's not going to tell anybody," assures John quickly. His face flushes. *Oops…if they didn't already know I told her, they sure do now. Is that what this is about? I was hoping they were going to ask me if I thought reunifying was possible.* John summons his will, knowing he must maintain a flow with the Life Field, surrender fear, and keep his attention tuned to the moment.

"No. We're not worried about that. She's a good woman. Loyal. We know," says Andy.

"Then what is it?" asks John.

"The team she's working with at her new job is looking into cell signaling pathways that promote differentiation in human embryonic stem cells," says Andy.

"You've lost me. That's her expertise, not mine." John knows exactly what they're talking about. This is a stall tactic, giving him time to recover from the shock of hearing it from them. He drops his shock into the flow and returns his attention to the moment at hand.

"Right," says Andrew, "Suffice it to say that, at their current pace of discovery, Emily's team could very well detect the Life Field at any time—if they haven't already done so."

"Wait, what?" exclaims John. "How do you know so much about—"

"John, how do you think Emily got her research job?" interrupts Andy.

John no longer attempts to hide his outrage. "No...you didn't..."

"We need her there. She's one of us now," declares Andrew exhibiting no concern for John's outrage.

"She most certainly is not!" John's stiffened body language is adamant.

"Listen, the minute you confided in Emily about the Life Field, you thrust her into our world, made her one of us," explains Andy. "What did you think would happen?"

"*This* can't be happening!" insists John.

"What do you fear is happening?" asks Andrew.

"You can't just assume Emily is gonna spy for you. Or have anything to do with you, for that matter."

"That's where you come in, John," says Andrew.

"No, no. I'm not putting Emily in the middle of this."

"Emily got herself into this when she took the job we set her up for," contends Andy. "Do you expect us to believe she didn't know these people might be on the verge of discovering the Life Field?"

"No. I mean, stem cell research was her passion long before she met me. And how, exactly, did you 'set her up?' She got that job because the CEO of her company saw her resume."

"And how do you think that happened?" asks Andy.

John looks at Andy, then at Andrew, back to Andy. "Och."

"We have people at the VC firm who made sure Carl got Emily's resume along with a strong recommendation to hire her," explains Andrew.

"So you know Carl?"

"Oh, we know Carl, alright. We've been watching him for some time now. He is not the guy you want experimenting with the Life Field," says Andy.

"Emily says he's a great guy. Brilliant. He nurtures his people. He built a company with the best work environment she's ever seen. Everybody's engaged, motivated."

"Yup, he's charismatic, alright. His staff are more like devotees than employees. That's one of the things we're afraid of," explains Andy.

"Son," interjects Andrew, "all we need her to do is give us an update every once in a while. Who knows, curing diseases might consume all their energy. They may never notice the Life Field because they aren't looking for it."

"What if they do notice?"

"We'll cross that bridge when we come to it. For now, we just need you to ask Emily to be on the lookout for it," says Andrew.

"No. I'm not doing anything, and neither is Emily…not until I know what you'll do if her team *does* discover the Life Field." *Oh God, I think I've let on that I'm not comfortable with their tactics.*

"What are you afraid of, John?" asks Andrew.

"I don't know. I just don't want anybody getting hurt." *Now I've done it. They must be able to sense my distrust.* Once again, the orange's aroma quickens John's senses, clears his mind, and allows him to surrender his dread to the flow and focus on the moment.

"What do you think we're gonna do, kill somebody?" asks Andy.

"Are you?"

"Nothing will happen to Emily," assures Andrew. "We know how much you cherish her."

Chills engulf John. Further conversation would be futile—and unwise. John's training provides everything he needs to respond appropriately. The Life Field flows through him. He surrenders his outrage, worry, and the horror invoked by Andrew's intimidating assurance of Emily's safety. His attention is perfectly tuned to the moment. He has tamed his reaction to Andy and his father as he had tamed the Cobra.

"Let me see what I can do," says John. "I'll get back to you in a few days."

John rises. Andy and Andrew follow John's lead. Miriam remains seated. She had been silent during the exchange, save for a few slurps while consuming her orange. He expresses his gratitude for her secret orange aid by taking her hand and kissing it as he had done when they first met. She offers a courteous smile while remaining seated.

John directs his attention to Andy and his dad. "Gentlemen," he says, nodding in due respect—but not bowing.

"Thank you, John," says Andrew. They shake hands, eyes locked. Andrew silently attempts to ascertain John's intentions. By dropping all his thoughts and emotions into the flow, John is able to thwart Andrew with a genteel smile and steady eyes.

"Good to see you again," says Andy. They shake.

"You, too."

"We're counting on you," interjects Andrew, snatching John's attention. Prior to his training, this would have interrupted the flow enough for Andrew to catch a glimpse of John's mind. Not this time. John, flow intact, captures both men's eyes at once.

"I'm sure you are."

Chapter Fourteen
Carl

CARL IS TIRED. Having given himself a little extra time to get to the VC's office for his 8:30 meeting, he refrains from extending his stride and increasing his speed to reach his usual city walking pace—a pace that normally invigorates him. Today, even the current pace is exhausting.

Carl's habit of walking fast arose out of necessity when he was a youngster trying to keep pace with his father, who found it unnecessary to slow down merely because he was walking beside a six-year-old.

Carl grew up in New York City. Like every other kid in his first-grade class, he walked to school unaccompanied until friends met up with him. Friday afternoons were special. When school let out, Carl walked with his buddies only as far as Mario's Barber Shop, where he waited inside for his dad.

Carl and his dad walked home together after Mario gave them matching crew cuts, expertly crafted using scissors, in the style of Carl's heroes: Alan Shepard, Mickey Mantle, Roger Marris. This exclusive ritual with his father elevated Carl's love of Fridays beyond the relief of being freed from school for the weekend.

And now my life has changed in so many ways. Carl's nostalgia for the music of his youth, for his school buddies, for Mario, for his dad, saps what little energy he has left. Breathing is a chore. Walking…no longer an option. His eyes close; hands reach for knees, folding his body in half. He draws a shallow breath and blows it out with fury. He knows he cannot continue down this dark vortex if he has any hope of keeping his lab and continuing his life's work. Only his sharp mind can save him now.

Mario charged 25 cents for my haircut in 1961. Adjusted for inflation that would be $1.63 today. My last haircut cost me $60. Even a kid's haircut costs $12 at Supercuts—and they don't have anybody remotely qualified even to shine Mario's shoes.

Mental calculations calm Carl, as they always do. Now he must banish Mario from his thoughts before the beloved barber can suck him back into nostalgia's vortex. He stands upright and draws a savage breath. The stinging cold, dirty air sharpens his focus on getting as much money out of these bloodsucking "vulture capitalists" as possible.

Carl has worked every day since his company received its initial VC funding. He cannot stop himself from dividing his base pay by the number of hours he's worked over the past 13 weeks. The result inflames his spleen. It's less than half the rate he's paying Emily, his newest employee.

I kind of like Emily. She's got that rare spark…so hard to find these days…and there's something mysterious about her. She'll be fun to unpack.

The prospect of getting to the bottom of Emily's mystery revives Carl, restoring enough energy to propel him to the VC's office in time for his meeting.

The heavy glass door resists being opened as if to protect Carl from the demons inside. A blast of hot air poisoned with the acrid smell of cheap, overheated coffee attacks Carl's face. Mrs. Danvers shoots her glare over her glasses without lifting her head.

"Good. You're on time," says Mrs. Danvers over the tappity-tap-tap of her vigorous typing. She looks back down at her heavy CRT monitor, still typing. "They're waiting for you in the conference room."

Her caustic voice is a dead ringer for Carl's fearsome third-grade teacher. He forces himself to swallow his queasiness, avoiding her beady eyes as he passes by her desk. The sickly-sweet smell of cheap perfume wafts past her humming monitor provoking a touch of vertigo. Carl slows his pace. He tries to decipher what the fervid voices emanating from the conference room are saying when Michael and his little brother, Sean, abruptly cease the animated conversation they'd been having with David. Making out words is unnecessary. The message is clear. David had flown in from the west coast, and nobody is happy.

"Good morning, Carl," says Michael, in the manner of a drill sergeant addressing his recruits. "You look like you need some coffee." He motions to the coffee machine as if he had just materialized it out of thin air. Carl pours the remaining black sludge into a styrofoam cup. He bleaches the sludge with the contents of six individual coffee creamers floating in a bowl of warm water that had been ice at 6 a.m. when Michael and Sean got to the office. Sean jumps up to make another pot of coffee.

"David has some concerns," says Michael.

"Well, then," replies Carl. "Let's address them."

"Please. Take a seat," invites David. He lifts a packet of papers. "Let's look at these numbers."

Sean had prepared the packets, placing each one strategically around the conference table. Carl grabs the papers lying in front of the seat intended for him, moves to the head of the table, sits, and reads. He says nothing.

"Your burn rate is higher than we projected," says Michael.

"Well, I told you those projections were low back when we put this deal together," replies Carl.

"Maybe so, but unless you start generating some cash flow, you'll be out of money—"

"In six months," interrupts Carl. "Yeah. You need to raise more money, like I said at the beginning."

"And I told you we needed to see results before we could commit any more money."

"Results." Carl pauses. He channels the rage burning within him to focus his mind and speak with a clear, calm voice. "We are on the cusp of identifying a number of crucial signaling mechanisms and pathways that program differentiation in human embryonic stem cells."

"*On the cusp* doesn't strike me as any sort of definitive result I can take to the boys on Sand Hill Road," says David, "especially if I'm to ask for more money."

Carl lowers the papers, puts his hands on the table, and looks David straight in the eye. "We're also experimenting with several technologies that might be able to reprogram an adult somatic cell to become a pluripotent stem cell."

"Again, with those words, *might be able*," complains David. "What do you expect me to do with that?"

"David, this would be a huge breakthrough enabling us to create patient-specific stem cells." Carl gathers Michael and Sean in his sights. "And it promises to free us from the nasty ethical problems of using embryonic stem cells for research. We could end up with a Nobel prize!"

David sighs. He looks at Michael, then Sean. Back to Michael.

"Have you thought about how any of this can be made into a product you can sell—or maybe a service?" asks Michael. "What's your plan for generating positive cash flow? What's your timeline?"

Carl fixes his gaze on Michael. "We are not going to generate *any* cash flow for *many* months. That's why we need more money," he turns to David, "to get to the point where we can sell something to doctors, hospitals, biotech, pharma." *I've got no clue what we might actually sell, but this is what they want to hear.*

"Do you have anybody working on products?" asks David. "What about that new girl Mr. Van Owen found for you?"

"Emily? She's smart. She's working with my A team. Like I told you: experimenting with ways to reprogram adult somatic cells to induce pluri—"

"You've got a good-sized payroll," interrupts Michael. "What do all these people do all day?"

"Research, damn it!" exclaims Carl. "Except for George and his poor suffering staff who slog through their days fulfilling the auditor's inane requests and writing reports for you guys."

"Have you thought about ways to incentivize your people to work faster?" Michael tags Sean with a roguish grin. "Maybe we should send Sean down there to light a fire under everybody's ass."

"Absolutely not. I don't want Sean anywhere near my lab or my staff," snaps Carl before he has time to gather his rage and focus his mind once again. "No offense, Sean. It's just…I don't think my people would get you."

"None taken," says Sean with a malevolent chortle.

"Do they understand what's at stake here?" Michael waves the papers. "How hard are they really working for these hefty salaries you have us paying them?" He slaps the papers onto the conference table.

"If you're not coming in on Saturday," says Sean.

Michael joins in, "Don't bother coming in on Sunday!"

Sean snorts. Michael laughs. David chuckles.

Carl dumped every penny of his small inheritance into his tiny company. He hired a few good people, nurtured a creative work environment, and dove into research. His patent application caught the eye of scientists at Van Owen's VC firm scarcely months before Carl's cash was about to run out. If he wanted to continue his work, Carl had to step into another world.

When he first met Michael and Sean, Carl was seduced by their cold, mercenary approach to business, assuming it was responsible for their financial success. He attributed his own perennial financial struggles to the fact that his inclination was nothing of the sort. Research, discovery, and healing were his only interests. Money was merely a means to fund research.

He tried wearing Michael's mercenary ethos like a leather bomber jacket. Carl credits *Michael's jacket* with toughening his negotiation skills and imbuing him with the character that convinced David to recommend funding Carl's company to Mr. Van Owen. It also torpedoed his marriage and estranged his children. Carl was now married to his work. Perhaps he always had been.

Michael sensed Carl's aversion to business and suggested one of their people serve as CEO with Carl as Chief Scientist. Carl refused, citing his success building a motivated, cohesive workforce and his connections with prospective customers. The VCs agreed under one condition: their man, George, would serve as Chief Financial Officer (CFO).

"My people are inspired by the thrill of discovery," explains Carl.

"Telling them we'll run out of money if they don't discover faster is only going to motivate them to find a job at a well-funded company before we run out of money. They're dedicated, not stupid."

Blank stares from David, Michael, and Sean alert Carl to raise the stakes.

"Look, the fact is we need enough money to last another year at the current burn rate. We've got enough for six months. If you can get the rest, we'll have a good shot at a major breakthrough that will be worth a fortune. So, what'll it be, hmm?"

David, Michael, and Sean redirect their eyes from Carl to each other. Nobody speaks. Carl knows the next person who talks in a situation like this loses the game of financing. He will not be the one to break the silence.

"I almost forgot," says David, "Mr. Van Owen wanted me to ask you about that patent application you withdrew."

"What about it?" asks Carl.

"Why did you withdraw it?"

"The machine doesn't work. At least not the way I thought it did. I've still got the thing hooked up in my office, but I figured you guys wanted me working on something we can sell. And we can't sell the damned thing if it doesn't work like the patent application says it does."

"What exactly is it?" asks Michael.

"It's an ultra-sensitive microplate reader with an accompanying uniform ELF-EMF generating device. It can be used to study—"

"If you get a patent on it, what could it be worth?" says Michael.

"That depends on a number of factors—"

"Van Owen wants you to fire the thing back up, tweak it, and see if you can get it working," says David.

"Really?" Carl cannot hide his surprise.

"Yup," confirms David. "If you can assure me you'll get it to the point where you can resubmit the patent within the next six months, I'm pretty sure I can get you the money for six more."

"Hang on," interjects Michael.

"It's OK, Michael," says David. "I got this."

"Alrighty then," says Carl. "You've got yourself a deal. Tell Van Owen I'm on it as soon as I get back to the lab."

Carl stands and extends his hand. David stands and shakes. Michael and Sean spring up. Carl savors the puzzled look on their faces.

"Sean, can you work up the numbers, adding money for another six months?" asks David.

"Sure, I guess," replies Sean looking toward Michael for approval.

"I'll get the legal docs started," says Michael.

Carl delights in watching Michael squirm.

"Thanks," says David. "We'll reconvene in say…a week?"

Michael calls out, "Mrs. Danvers?"

"Yes?" replies Mrs. Danvers from her desk, her remote voice sending chills of dread through Carl.

"A week from today work?" asks Michael.

"All set," replies Mrs. Danvers over the beat of her typing.

"Well…there it is," says David.

Carl speaks directly to David, "Thank you." He shakes David's hand again. "See you guys in a week."

He shakes with Michael, shakes with Sean, and leaves.

"It's a good thing we've got George there," says Michael hardly above a whisper.

"Like we've always said," adds Sean, "a CFO's job is to keep a string around the founder's balls with a slip knot ready to pull on our command."

Sean, Michael, and David chuckle.

Chapter Fifteen
The Machine

EMILY JUMPS. Her vibrating phone startles her out of the trance like concentration induced by analyzing data at the computer all morning.

"My office, please," is the text from Carl.

"On my way," replies Emily.

I wish he didn't think I was a genius. I've only been here a few months. What does he expect I should have discovered already?

Carl is sitting at his computer. He waves Emily in as she approaches the glass door to his office.

"Come. Look at this," commands Carl before the door shuts behind her.

Emily peers over Carl's shoulder. "What am I looking at?"

See…I'm obviously not a genius.

Carl points to a spike in the graph. "Right here."

"Is there something wrong with your ELF-EMF generator?"

"That's what I thought. But this disturbance doesn't always show up, and the self-test reports all systems in working order."

"Looks like its duration is less than a nanosecond. Are you sure it isn't some kind of interference?"

"Well, that's the problem. I can't tell if it's hardware related—calibration or shielding—or a software glitch."

"Can you replicate it?"

"Sort of. That's the other thing. These samples are all from the same stem cell line." Carl points to the spike again. "But this only shows up once in a while."

"Is it always at this frequency?"

"Shit!" Carl scrolls too fast for Emily to catch anything. He stops at another graph.

"Guess not," says Emily. She retracts a little from her position over his shoulder to avoid bumping heads as he turns to look at her.

"You really are a little genius," says Carl in a throaty whisper. "Give me 20 minutes to look at some stuff. I'll text you when I'm done."

"Okay…" whispers Emily.

"Close the door," says Carl, his eyes glued to the screen.

Emily strolls to the kitchen and pours herself a cup of coffee. Her growling stomach reminds her she hasn't eaten anything today.

Twenty minutes isn't enough time to get to the deli and back. Anyhow, the last thing I want to do is eat in Carl's office.

She grabs a homemade chocolate chip cookie from the tin on the counter labeled "4 EVERYONE 2 ENJOY!"

"So…you've had your Carl moment?" asks Rox, who has arrived at the kitchen to retrieve her sushi from the refrigerator.

"What?" says Emily.

"He calls you in to look at something, picks your brain for a couple of minutes, then kicks you out while he goes off on a tangent inspired by something you said."

"Uh, yeah, I guess."

"That's because he's a true genius. That's how they work, you know. Some little thing you say sparks a crazy idea, and they chase that idea like a dog after a rabbit. One day, one of those rabbits will lead to a major breakthrough, and we'll all be able to retire on our stock options."

Rox smiles, pivots, and scurries back toward her desk at the same brisk pace she had taken while escorting Emily on her first day at work. Emily eats another cookie.

"Come look." Carl's text arrives after only 12 minutes. Emily hurries to his office. Carl is standing in front of the computer, his hands on his head. He waves her in excitedly.

"I took each sample that registered a disturbance and plotted its frequency and duration. Now, what do you see?"

"I see a sine wave."

"Exactly!" Carl is overcome with excitement. "A waveform. It's as if those little samples are resonating with some unknown energy field. And every once in a while…something in the samples…or that energy field…whatever it is…decides to interact with the electromagnetic field… for whatever reason…at some frequency. It seemed random until I plotted the frequency and duration together. You are such a genius!" Carl spontaneously hugs Emily. "Oh, sorry. Was that inappropriate?"

"No, not at all."

Emily smiles like a mother telling her little boy he can have another cookie. The force of Carl's chest and strength of his arms had invoked a tingle within her. It lingers. Her intuition confirms the impetus for Carl's hug was pure excitement and camaraderie, nothing more, much to her dismay. *He doesn't find me attractive?*

After her interview with Carl, Emily had imagined kissing him, her kiss coaxing Carl's heart to venture out beyond the fortress he had built with his brilliance and his workouts to protect him from the pain inflicted by most of his relationships. Carl had buried his torturous pain more deeply than most people.

Ever since Emily had gained access to Ashley's "lunatic sanctum," she would plunge through a friend's defenses the instant she spotted an opening. She simply could not resist any opportunity to touch someone's heart and melt a little pain.

Nothing short of a kiss would have much chance of reaching Carl's heart. She knew she could never permit her fantasy to become reality. A kiss bore many obvious dangers. And any contact with Carl's volatile pain was likely to unleash unforeseeable consequences.

"But *I* didn't think to plot those values. You did. You're the genius, not me," contends Emily.

"Ahh…but you noticed the duration. You asked whether I could replicate the disturbance. You asked about the frequency. What on Earth gave you the idea to focus on those things?"

"Not sure."

"Genius, that's what."

"Whatever. So, now what?"

Carl closes the door, leans against it, and folds his arms. "Here's the thing." He glowers at his petulant invention sitting on the table looking like an innocent microwave oven. "I've been getting these pesky disturbances from that contraption since it first registered the effects of EMFs on embryonic stem cells. I tested hundreds of samples from the same line and only saw the disturbances once in a while. So, I went looking for the source of the problem in the hardware and software. It never occurred to me that the stem cells might be involved in causing the disturbance."

"Honestly, Carl, it didn't occur to me either."

"Anyhow, I pulled the patent application and pretty much forgot about it. I only started fussing with the thing again right after you got here. My investors want me to resubmit the patent. But that'll take months. We can't spend months on a patent application when *this* is staring us in the face. Like Eddington said, 'something unknown is doing we don't know what' and we are looking straight at it." Both hands point to the computer screen. "This is big."

"So, how can I help?"

"Your husband, what's his—"

"Boyfriend."

"Right. Sorry."

"John. His name is John."

"Right. John. I understand he's a bit of a genius when it comes to software, especially pattern recognition and AI, Hmm?"

"I guess you could say—"

"Would he be interested in some side work?"

"Oh, I don't know. He's—"

"Look…Emily," Carl gestures toward the computer, "if we're going to figure out why some samples generate the disturbance and others don't, we need to analyze this mountain of data." He aims at the machine. "At the same time, we need to start tweaking that thing and collect an-other mountain of data." He fixes his gaze on Emily. "We may not know exactly what we're looking for but, believe you me, there's a pattern in there somewhere. I can feel it."

"But John has a full-time job. He works for—"

"Emily, we need somebody we can trust. I assume we can trust him, right?"

"Absolutely. John is the paragon of discretion."

"Good. When can he start?"

"I'd have to talk to him about this first."

"Of course. Call him."

"Now?"

"Will he pick up?"

"Probably."

"Good. Call him. We have no time to waste."

Emily calls John.

He answers, "Hi Babe. What's up?"

"John, I'm here with Carl. He wants to ask you something."

"Me?"

Emily offers her cellphone to Carl. He snatches it, flashing a scolding glance.

"Good to meet you, John. Carl here. Emily says you'd be up for a challenge."

"Carl!" chides Emily.

"Oh, did she?" replies John sarcastically.

"Look, we're on the brink of a major breakthrough and we need somebody super smart to find a pattern amid a ton of data. Needle in a haystack, really. Now, I understand you're one of the top guys in this pattern finding business and—even more importantly—we can trust you." Carl pauses. He glances at Emily. "We *can* trust you, right John?"

"Trust me with what?"

"Keeping what we find quiet. At least until we figure out what to do with it."

"Sure."

"Good. I'm allocating plenty of resources for this, John. You'll be well paid."

"Okay, but—"

"I'll get you credentials for my servers, so you can work from home. Emily will fill you in on exactly what we're analyzing. Just keep me in the loop with anything you find, OK?"

"I can't just drop everything and—"

"Of course not, John. When can you start?"

"I don't know. I could probably have a look on Saturday and see—"

"Excellent. Emily will get you squared away in our systems, and I'll send her home with your first check today as a start-up bonus. Welcome aboard, John. We're going to do great things together!"

Carl hands the phone back to Emily.

"What just happened?" asks John.

"Let's talk when I get home."

"Fine."

Chapter Sixteen
The Wrong Hands

"CAN WE HAVE THAT BOOTH all the way back there?" asks Emily, pointing only with her eyebrows.

"Certainly," replies the hostess. She ushers Emily and John to the back corner of a large Chinese restaurant. It's three in the afternoon, offering plenty of privacy. After they're seated, the hostess hands a giant menu to Emily and another to John. "Tea?"

"Please," answers Emily with a gracious smile.

"So, you're my agent now?" asks John.

"I'm as astounded by Carl's request as you are."

"Well, what do you think?"

"What do I think?" Emily leans across the table. John meets her in the middle, tête-à-tête. She falls into her sultry, throaty whisper, "I think he's discovered the Life Field. That's what I think."

"Whoa!" John retracts as if acceleration has plastered his back against the booth.

The hostess returns. A stylishly painted china teapot steams on her tray flanked by two matching teacups. Her graceful hand places a teacup in front of Emily and another in front of John. With one fluid motion she pours hot tea into each cup and places the pot near the edge of the table. She adjusts it once; then glides out of sight. The whole episode plays like an ancient ritual dance.

"He doesn't know what he's discovered yet," says Emily, her eyes darting around the dining room. "That's why he wants your help."

"Holy sh—"

"John, you have to take Carl up on his offer and find a way to point him in another direction. Besides, it pays really well. We could get a nicer apartment."

"What's wrong with our apartment?"

"I don't know...peeling paint, leaks, roaches...oh my God, the window shades—"

"Sorry I asked. So, where do you think I can point Carl that will distract him from the Life Field?"

"Not exactly sure...at least not right now. We'll figure it out. You were all set to do this sort of thing for The Faithful only a few months ago."

"Yeah, but—"

"But nothing, John!" Emily pauses, gathers her thoughts, lowers her voice. "Who knows what'll happen if Carl realizes he's discovered the Life Field. He's really unpredictable, you know."

"Geez, you sound like Andy...Listen, I need to tell you something."

Emily shoots a disapproving look at John, reminiscent of when his mother was about to scold him.

John gulps some tea. "It turns out you did have help getting that job."

"What? I thought you said Jimmy—"

"No, it wasn't Jimmy. It was Andy. The Faithful. They've got someone at the VC firm that's backing Carl's company. And, evidently, he gave Carl your resume. They want you there to do exactly what you've just done."

"Wait, what? When did you find this out? When were you going to tell me?"

"I'm telling you now. Andy told me when I met with him a few weeks ago. They wanted me to convince you to spy on Carl and let them know if he got close to discovering the Life Field."

"Jesus, John."

"I know. I know." John pauses, slurps more tea, "There's more."

"More? What more could there possibly be now?"

She's already mad, so I might as well... "I saw Sophia. She just showed up in the café."

"Oh, John. I've known about that since the day you two met. She called me right after she left you. I was wondering when you'd have the cojones to tell me."

"So, wait. You two just talk about me behind my back?"

"John, you're in no position to accuse anybody of anything right now. What did you tell Andy?"

"Nothing. I dodged it. And I've been stalling ever since. But you've just done what they asked me to convince you to do…all on your own."

"So now what?"

"I need to think." John runs a hundred scenarios through his mind in about 90 seconds. In between each scenario, John is distracted by the thought of Emily and Sophia commiserating about him. "What do you and Sophia talk about anyhow? Have you seen her?"

"John! Focus!"

A waiter approaches. John and Emily snatch their menus.

"We'll have your sampler for two, please," instructs Emily. She hands her menu to the waiter. He looks at John for confirmation. John hands him the menu and shrugs. The inscrutable waiter nods to John, nods to Emily, pivots, and leaves without saying anything.

"Let me get into Carl's data," says John. "If I find anything, we'll deal with it then."

"I can tell you what you'll find." Emily leans in and lowers her voice. "A disturbance will show up just before a stem cell begins to differentiate. And the disturbance will be a slightly different frequency and duration depending on what the cell is about to become."

John's face contorts.

"You know…a heart cell or a bone cell or a toe cell or a blood cell or a brain cell or anything else," explains Emily.

"You're sure about this?"

"Of course, I'm sure. I could have told Carl all this when I was in his office. But something told me to keep it quiet and tell you instead."

"So, you think Carl has discovered the point at which the Life Field triggers stem cells to differentiate?"

"Exactly. He doesn't know it yet, but his machine detected it. Now, if somebody gets their hands on that machine, how long do you think it would take them to go from detecting the Life Field to amplifying it, focusing it."

"You mean like a laser?"

"Yes. Like a laser amplifies light, Carl's machine might be modified to amplify the Life Field and focus its power. Don't you think that machine in the wrong hands would be dangerous?"

"And you think Carl's are the wrong hands?"

"Not sure. But he's kinda volatile. And his investors want him to patent the thing. Then his discovery will become public knowledge."

Chapter Seventeen
The Experiment

James Douglass had no intention of retiring merely because he had turned eighty. The last sixty years of tech innovation had been a good warm-up. Now, the real fun was about to begin, sparked by John's arrival on the scene.

John's response to the job offer was delightful. Amid the struggles of the past two decades, Jimmy had forgotten how much joy arises from helping young people chase their dreams and unlock their true potential. Not to mention the pleasure of watching slices of life fall into place. His clients get the Artificial Intelligence systems they've been hounding him for—and building them prepares John for his encounter with the Conscious Internet. Best of all, absent his family's relentless career scrutiny, John was finally able to focus on finding joy. And, as luck would have it, working from home gave John the flexibility he needed to take on Carl's project. Or, perhaps, it wasn't luck at all.

A flurry of random dots emerged when John plotted every disturbance the machine captured. Carl's intuition about an energy field had been spot on, but the sine curve was a coincidence, not evidence of it.

The true evidence was downright revolutionary—and exactly as Emily had predicted. Carl's machine registered a disturbance at the instant a stem cell showed its first signs of differentiation. Also, as Emily had predicted, the frequency and duration of the disturbance did, in fact, correspond to the kind of cell it would become.

Emily's brilliant inference was prophetic. The Life Field not only triggers differentiation, it also directs the cell's outcome. John's eyes closed. He'd been staring at the first scientific measurement of the Life Field! Jimmy's assertion that the Life Field is what coaxes a stem cell to choose what kind of cell it will become was now confirmed. So was The Faithful's fear of stem cell research.

Why am I not thrilled? Anybody else would be calling friends, alerting the scientific community, scrambling to verify findings. But here I am, concocting a plan to squash the most profound scientific discovery of a generation. Something I vowed never to do.

A new puzzle coaxes John out of his self-loathing quagmire. Carl's intuition. Carl hadn't been looking for the Life Field at all. Thousands of brilliant people throughout history had missed the Life Field simply because they were focused on something else. Not Carl. Why not? Carl was brilliant and driven—driven by his intellect, not his gut.

John flashes on how Emily can help him solve this riddle. He calls her cellphone while she's at work.

Emily answers, "Hi John. What's up?"

"Am I on speaker?"

"No. Everything OK?"

"Oh yeah. Fine. I've got a theory to test, and I need your help."

"A theory about the machine?"

"Yes, but there's a catch."

"Catch?"

"You and I need to test the machine without Carl in the office."

"Oh."

"Can you make that happen?"

Alone in her office, Emily rotates toward the wall and lowers her voice, "That's going to be tricky. Carl locks his office when he's not here. And the machine keeps a log of every time it's used. It'll be nearly impossible to hide our use of it from him."

"Got it. I'll get back to you."

John hangs up and calls Andy.

Andy answers, "Hi John. Good to hear from you."

"I have news."

"Not over the phone."

"OK. Your place?"

"I'll be here all day."

"Give me 30 minutes."

"See you then."

Emily and John enter MGH together.

"Well, hi there, John!" Rox greets him with a genuine smile. "Glad to finally meet you. You're pretty famous around here, ya know."

"Am I? I mean, thank you. Good to meet you too."

John extends his hand over Rox's desk. Rox stands and shakes with a firm grip, her eyes locked on John's eyes in an attempt to take the full measure of Emily's beau.

Something's up with these two.

Rox takes a key out of her drawer and offers it to Emily. "Carl left his office key for you."

"Thanks," says Emily, grasping the key.

Rox refuses to let go. Her eyes fix on Emily's. "You *will* return this to me before you leave."

"Absolutely," confirms Emily. Rox releases the key and sits. Her eyes follow Emily and John down the hall.

John whispers into Emily's ear, imitating Alec Guinness, "These aren't the droids you're looking for."

"Stop!" whispers Emily. "She's very protective of Carl. That's a good thing."

"Kinda low tech, though," sneers John. "She couldn't program your keycard to open Carl's door?"

"This can't be hacked." Emily turns the key as if unlocking the air in front of her. "And Rox will guard it with her life."

"She doesn't look that hard to subdue. And her Jedi mind trick won't—"

"Don't let her size fool you," interrupts Emily. "Rumor has it, she holds a seventh-degree black belt."

"Oooookay…"

"How'd you do it, John?"

"Do what?"

"Don't play coy with me. Three days after you tell me we need private access to Carl's office, he's called to the west coast for an emergency meeting? That can't be a coincidence. Especially since he specifically asked me to run some tests on his machine while he's gone."

"I told you before. Andy has someone at the VC firm. I asked him if he could get Carl out of the office so we could test my theory."

Emily stops at Carl's office door. She shoots John a fierce look.

"What the—"

"Not here," interrupts John, "Open the door."

Emily unlocks the door, ushers John in, slides in after him, shuts the door, and sets her hands on her hips, "You told Andy about this?"

"Yeah, I did. It was the perfect opportunity to make him think I had convinced you to spy for him. I couldn't stall forever."

"John, I'm not spying for them!"

"Didn't you tell me we couldn't let Carl discover the Life Field? He couldn't be trusted with that knowledge? And his patent might reveal it to the world?"

"Yeah. I told *you,* not *them!*"

"Didn't you ask me to find a way to point Carl in another direction? To distract him from the Life Field? Exactly what I would have done if I'd chosen to join The Faithful?"

"Well, somebody has to."

"Emily, we talked about this. You supported my decision to study with Jimmy. And you know Jimmy's distaste for obstructing scientific discovery."

"I did support your choice. But I didn't think *this* would happen. Not now. Not Carl. And certainly not a patent. John, we've got to do something!"

"Fine. We're here now. Let's test my theory, OK?"

"Sure. What's this mysterious theory of yours?"

"If I tell you, it'll taint the results."

"Oh, so I'm the subject?"

"One of them."

"Fine." Emily rolls her eyes. "I prepared the cultures the way you asked. What do you want me to do?"

"Put one in the machine and while you're doing so, guess whether or not we'll see a disturbance. Then turn the machine on and we'll have a look."

Emily selects the top petri dish from one of several stacks, opens the machine's door, positions it in the center, and closes the door. "For this one, I'll say no."

"No disturbance," confirms John.

"That's right. No disturbance." Emily presses some buttons on the machine's LCD keypad. A few seconds later, a disturbance registers on the computer screen. "Guess I was wrong."

"OK," says John. "Let's do another one."

Emily removes the culture, sets it aside, and loads the next one. This time, she predicts they will see a disturbance. And they do. Emily tests 100 cultures, finding a disturbance in 33 of them. After her first incorrect guess, Emily guesses correctly every time.

"See what happened?" asks John.

"So, I got pretty good at guessing."

"99 out of 100. That's better than pretty good. How'd you do it?"

"Not sure. I just felt like I knew…like I wasn't really guessing." Emily's intuition detects a vital change in John. He is clear, calm, resolute; his attention intensely focused on her; his perennial insecurity gone. It had been lessening gradually over the past few weeks. Now, it has abruptly vanished. Most peculiar of all, the incessant questioning that normally fills John's head and clouds Emily's intuitive sense of him has also vanished. She can see right through to his heart. The glow at the center of his being takes the shape of a butterfly.

"What's going on?" asks Emily.

"Nothing to fear." John waits for Emily to take a breath. "The experiment proves my hypothesis. Your intuition is enhanced by being in the presence of cells resonating with the Life Field. It explains why Carl felt he had discovered an energy field, even though he wasn't looking for it."

"Yeah, Carl's not the kind of guy you would normally consider intuitive."

"Yet his intuition was spot on. And it led him straight to the Life Field."

"But disturbances last for less than a nanosecond—and we only detected 33 of them. How could they have such a profound effect on anything?"

"Your intuition was enhanced after the first disturbance was detected."

"Sensitive dependence on initial conditions? You're saying intuition is a chaotic system?"

"That conclusion would be supported by the data, wouldn't it?"

Come to think of it, what I see in John looks a lot like the Lorenz attractor—the butterfly effect. "Yes. Yes, it would." Emily pauses, lost in thought for a few moments. "So, this finding would predict Carl will know he's discovered the Life Field as soon as he returns. How do we stop that?"

"Not sure. But even if we do…what's to prevent every other stem cell researcher from being affected the same way as Carl?"

"Because they don't have his machine. I follow the work in this field very closely. Nobody else is investigating the effects this machine has on stem cells."

"Emily, you know that lots of people work with stem cells, and some of those stem cells are bound to resonate with the Life Field—machine or no machine. Wouldn't that resonance enhance the researcher's intuition too?"

"Maybe. Or maybe…without the machine, the effect is so weak it goes unnoticed. Or maybe their intuition is focused on something else. Like why their boyfriend didn't tell them about his meetings with Andy and Sophia."

"Hey. That's not fair!"

"No, it's not. John, you've gotta stop keeping things from me."

"OK. I'm sorry…"

Emily's phone rings. She checks the caller ID. "It's Carl."

"Better get it." John eyes the ceiling.

Emily answers, "Hi Carl. How's the other coast?"

"Dry and brown. They call it golden. Hey, I see you've run some tests on my machine. What did you find?"

Emily looks at John as if to ask, *how does Carl know this?* She puts the phone on speaker mode and lays it on Carl's desk. "I'm here with John."

"Hi John. How do you like our cozy little lab?"

"I like it. Very artistic. Inspiring."

"Good. So, what do you two geniuses have for me?"

Emily and John stare at each other, flustered. John mouths the word, "Stall."

"We found a disturbance in 33% of the cultures," says Emily, moving her head closer to the phone. "John's looking for a pattern among them—and among the ones you tested before."

John extends his hands in a giant shrug and shakes his head.

"It'll take him a few days." Emily knows this is a lie. She had convinced John not to tell Carl about the correlation he found between the disturbances and differentiation. She's quite sure John will find the same correlation in the dataset from today's testing, probably in a couple of hours. *I don't know how long I can convince John to keep hiding this from Carl.*

"You saw the results I sent you showing the sine curve was a co-incidence, right?" adds John, uneasily propping up the lie.

"Yeah. But something is going on there. I can feel it. I'd really appreciate anything you can do to speed up your analysis, John," insists Carl. "I don't believe in coincidence. Ask Emily."

John and Emily have the same thought, *did this experiment boost Carl's intuition from 3,000 miles away?*

"Hey Emily…" Carl's disembodied voice interrupts the silent dialogue Emily and John are attempting.

"Yes?"

"Tell John how this machine ended up saving my company even though I thought it didn't work. You really think that's a coincidence?"

"Probably not," offers John. "She told me the story. Fascinating."

"More than fascinating, John. It's a revelation." Carl pauses. John and Emily remain silent. "Here's the other thing. Van Owen's got a guy. Specializes in getting patents approved. Has connections. Pushes 'em through."

John and Emily share a sense of dread.

"Oh," they blurt out in unison, pretending to sound encouraging.

"Yeah. Really exciting. So, I've sent him the application. Don't give him access to my server, but send him all the results we've gotten so far. Send him today's results too. And whatever John finds ASAP. Anyhow, he wants to see the thing in action."

John and Emily roll their eyes.

"He's coming by there next Tuesday," continues Carl. "Emily, can you give him a whiz-bang demo?"

Emily knows this is an order, not a request. "Sure. I'd be honored."

"Good. Coordinate with Rox. I'll be back by the end of next week. Van Owen wants to take me to wine country. Think he's got a vineyard or something. Hey, gotta go. Van Owen just walked in." Van Owen's voice is heard in the distance. The call ends.

Chapter Eighteen
Croissants

Jimmy was right. Seeking beauty and finding joy did, in fact, raise John's consciousness to higher levels, and exposure to Carl's machine was like flooring the Cobra's gas pedal. Each new level came faster than the last, accompanied by new revelations and new challenges.

John's rapid growth uncovered a talent to sense the inner feelings of people he encountered—a talent Emily had uncovered many years ago. John was finally catching up. Simon showed John how to nurture and tune his newfound psychic sense. For John to heal people, he had to see their potential, visualize their new reality, and spot whatever was blocking them from realizing it. Tuning his psyche led to a more potent connection with Emily, which, in turn, boosted her intuition, further refining John's tuning process—the experience giving John his first taste of a virtuous cycle. Like ice cream and salt, the taste was addictive. As his psyche gained power, so too did his craving.

Establishing a flow and maintaining resonance with the Life Field became almost routine…almost. Whenever he strayed from mindful attention to the moment, doubts interrupted his flow. Sometimes, he spotted the doubts, dropped them into his flow, and resonance resumed. More often, though, his mind went racing off to collect a thousand reasons why he was engaged in the wrong activity, walking the wrong path, or pursuing the wrong goal.

Focusing on a complex task—like finding patterns in Carl's data—allowed doubts to brew in the background for a while, undetected. Finally, the brew boiled over and manifested as a headache, chest pain, or nausea. He learned to recognize those symptoms as a call to stop, breathe, and surrender. Most often, the flow returned within minutes.

Not lately. For the past three days, flow and resonance have been elusive. John was stuck. Doubt was king. Fear was his queen.

Is this it? As high as I can go? After all my work and the boost from exposure to the machine, I'm still nowhere near the level of consciousness I reached singing in the café with Sophie. Was that a one-off? A fluke? Maybe it's time to admit I'm done.

It was time to see Jimmy D.

"Good morning, John." Jimmy's friendly greeting sets John at ease. "Come in. I have a treat for you."

"Thank you for making time for me on such short notice."

"Not at all, my boy. That's what I'm here for."

Jimmy ushers John into his kitchen. Comforting steam rises from the French press. The coffee's aroma weaves its way through John, evaporating much of his anxiety.

"I believe they're done," says Jimmy as he opens the oven to unveil four golden brown croissants. A wave of nutty, buttery, sweet, warm air blends with the coffee's aroma, cultivating an altogether hypnotic atmosphere. Jimmy nimbly lays each croissant into an intricately woven basket lined with a white linen cloth.

"These were frozen unbaked in France and sent to me by an old friend with instructions for baking them," says Jimmy. "Looks like the instructions were spot on."

"Thank you, Jimmy. They smell superb."

"Try a little confiture on it," says Jimmy, sliding the jar toward John.

John gingerly lifts a croissant out of the basket. Removing one curved end triggers a crisp, wispy crunching sound. Steam escapes from the soft, buttery, silky inside. He spreads raspberry confiture on the inside and savors his first delightful bite—the experience dissolving his planned launch into the source of his troubles. He sits back in his chair and smiles.

"You are a true master," says John.

"Oh? What makes you say that?"

"I came here after three days of torture, and your warm welcome and simple, elegant breakfast set me right."

"How so?"

"Your smile. The aroma. The warmth. Even the sounds. These amazing croissants—like nothing I've ever eaten before. I see why you had to get them from France. It all…blended like a symphony of pleasure; and now I have my flow."

"And why do you think that is?"

"Not sure, really."

"You are present in the moment, John. The same way you were present while driving the Cobra and drinking in salt air at the beach. The croissants are nothing more than a reminder. A catalyst, perhaps."

He's right. Why couldn't I do this without the catalyst?

John logs this moment—and this question—for later study.

"Now, what's on your mind, my boy?"

"We have a problem."

"That machine of Carl's I suppose?"

"Exactly. And then there's Emily. She might as well be working for The Faithful."

Jimmy chuckles. "She doesn't want Carl to discover the Life Field."

"Not at all. And she's adamant. She expects me to stop him."

"That is a sticky wicket, alright."

"So, what do you think I should do?"

"Well, that depends on a number of things."

"Like...?"

"For starters, what do you think Carl will do with his machine after he discovers it's detecting the Life Field?"

"No idea. He's unpredictable. That's what scares Emily so much."

"Ah, there it is again. Fear. Making decisions for us."

"Emily's right. Carl is driven. And he needs money. His investors want him to patent the thing. Then he'll sell the patent to raise money for his research."

"Isn't Carl's research focused on healing people?"

"Yeah, but who knows what the buyer of the machine and the patent will do."

"Why don't we cross that bridge when we come to it? Carl's not yet ready to re-file the patent. He's got a long way to go before that contraption is worth any real money."

"And how do I calm Emily down in the meantime?"

"Emily is a brilliant scientist with a strong psychic sense. Perhaps she can point Carl in another direction."

"What direction would that be?"

"Didn't Emily tell you her team is working on a way to reprogram a person's blood or skin cells so they can become stem cells?"

"Yes. She's tremendously excited about this. If they're successful, it will revolutionize the treatment for all sorts of terrible diseases. It could even lead to cures. It's the kind of discovery that could win a Nobel Prize."

"And wasn't this Carl's main focus when he started his company?"

"According to Emily, it was…until he got distracted by that damned machine."

"Do you think you and Emily, together, could get Carl's focus off the machine and back onto his original purpose?"

John ponders Jimmy's question until it sparks an idea. "You know, we might. We just might."

Chapter Nineteen
The Hoax

Francis Xavier Cummings, III reminds Emily of Orville, only smarter. Unfortunately, his superior intelligence comes with a heightened air of entitlement surpassing even Orville's. Worst of all, Frank (he's fond of interrupting to say, *Please call me Frank*) is handsome, impeccably dressed, and charming. His congenial smile, baby blue eyes, sandy hair, suave demeanor, and smooth voice disarm most people within seconds. Not Emily. She sees a snake. A devious, unctuous, scoundrel, who would sell his mother into slavery for thirty pieces of silver. Everything out of Frank's mouth strikes Emily as condescending, even as it is polite and well spoken. Two and a half hours trapped in Carl's office with this man has Emily dying for a reprieve.

"Now, these disturbances, Carl spoke of. What do you make of them?" asks Frank.

Emily is cognizant of how carefully she must tread. She wants to give Frank enough information to support Carl's patent application without divulging the discovery.

"So, at first, Carl thought the machine was detecting some sort of energy field, but upon further analysis, we determined that was not the case."

"Did your analysis discover anything else?"

Heat is making its way to Emily's cheeks. *He's going to know I'm lying.* "Let's take a restroom break."

"Good idea," replies Frank. "I'll have your girl get us more coffee."

Rox is a full-grown woman with a seventh-degree black belt, is what Emily would like to say. "No. I'll get it. Rox is very busy today. Follow me."

Emily leads Frank down the hall, points out the men's room and darts into the ladies' room to send John a text message.

"You done?"

"Almost"

"Need it NOW!"

"5 min"

"K"

Emily was relieved and hopeful when John returned from Jimmy's with such an elegant, clever scheme.

What had convinced him it was the right thing to do? It's probably better not to ask.

She prepared 100 new cultures and, ever so slightly, altered the DNA in about a third of them. John modified the machine's software, telling it not to report resonance with the Life Field. Instead, it registered a disturbance when it encountered the altered DNA. For good measure, she prepared and tested another 100 cultures. Plenty of data now "proved" the disturbances resulted from "unusual" DNA.

All that remained was for John to alter the mountain of data the machine had already collected and hide his hacking—no small feat. Carl's extraordinary intelligence and growing intuition amplified the challenge. John found it invigorating, the excitement enhanced by the rush to complete his deception in time for Emily to give the doctored data to Van Owen's "guy" Frank.

John had worked through the night, knowing Emily was to meet with Frank this morning. When she awoke, John was not yet done. A confounding snag had stymied his plan. He asked her to stall as long as possible. Her response was to kiss him firmly on the lips; then clasp his head in both of her hands, holding him so close her vivid green eyes were all he could see.

"You can do this," she said lovingly. "You have to. I'm counting on you. Humanity is counting on you." She kissed him again, longer and deeper than before, moving one hand to caress the back of his head while the other caressed his neck. "No pressure, my love."

She smirked, mussed his hair, grabbed her purse, and hurried out the door.

John's heart quickened. His head cleared. Energy returned as if he'd awakened from a good night's sleep. The flash of an idea struck. He knew how to solve the problem.

"Done" is the text stopping Emily's foot from tapping a beat in time with her fingers while hiding out in the bathroom. "Check ur email."

Her phone indicates a new email has arrived. It's a long email from John with several attachments. "Yes!" she says silently, grabbing the air and pulling it down like a trucker honking the horn. She pushes the bathroom door open. Rox is in Carl's office having brought in coffee.

That prick. I told him not to bother Rox.

"Thanks, Rox," says Emily as she pulls Carl's office door open. "I could have gotten us coffee."

"Oh, no problem," replies Rox. "We were just chatting at my desk while he waited for you. I offered to get you guys coffee." Rox twirls round and scampers off.

He's such a conniving charlatan. Makes my skin crawl. "So, Frank, you were saying?"

"Yes, your research. What did it finally uncover?"

"The machine reacts to a very slight difference in the DNA of some cultures. My boyfriend's been analyzing all the data and just sent us updated results."

"John. Yes. I've heard about him. Carl tells me he's quite the genius."

"Yes, he is." Frank's esteem for John's genius makes Emily's blood boil, much to her surprise. A breath and focus on the task at hand summons enough calm to prevent rage from flushing her face. She uses the computer on Carl's desk to open the email John had sent. "Do you want me to print this for you?"

"No. Forward it to me." Frank hands Emily his business card. "Send me all the raw data too."

Shit, I was hoping he'd only ask for the email. I sure hope John was able to hide his hacking. She slows her movements, using the mouse to steady her trembling hand.

"Emily?" Rox's voice squawks from the telephone speaker.

Emily pushes the intercom button. "Yes?"

"There's a guy here named Alphonse for Mr. Cummings?"

"Ah, yes," says Frank, projecting his voice to be heard over the intercom. "That's my driver. Send him back."

Emily shoots Frank a quizzical look.

"He'll pack up the machine. I need to get going."

The intercom line is still open. Rox is silent on the other end. Frank raises his eyebrows, nodding as if to indicate Emily has no choice but to comply.

"Okay," says Emily reluctantly. "Send him back." The intercom line goes dead.

"What's going on?" asks Emily.

"Mr. Van Owen asked me to bring it back there."

"You can't just check this as baggage on your flight."

"I fly private, my dear."

Of course, you do. And I'm not your dear. "Carl didn't tell me you were taking his machine."

"Nothing to worry yourself about. We'll take good care of it."

"I need to check with Carl."

Emily calls Carl. It goes directly to voicemail. She leaves a message, "Call my cell the minute you get this. It's an emergency."

Alphonse approaches the glass door carrying a large metal case. Frank waves him in.

"There it is," directs Frank, pointing to the machine.

Alphonse offers a respectful nod to Emily. "Ma'am." He moves past her toward the machine.

"Hold on," instructs Emily.

Alphonse looks at Frank, who motions for him to continue his work. He sets the case on the floor, unlatches the top, and removes some packing materials.

"Frank, I cannot let this machine out of this office without explicit instructions from Carl," declares Emily.

"Reaching Carl now is unlikely. He's at the vineyard with Mr. Van Owen."

"Has it been powered down properly?" asks Alphonse, "so I can unplug it?"

"Yes. I mean, no. You can't take it until I reach Carl!" insists Emily.

Alphonse raises his hands as if someone has pointed a gun at him. He glances at Frank. Frank motions for him to continue. Alphonse unplugs the machine.

Emily stands. "Frank!"

Frank remains seated. "I don't know what to tell you, my dear. Mr. Van Owen wants the machine at Sand Hill Road while we put the finishing touches on the patent application."

"Yeah, and I work for Carl. He said nothing to me about you taking the machine."

"Must have slipped his mind."

"Are you telling me there's no way to reach Carl?"

Frank looks at his phone. "Not likely." He asks Alphonse, "Are you ready?"

"Almost done, sir."

The caustic, ripping sound of packing tape infuriates Emily. She imagines Rox taking these guys out with a few of Bruce Lee's signature moves.

Should I ask Rox to help me prevent them from taking Carl's machine? She probably wouldn't even need my help. I wish I knew what Carl wanted.

Emily's heart rate quickens. Her intuition cannot overcome her panic at the prospect of making the wrong choice in this moment. She moves to block the door.

"Well then, Frank. We'll just have to wait until we *can* reach Carl."

"I am a patient man, Emily. But you are beginning to tax the limits of my patience." Frank stands, gesturing at the surroundings like a ringmaster introducing the latest sensation. "You do understand that Mr. Van Owen is bankrolling all this."

"That may be. But this is Carl's machine."

"That Mr. Van Owen is paying for, my dear. Alphonse, are you quite ready?"

"Yes, sir."

"To the car, then." Frank moves toward the door. Emily obeys her urge to stand aside. Frank pushes through the door. Alphonse approaches, barely managing to carry the heavy case, his head tilted back so he can see over its top. His foot prevents the door from swinging completely shut. He backs into it like a waiter with a full tray exiting a kitchen, something Emily has done a thousand times.

Emily recovers from her momentary daze and follows. She calls Carl while walking. Voicemail. She picks up her pace while texting Carl, moving past Alphonse and Frank to reach the front desk before they do.

"Rox," whispers Emily, "did Carl say anything to you about Frank taking his machine?"

Rox darts from behind her desk. She positions herself between Frank and the door, striking a warrior stance. With her back straight and arms extended, she stares Frank down. He will not get past her.

"That machine does not leave this building."

Frank sighs, "Emily?"

"Hold on," replies Emily. "Carl just texted me." She stares at her phone longer than it takes to read the text, long enough to hide her surprise.

"It's okay, Rox," says Emily.

Frank waves Alphonse ahead. "Keep your phone on and close by all night," he says to Emily. "I may need to call you after I review this material. It'll show up as an unknown number."

I didn't give him my cellphone number. What the fuck?

Still carrying the bulky case, Alphonse backs out the first door, backs into the second door, and holds it open. Frank pushes through the first door and sweeps by Alphonse, who follows Frank, passes him, and reaches the car ahead of Frank. Alphonse sets the case gingerly on the sidewalk, opens the car door, and closes it after Frank slides nonchalantly into the back seat. Emily and Rox glance at each other; then stare outside. They shake their heads as Alphonse hefts the case into the trunk before driving away.

"What a dick," they say in unison.

Chapter Twenty
The Party

THE TUXEDO FITS PERFECTLY. It must have been tailored specifically for Carl. Normally, Sonoma Valley partygoers dress casually. Not tonight. Carl has been instructed to prepare himself for an altogether lavish affair. Van Owen's guest list includes U.S. senators, members of the British Parliament, royals from several countries, titans of industry from around the globe, and—because it's California wine country—a smattering of fashionistas and movie stars. Nobody, who had finally secured a coveted spot on Van Owen's elite guest list, would refuse an invitation to one of his legendary soirées.

Tonight, they are coming to meet Carl, Van Owen's new biotech star. Van Owen continues to expand his tremendous fortune by promoting a scientist or inventor as the next big thing. For this evening, Carl is the next big thing.

In an attempt to forestall any tendency Carl might have to get starstruck, Van Owen told Carl, at breakfast, that he'd invited some friends, prospective investors, and a few "interesting people" without disclosing who they were. Van Owen then offered Carl a tour of his vineyard followed by an extraordinary luncheon of foie gras, goat cheese, oysters on the half shell, grilled octopus salad, an assortment of fresh and pickled vegetables, and warm, freshly baked bread—all paired with the finest wines from Van Owen's private collection and served by three waiters at an elegant table on the estate's veranda overlooking the sprawling vineyard below.

During lunch, Van Owen asked Carl about the disturbances his machine detected. Carl speculated about some new energy field. Van Owen insisted Carl stick to cellular reprogramming technologies when speaking with tonight's guests and avoid any mention of the machine.

Relaxing is not Carl's forte. He is irked by Van Owen's advice to "unwind" in his guest room before attending tonight's party. The room's luxurious splendor—rare antiques, original impressionist paintings, gold fixtures, a shelf of rare books—is lost on him. He longs for access to a computer connected to the internet, something that would "spoil the getaway" according to Van Owen.

What am I to do for another two-and-a-half hours dressed in this monkey suit?

The task of relaxing is made all the more stressful by Van Owen's directive not to speak of the machine.

This could be the biggest discovery since black holes. I know; I know...Van Owen's a master at raising money—and tonight is about raising money, so I'll go along with him. But only for tonight.

Carl checks his phone. Plenty of bars. He calls Emily.

She answers, "Hi Carl. You know it's 8:30 here, right?"

"Yeah. Sorry. Listen, I haven't heard anything from you today.

How did it go with Van Owen's patent guy?"

"I told you in the texts, he took the machine."

"What? What the f—"

"I called you twice. Left messages. Then I texted you. It was all a few minutes after noon my time. Would have been—"

"Just after nine my time. I was in the vineyard with Van Owen's winemaker. I didn't get any calls or texts from you!"

Emily puts her phone on speaker while she checks her text message thread. "Carl, I'm looking at the texts right now."

"Wait a minute." Carl does the same, revealing the same thread. "That son-of-a-bitch Van Owen!"

"What's going on?"

"Somehow he must have gotten hold of my phone. He said I dropped it while touring the vines, and he handed it back to me just before we had lunch, but there was no cell service there either. I never heard it ring or beep or anything."

"So, you didn't want me to let Frank take the machine?"

"Of course not! She's my baby. I told you we're on to something big! What on Earth were you thinking?"

"Carl, I called. Left messages. Texted. And you texted back, or so I thought."

"That son-of-a-bitch Van Owen!"

"Carl…Listen…I actually have some good news. My team had a breakthrough this afternoon. We might have found a combination of genes that can reprogram fibroblasts into pluripotent stem cells."

No reaction from Carl. The line is dead.

"He is not a happy camper," says John. Carl's call had interrupted his dinner with Emily in their kitchen.

"No. He's not," confirms Emily woefully. She pushes her half-eaten bowl of capellini pomodoro away and shakes her head.

"But this is what you wanted, isn't it?" asks John.

"What…you think Van Owen is in cahoots with Andy?"

"How else could you explain what just happened? Van Owen is probably Andy's guy at the VC firm, and Andy probably told him to get the machine out of Carl's hands, pronto. Actually, it makes our job a lot easier."

"Really? What about *my* Job—the one that makes *real* money? Carl is obviously furious with me?"

"He'll get over it. And without his machine, he won't be able to test his own cultures and find a connection with the Life Field. Without more testing, it'll be next to impossible for Carl to detect my tampering."

"But he's devastated."

"Oh…so now it's 'poor Carl?' What happened to 'We can't trust Carl with discovering the Life Field?'"

"You don't have to work with him!"

"Look, you were about to tell him what your team found today. He'll be stoked when he hears that! This is exactly what we're looking for; what you asked me to find; a new direction for Carl. Actually, didn't Carl start his company with an eye on figuring out how to do what your team is on the verge of doing?" John twirls a large forkful of capellini and delivers it to his mouth.

"Yeah…he did."

"Good. So, we've accomplished the task you asked me to help with," says John with his mouth full. He swallows, wipes his mouth, and drapes his arm around Emily's shoulders. "Babe, this was a great day."

Without smiling, Emily's face betrays begrudging acceptance of John's point. Leaving his arm around Emily, John slides her bowl of capellini in front of her.

"Now, eat," says John. "This could be the best pomodoro I've made. Very fresh. Got the tomatoes, basil, and cheeses at Savenor's when I picked up the lamb racks for your birthday dinner. It won't be that good left over." He eats another forkful.

We can't afford lamb racks. And we certainly can't afford to shop at Savenor's!

Emily catches her instinctual objection before it escapes through her lips. She allows John's caring spirit to seep in. Warmth rises from her chest, sending a gleam to her eyes and a smirk to her mouth. She grabs John's head with both hands and plants a deep kiss. John's typically delicious lips blend with fresh tomatoes, basil, and olive oil. The exotic flavor sends chills up Emily's spine...and down again.

John gulps, steals a breath, and returns to Emily's bewitching lips. He lifts her T-shirt. She assists, tossing her top with the flair of Salome. Her mouth attacks John's neck, licking, biting, sucking. She yanks his shirt up. He raises his arms. She flings it over his head. Her hands rush over John's bare upper body. His nearly hairless chest flushes. Heat streams through Emily's hands. A tingling wave surges through her arms into her shoulders, up her neck to the top of her head.

John unclasps her bra and heaves it upward. Emily's creamy white, Venus de Milo breasts revel in their freedom. The tingling wave engulfs her chest. It cascades down past her velvet, flat belly, gaining strength as it thrusts her onto the table.

Bowls catapult toward the ceiling. Capellini strands and cherry tomato halves rain down onto Emily's satin skin, complementing her bright pink nipples. John licks her silky, salty body clean. The tingling wave quivers with each revolution of John's tongue around her stiff, engorged nipples. Emily and John allow the wave to carry them away while shattering ceramic and clanging silverware reverberate off the hardwood floor. Their love banishes all doubts, all fears, all thoughts. Ecstasy reigns.

Carl erupts into the hallway, accosting the first person he encounters. "Where's Van Owen?"

"I believe he's in the kitchen, sir," replies the short, startled, young woman with a French accent, dressed in the catering company's uniform.

"Where's that?"

"The kitchen?"

"Yes, the kitchen. I need to speak to Van Owen now!"

"Down the stairs and to the right; then down the hall."

Carl bounds down the stairs, taking two at a time.

"But sir, Mr. Van Owen does not like guests in his kitchen."

"What the fuck, Van Owen!" yells Carl as he bursts through the door.

"Excusez-moi?" says the handsome, white-haired pastry chef with an accent Carl remembers hearing in Geneva. He is holding a pastry bag ready to pipe white icing on top of hundreds of layers of puff pastry and vanilla cream.

Carl apologizes instinctively in French, "Je suis désolée!" He admires the pastry chef's crisp white coat, astoundingly clean for a man whose finished delicacies reveal he's been working for hours.

"Mister Van Owen has left the kitchen," says the pastry chef in his Genevoise accent, without any hint of alarm. "Perhaps you would like me to send for him?"

There is no response from Carl.

Using only his head and eyes, the pastry chef signals to a young apprentice, who scurries off to locate Van Owen. Carl's eyes remain on the pastries.

"Would you like a taste?"

Carl is now thoroughly disarmed. "Well…sure."

The chef selects a Napoleon pastry from behind him, places it on a plate, and hands it to Carl. "For you, please."

Carl accepts the plate with a courtly nod and takes a bite. Sweet cream, crisp pastry, rich chocolate, and velvet vanilla icing explode in Carl's mouth, transporting him back to his glorious year in Geneva as an exchange student. He closes his eyes, lost in bliss.

"I understand you're looking for me?" Van Owen's shrill voice punctures Carl's perfect moment from behind.

Carl gulps before he's finished chewing, whips around. "What did you do with my machine?" He coughs on flaky pastry caught in his throat.

"Perhaps we should continue in my study," invites Van Owen. He holds the kitchen door open and motions for Carl to pass through.

The pastry chef is back at work expertly piping his icing.

"Merci. This was…magnifique!" exclaims Carl with a flourish. The pastry chef nods, graciously accepting Carl's compliment without disturbing the surgical precision of his hands.

"This way," instructs Van Owen. They step into the hallway lined with photos of Van Owen through the decades posing with kings and queens, prime ministers and presidents, movie stars and rock stars—all of which Carl had failed to notice on his way to storming the kitchen.

Van Owen opens a tall rosewood door with Rococo carvings and holds it for Carl to enter the study. The sheer majesty of the rotunda slows Carl's pace as he wanders in, head back, eyes wide, mouth agape. Two stories above, a walnut library ladder leans against rosewood paneling. Scores of shelves filled with a thousand books line the walls. Golden chards flung by the reclining sun hurtle through towering windows to lash a perfect replica of the resolute desk. Their wicked dance mimics the roaring fire in the hand-carved, Italian marble fireplace. Top shelf liquors stand proudly on floating backlit glass behind a serpentine bar carved from a single redwood slab. A huge blue domed ceiling with zodiac detail in gold leaf invites Carl to stand under its oculus and gaze through at Venus, flaunting her brilliance as the only star visible in the deep blue, early evening sky.

Marble pedestals and ornately carved giltwood tables display sculptures and busts. Aristotle, Homer, Beethoven, Lincoln, Einstein, and others Carl does not recognize. Carl does recognize two sculptures: a Buddha, and Rodin's Eternal Idol. Photos signed by The Beatles, Rolling Stones, Led Zeppelin, U2, and others, including Milton Glazer's iconic Dylan poster adorn the walls, artfully placed next to what Carl suspects might be originals by Matisse, Degas, Cézanne, Frida Kahlo, Georgia O'Keeffe and one signed photo by Alfred Stieglitz.

So…a mansion full of rooms like this and a French chef and a household staff and a two-thousand-acre vineyard and half my company. This is what a billion dollars buys you.

Van Owen closes the door and makes his way behind the resolute desk. He sits, motioning for Carl to sit. "Don't worry, Carl. Your machine will be safe here with me."

The rage that had incited Carl to storm the kitchen had been partially melted by the pastry and is about to be altogether evaporated by the grandeur of Van Owen's study when Carl resurrects it by refusing to sit. His verbal attack had missed its mark in the kitchen. Before re-launching it now, he considers focusing his rage to sharpen his mind might be a more fruitful approach.

"Look, Mr. Van Owen, I'm on to something. My people ran some tests and just finished analyzing the data. So, why don't you give me access to a PC with internet and we can have a look?"

"I'd be glad to, Carl. But first, I beg your indulgence for a moment." Van Owen motions toward the Chesterfield ruby leather wingback in front of the desk, "Please. Sit."

Carl takes a deep breath and warily lowers himself into the chair. Its seductive comfort is dangerous. Even though Carl is taller, the wingback places him below Van Owen, who commands the intimidating desk from his Gunlocke JFK Oval Office chair. Carl sits up straight and leans forward. "Alright then. What's so important?"

"Carl, you can no longer trust Emily or that boyfriend of hers."

"What? No. I can trust them. I'm quite a good judge of character, you know. They'll keep their findings secret."

"Oh, they'll keep their secrets, alright. They've been doing so for some time, as evidenced by the fact they haven't told *you*."

"What are you talking about? They've shown me their findings. Emily's the one who got me pointed in the right direction in the first place."

"Mm-hmm. And right after breakfast, Frank emailed me the analysis she gave him. The same analysis they prepared for you. I sent it along to my hacker guy to have a look. It's been doctored, Carl.

"Doctored?"

"Whoever did it is extremely clever; one of the best jobs we've ever seen. But my guy is the best—and what he found is astonishing."

"So you just hijacked my entire project?"

"Your gut was right, my friend." Van Owen leans forward. He places his hands on the desk, palms down, locking in Carl's gaze. "Carl, your machine has detected an energy field. A very powerful one. Indeed, the most powerful force in the universe." Van Owen stands. He shimmies toward the bar. "Brandy?"

"I knew it!" Carl bolts up. Drinking before the party could be risky. He'll need his wits tonight. But Van Owen is pouring from a bottle of Louis XIII cognac. "Sure. Why not?"

Van Owen hands Carl a snifter of brandy. He pours another for himself and raises his glass to offer a toast. "To the man of the hour."

Carl looks around, feigning a search for *the man of the hour*. "You can't possibly be talking about me?"

Van Owen swirls the brandy, holding his glass at chest height and draws a breath through his nose. "It's all you, Carl. That machine you built will revolutionize life as we know it!"

"Then why don't you want me talking about it tonight?"

Van Owen raises his glass to chin height, takes a whiff, eyes closed, "Because these people are philistines." The eyes open. "Oh, they may be high born, or just wealthy enough to think themselves cultured and successful. But not one of them is capable of comprehending the truly profound nature of the energy field your machine detected. Unveiling that discovery must be done strategically in order to maintain control over its formidable power." He offers a nod of respect, raising his glass again. "Now, thanks to you, that control rests with me. And I intend to keep it that way." Van Owen takes a tiny sip.

"You?" Carl takes a deep breath, quashing his impulse to throw the four-thousand-dollar brandy in Van Owen's face. "That is *my* invention. *My* name is on the patent application. You didn't strike my name from the revised application, did you?"

"Good heavens no, my friend." Van Owen returns to his seat, leans back in his chair, and reaches out across his desk motioning for Carl to sit. "Please. I'm quite sure we can discuss the future of your invention as civilized men." Another sip. "How do you like the Brandy?"

"Well...it's extraordinary...But—"

"I knew you were a man of distinction. You're a scientist, an inventor. I'm an entrepreneur. There's a distinction, hmm?"

Carl finds Van Owen's wordplay exasperating. "Of course. But—"

"Carl, I'm about to make you richer than your wildest dreams could possibly have imagined."

"Och."

"Oh...? You don't like money?"

"Well, I'm not about to move to California and buy a vineyard."

"You can buy a vineyard in France if you'd prefer. I mean...since you speak the language. And Carl, you'll have plenty of money for that soon enough. I'll connect you with some people who can help you find a good one." A third sip.

Carl knows it is unwise to scoff at a financier's offer of an outrageous sum of money—especially since this particular financier happens to be bankrolling his financially strapped company.

Let's see if I can convey my true ambition without insulting him. "Do you have any idea why I started MGH?"

"To develop novel treatments for diseases that afflict millions of people?"

Wow! Money really is all he thinks about. Here goes nothin'. "Cures, actually. Healing is the true goal. But my greatest dream is to solve one of the most profound mysteries in all of biology."

"And that is...?"

"What coaxes a stem cell to differentiate?"

Van Owen lays his glass on his desk and raises his eyebrows.

"You know," continues Carl, "how does it decide to become a heart cell or a bone cell or toe cell or a blood cell or a brain cell or anything else?"

Van Owen leans back in his chair and smiles. "Well, my friend, you've come to the right place. I can answer that question for you. But first, you must get rid of Emily and her boyfriend."

Carl's entire body of cell biology knowledge crashes into his experience raising money and plows into his encounters with Emily and John. It's as if he's trapped in a 20-car pileup halfway through a deep tunnel under a forbidding mountain. Only a single word escapes, "Why?"

"Because they're members of a secret society determined to prevent the answer to your question from being discovered. They doctored the findings to make it look like your machine detected a DNA anomaly. But, in reality, it detected the answer to your question."

"I don't understand. *You* told me to hire Emily!"

"Yes, I did." Van Owen takes a longer sip of brandy. "I have a confession to make." He sets the snifter on his desk. "I was once a member of that same society. I once shared their determination to keep mankind in the dark. But I have seen the error of my ways. You, my friend, and your machine have inspired me to seek another path—a path of enlightenment."

Carl trains his focus on a pinpoint of light at the end of the long, dark tunnel. "So, you're telling me the answer to this great mystery lies in the data from my experiments with my machine?"

"Well...the answer has been known—and kept secret—for some time. Your machine provides the first scientific proof of it."

"Alrighty then, let's have a look at that data!"

"All in good time, my friend." Another luxurious sip. "Look, I realize this is a lot to digest." He leans back in his chair, swirling his brandy. "The life you've been living is over. Your financial struggles? A thing of the past. Tonight, you enter a new world as a new man—a very successful, wealthy, *desirable* man. And your success will be compounding every day for the foreseeable future."

Carl pretends to relax in his chair. He takes a long, slow, deep breath and stares down at the brandy swirling in his glass. His careerlong quest is within his grasp, but Van Owen insists on delaying. *Why?*

Van Owen had just betrayed the answer. Look at his self-satisfied smirk. The one thing he craves more than money is power. Delay is part of his game—a control tactic, a power play. What if Carl were to mosey on over to the fireplace and keep Van Owen engaged in conversation while adjusting logs with the tall poker? Once the poker is good and hot, he could whack Van Owen's head off before he knows what hit him. For that matter, given his greater stature and superior strength, Carl could lunge across the desk and snap Van Owen's neck with his bare hands. But what then? Van Owen knows the answer to the mystery. His hacker guy knows how John altered the data. And he's got the money needed to fund continued research. Carl needs Van Owen.

But why does Van Owen need me? He's got my machine, my data. He already owns half my company. What am I missing?

A strategy for answering this question flashes behind Carl's eyes. He abandons his brandy to catch Van Owen's eye. "So, what would you have me do?"

"Be your charismatic self tonight. These people are easily seduced by confidence and charisma. And you, my friend, are eminently capable of exuding both when you want to. They'll eat it up."

"And what about my machine? My data?"

"I can get plenty of these people to invest without any mention of the machine. Tonight, I'll raise enough money to thrust your company into the forefront of stem cell research and set you on your way to becoming ridiculously wealthy."

"But didn't you say I've discovered a new energy field?"

"Indeed…the machine detected an energy field."

"Wouldn't tonight's people be interested in my discovery? Wouldn't it make an investment in my company more attractive? Wouldn't we get a better deal?"

"Oh, they'd be interested, alright. Interested enough to concoct a scheme to take it from me." Van Owen finishes his brandy, sets his snifter down, and leans back in his chair. "You see, these people are eager to be associated with the leading edge of science," he gestures toward Carl, "and delighted to profit from it, with my help, of course," his head and hands feign modesty, "but if they get wind of a chance to gain control of this energy field," he puts his hands together at the fingertips, "they will stop at nothing to do so."

"I don't understand. You've got everything you need to maintain control. What could they possibly do?"

"Oh, my dear, Carl. Do not play at naïveté. You know perfectly well how powerful people do whatever is necessary to maintain and enhance their power. They'll pretend to share your devotion to discovering new treatments, but there's only one thing that truly captivates their interest."

"Cures, dammit. Healing. Not mere treatments!" Carl reigns in his frustration before it overflows. "Anyhow, what plans do you have for my machine?"

"Let's talk about that tomorrow, hmm? Tonight, we focus on you. Your cures, your company, your future, your wealth."

"Fine."

"And don't call Emily before we have a chance to talk tomorrow."

"You got it."

"Excellent." Van Owen rises. "Now...let's go introduce you to some interesting people."

The party—and the grand ballroom—were more extravagant than Carl could possibly have imagined. The food. The wines. The champagne. The live music. The guests!

Following Van Owen's dictum to exude confidence and charm

suppressed any tendency to be starstruck until after Carl had collapsed in his room, at which point he couldn't possibly sleep with all those famous people traipsing through his head.

At first, Van Owen's constant praise unnerved Carl. An hour or so later, he had become so inured to it that he was startled when introduced to Van Owen's brother without any accolades whatsoever. The reason for Van Owen's unusual presentation unveiled itself when his brother, who conspicuously showed no interest in Carl or his work, immediately launched into improbable tales of his own heroic exploits and sexual conquests. After four or five minutes that felt like hours, Van Owen rescued Carl by whisking him away and presenting him to the Senate Majority Leader, employing his typical laudatory introduction.

Carl lies awake, staring out the giant window at the deep blue light seeping into the black sky. All night long, he'd mingled effortlessly with some of the most famous and powerful people on Earth. Every one of them had been captivated by his charm, fascinated by his work. He basks in the honor, glory, and power bestowed upon him...and he craves more.

Chapter Twenty-One
The Partnership

"GOOD MORNING, SIR," says the butler as he pulls a chair away from the breakfast table, inviting Carl to sit. Carl obliges. "Coffee or tea?"

"Coffee. Thank you."

The butler pours steaming coffee into an elegant china cup from a sterling silver pot. He motions to the silver pitcher of cream and silver bowl of sugar cubes with silver tongs on a silver tray at the center of the antique mahogany table. "Mr. Van Owen will join you presently."

Carl empties the dainty little cup of black coffee in 3 gulps, at which point the butler appears, seemingly out of nowhere, to refill it. The butler motions to the uniformed maid standing by the buffet. She dashes off. Carl smiles at the butler. He downs the newly poured, slightly cooler coffee; this time in 2 gulps.

I hope she's getting more coffee. It'll take plenty to get me going this morning.

The butler suddenly comes to attention.

"Well, good morning, Carl," says Van Owen as he bounds into the dining room with more than enough joviality to crank up the volume of Carl's headache. "What a night we had, eh?" He rubs his hands together.

Carl swallows his wooziness and rises. "Good morning."

"Oh, please…sit." Van Owen sits at the head of the table. He nods to the butler, who cruises to the kitchen.

Carl sits, still fuzzy. "So last night was…successful?"

"A banner night, indeed, my friend. You were quite the sensation."

"Glad I could help."

"Listen, I took the liberty of dropping the first million into your personal account just now. The rest will be along in due course."

"What?"

"And I had another look at your books. Carl, you need to start paying yourself a respectable salary."

The butler and maid return. The maid sets a silver coffee pot on a silver tray, striking a clear, bell tone ring.

Ahh…the sound of wealth.

The butler sets half a grapefruit at each of their places, returning a moment later with coffee. Van Owen removes a section of grapefruit with his pointed grapefruit spoon and eats it.

Carl sips the scorching coffee, hoping it will help him recover from the million-dollar shock. "I don't know what to say."

"Nothing *to* say, my friend." Van Owen gives Carl a serious look. "You know…you ought to have a Swiss bank account. We'll get that set up for you after breakfast." He slurps down another section of grapefruit.

Carl locates the grapefruit spoon amid the array of silverware before him. He timidly pokes it into the grapefruit. Juice squirts into Van Owen's eye.

"Oh, I'm so sorry!"

Van Owen gropes for his napkin and dabs his eyes. "No worries." He wipes his face. "Perhaps grapefruit is not your breakfast." He motions to the butler, who vanishes into the kitchen.

"No, it's fine. I'm just a little—"

"Not a lot of sleep?"

"Well…no, actually."

Van Owen attacks his grapefruit. With slow, deliberate strokes, Carl carves around the edges of one grapefruit section.

A few moments later, the maid removes the grapefruit dish from Van Owen, who had gobbled up the whole thing, and Carl, who had mangled one section but eaten nothing. The butler lays a plate with a silver cover before each of them. At precisely the same moment, the butler and maid remove the covers.

"Enjoy," says the butler.

Carl marvels at the beauty of his plate. A French omelet with a smooth, glistening surface artfully arranged with a small piece of toasted French bread, two slices of fresh avocado, fresh sprigs of parsley and thyme, and three small tomatoes—gold, red, and purple—each sliced in half.

"All this is grown here, and the eggs are from our chickens," explains Van Owen. "Dig in, my friend. We've got a busy day ahead."

Scents drift up from the plate. They blend into an enticing aromatic, dissolving Carl's headache and arousing his hunger. He laments having to ruin the chef's visual splendor in order to eat. His fork carefully slices a bit of omelet. It takes 90 seconds for the creamy, soft, buttery eggs to melt in his mouth, and lift him into a state of bliss with his eyes closed.

Van Owen devours his entire breakfast with a few huge, brutal bites. Carl picks up his eating pace. He snickers secretly, recalling how he felt as a little boy struggling to keep a walking pace with his father.

As if watching from the ceiling, Carl observes himself gradually being seduced by Van Owen's opulent world. The sensation is reminiscent of his experience wearing *Michael's jacket.*

What am I doing here? What will this new life do to me? How can I remain dedicated to healing?

"Last night, you mentioned you have a strategy for revealing what I've discovered," says Carl. "Can you elaborate on that?"

"Yes, I can. And we'll dive right in after we sort out a few details of the investments I secured last night."

Carl stands. "Ready when you are."

Van Owen leads Carl to his study. He presents Carl with papers to sign. Hiding his distress becomes more difficult with each page Carl reads. He'd already traded away a majority stake in his company and his machine in return for another six months of funding. Now, Van Owen wants him to sign a non-disclosure agreement (NDA) banning Carl from telling anyone about his discovery.

"I have some concerns here."

"Please...elaborate."

"You want me on the board of your new educational foundation? I figure David didn't tell you how much I loathe boards and committees. It took over ten years of consternation for me to discover that non-profits are designed to serve the needs of the donors. If I hadn't wasted so much time with those damned boards and fundraisers, I could have had my machine patented in the 90s."

"It's just a formality, my friend. We need your degrees, not your time. One or two meetings a year. And believe me, you'll enjoy the meetings. Did you enjoy yourself last night?"

"Well...sure..."

"Good. It's settled then. I'll deal with donors and fundraisers and all the nasty details of running a foundation. You just come to a couple of parties, sign some papers, and that'll be that."

"Fine…But why the NDA?"

"Carl, like I said last night. You're a scientist. I'm an entrepreneur—and a PR pro. You focus on the science, the treatments, the cures. I'll focus on educating the world about the energy field. We can't have people just blurting it out, you know. Communication with the public must be handled with the utmost care."

"But I'm not just anyone 'blurting it out.' I discovered it. You can't muzzle me."

"My dear, Carl. It's not a muzzle at all. Think of it as another way to protect your time. Do you really want to waste your days away dumbing your discovery down to the point where it can be explained to talk show hosts and bureaucrats?"

"I couldn't explain it even if I wanted to because I don't know what it is." Anger bleeds through Carl's voice. "You supposedly know what it is, but you won't tell me. Assuming you finally do tell me, I won't be able to confirm your hypothesis because you took my machine away!"

"Calm down, my friend. I told you we'd get to discussing your machine…and we will. We just need to put all this business paperwork behind us first."

The admonition to calm down has always incensed Carl and this time is no exception, made all the more infuriating by Van Owen's deadly calm voice. Visiting Van Owen's estate has given him plenty of practice focusing his rage to sharpen his mind—practice that comes in handy at this juncture. He slaps the file folders closed and holds them up. "I need my lawyer to look at these."

"I've already emailed everything to Stan. He'll call you later today and talk it over with you."

"Boy, you really do think of everything."

"That's my job, Carl. Now, let's get your Swiss bank account set up." Van Owen starts typing.

Carl knows he's being played. *What have I got to lose?* "Mr. Van Owen," he clears his throat, "I really do appreciate your generosity…and your help with opening a Swiss bank account. But can you please tell me about this energy field I've discovered and your strategy for informing the public?"

Van Owen stops typing. "Certainly. What would you like to know?"

"Why don't you start by telling me what you know about the energy field."

"Alright." Van Owen leans back in his chair. "Simply put, Carl, it is the source of life. It is what coaxes a stem cell to differentiate. It lies at the root of the placebo effect. All those stories you may have heard about miraculous healings are, in fact, encounters with this energy field."

"Whoa…" Carl's anger, doubts, and frustrations vanish. His mind is clear, focused on this single revelation. Shivers race up his spine. "You're implying…my machine detected the energy field at the instant stem cells began to differentiate."

"That is entirely possible."

"Is that what the data show? Before being doctored, I mean?"

"My guess is yes, which is why they felt the need to doctor—"

"Gimme a couple hours with that data, and I'll confirm it for you." Anticipation surges through Carl like an Olympic runner awaiting the starting gun.

"After your chat with Stan, there'll be plenty of time for you to inspect the data."

"So, you're holding my machine and my data hostage, now?"

"That's an awfully hostile characterization of our partnership."

"Partnership, huh? Is that really how you see it?"

"Why yes. Of course. Carl, we are about to usher in a global revolution on par with the discovery of electricity. But our revolution will change the world much more quickly…which is why it must be managed so very carefully. And that is going to require the both of us, working together, each of us understanding our own role while appreciating and respecting the role of the other.

"We've talked about this, Carl. Your role is chief scientist, inventor, healer. My role is…well…everything else, essentially. Honestly, Carl, do you really think you're suited to managing all the politics and PR involved in a worldwide scientific paradigm shift?"

"And you are?"

"Let's hope so. Unless you've got someone else in mind…"

Carl shrugs. He's enthralled by the prospect of being free to focus on his research without constant financial worries and insufferable investor meetings. Yet something deep within him is ringing out a warning. The specter of losing control over his machine—his discovery—hammers at his side, tightening the muscles below his waist into a knot.

Van Owen can characterize this as a partnership all he likes, but it's certainly not an equal one. He's pulling all the strings. This is what a billion really buys you!

Chapter Twenty-Two
A New Reality

"STOP RIGHT THERE!" commands Rox. She shoots up as Emily strides through the MGH doors.

The sight of a box with her name on it sitting on the front desk sends a chill through Emily. "What's going on?"

"Carl has instructed me to tell you..." Rox looks down at the box, then back at Emily and continues in a softer, lower pitched voice, "that you are no longer welcome here."

"What? Why?"

"He didn't say."

"What the f—"

"I'm sorry, Emily. Personally, I've liked you from the day you walked in here."

"But—"

"I have your final check here—and some papers for you to sign," says Rox trying to affect a friendly tone.

"I'm not signing anything! Where's Carl?"

"Carl got in late last night." Rox lowers her eyes. "He's not here…yet."

Emily grabs her cellphone and calls Carl. Voicemail.

"I doubt he'll answer," says Rox without looking up.

Emily's face heats up. She figures her cheeks will soon be pink enough for Rox to notice. She whips around and throws the door open.

"Wait…Emily. Your stuff."

"Hold onto it," yells Emily without turning around, "I'll be back!"

Emily's phone rings as the door closes behind her. It's John. Her heart races. She answers angrily, "What!"

"Are you at work?"

"I just got fired."

"Well, I guess I did too. I can't get into anything. Access denied…everywhere!"

"What's happening, John?"

"I'll get into it. Come right home!"

Emily ends the call and tramps toward the T station. She dreads going home even as she's compelled to continue walking. An old man in a dark fedora approaches on the sidewalk. The small dog he's leisurely walking scurries back and forth in front of him as if sweeping clean a path for his master's stroll.

How can anyone be so nonchalant at a time like this?

Emily's pace quickens. She calls Becky, the leader of her lab team. Voicemail. She hangs up and calls Frank. Voicemail. Emily stops. She yells into the phone, "Fuuuuuck!"

The old man crosses to the other side of the street and stares back at Emily. She shouts at him, "Good idea to keep that mangy mutt away from me. I bite ya know!"

The old man picks up his pace, dragging the dog behind him.

Emily marches on. She calls Ashley.

Ashley answers instantly, "What's up, girl? It's been a while."

"I really need to hear a friendly voice."

"What's wrong, hon?"

"I just got fired."

"From your dream Job? Oh, Emmy. I'm so sorry. What happened?"

"I really don't know. Something's not right. I can feel it."

"Everything okay with John?"

"Yeah, I guess."

"Oh my. You sound terrible."

Emily does not respond.

"You know," continues Ashley after another beat, "I've got some vacation days saved up. How about you and I go visit my dad in Honduras for a week? It's warm. It's beautiful. It's quiet. We can get away from it all."

"Wow, Ashley. That sounds amazing. But I can't just up and leave. Not now."

"Why not? You don't have to go to work."

"Exactly. And I won't be getting paid either. Shit…John and I are looking at new apartments. Guess we'll have to put the kibosh on that."

"I thought you said John was making decent money."

"Yeah…better than the restaurant. But we live in Cambridge… and without my income…besides, I've got to figure out what's going on?"

"Emmy, tickets are cheap now. And a week in the middle of nowhere might be just what the doctor ordered for getting your head together. You know how it's worked wonders for me."

"Ashley, the problem isn't with my head. It's—"

"You're right. It's with your heart."

"What?"

"Can you hear yourself, girl?"

"Huh?"

"You sound heartbroken."

Emily cannot hold back her tears. She puts the phone to her chest, averts her eyes from the crowd pouring out of the T station, and darts into a coffee shop in search of an empty table.

"Emmy? Are you there?"

Emily curls into a ball in a corner booth, crying softly into the phone, "I'm here."

"You know I'll always love you."

"I know," sobs Emily, "I'll always love you too."

"You'd better," a touch of despair seeps into Ashley's voice, "You're the only one I can trust."

"Uh-oh. Everything okay with—"

"Don't. Just don't. Don't say his name."

"Oh, I'm sorry."

"I'm not. You were right. He turned out to be a first-rate dick!"

"Isn't that his—"

"Stop!" Ashley laughs until a sob creeps through.

Emily laughs through tears. "Okay. Let's do it. I'll talk to John when I get home."

"I'll book flights. Don't you let him talk you out of—"

"I won't. Don't worry. See you soon."

"See you soon, love."

The hint of Ashley whispering, "Yes!" floats through the phone before the call ends. Emily closes her eyes.

What have I done? What did I agree to?

Heading out of the coffee shop, Emily spurns the sounds, smells, and sights of the city. With each step down into the T station, she retreats farther into her inner world. By the time she enters the subway car, Emily, like most other commuters, is barely cognizant of her surroundings. Face dry. No sign of tears or the pain that had prompted them.

Ashley's wrong. My heart is fine. I just have to figure out what made Carl so angry he'd want to fire me. Was it because I let Frank take the machine? What else could I have done? What if he somehow figured out we doctored the data? That would explain why John is locked out too. Does it also mean Carl knows his machine detected the Life Field? Oh, what a disaster.

The train squeals. Thoughts subside like receding flood waters, leaving only ruin and despair in Emily's heart, confirming Ashley's diagnosis.

The PA's unintelligible squawk announcing Emily's stop startles her out of her stupor. She has no memory of the past few stops and almost missed this one. The braking train tugs an ache from her chest. Nobody is standing by the door. Emily slides into place, leaning into the forward pole flanking the exit, determined to be first to hit the platform. When the doors open, she walks like a zombie, dread intensifying with every step.

Emily opens the apartment door with the same care she took when John was recovering from his mystery meeting. She peers down the short hallway. John is at his computer, his emotionless face hardened by the stark, bluish-white glow from the screen. He fails to acknowledge her as she approaches.

"What a fine mess you've gotten us into now," says John in a quiet monotone, still facing the screen.

"What? What did you find out?"

"Nothing. Absolutely nothing. I'm locked out of everything. Carl won't return my calls, texts, emails—nothing!"

"He ghosted me too."

John leans back his chair and glares at Emily. "And why do you think that is?"

"I don't know. Maybe you didn't hide your data manipulation well enough."

"Oh, so this is all my fault?"

"I don't know. Maybe he had help."

"If he saw through my mods, he must have had help. Smart help. Carl's a genius...at biology. There's no way he has the hacking skills to catch—"

"So what do we do now?"

"We? There's no we here, Emily. This is your problem. You fix it."

"Really? Wasn't doctoring Carl's data your idea?"

"Only because you forced me to *do something* to prevent Carl from realizing he'd discovered the Life Field."

"We wouldn't have had to worry about that if you'd gotten a *real* job in tech—the thing you obsessed about every day since I met you. And you'd be paying off your six-figure student loan. But no. You had to go join Jimmy's goddammed cult."

"Yeah...well if I hadn't tracked Jimmy down and met Andy, you wouldn't have gotten the job with Carl. You'd still be working in a restaurant!"

"My job as Orville's top manager is the only reason we could afford this apartment. We certainly couldn't have done it on your paltry tips."

"I'd have been perfectly happy in the dorm. You're the one who convinced me to move into this expensive place. And now you want to move again—to a more expensive place. Nothing is ever good enough for you!"

"We moved in here so we could be together! I thought that's what you wanted. But it doesn't matter now. We're not gonna be able to afford a new apartment anyhow."

"Thank God! I am so sick of getting dragged around this city every night, every weekend, looking at 3rd floor walkups we can't afford even with both our incomes."

"Is that what I am to you? A burden? I thought we were in this together."

"No Emily. You roped me into this Carl caper against my better judgment—and my warning, if you remember. I'm done." John gets up, grabs his coat.

"Where are you going?"

"Out."

"No, you don't. Not again. You are not going to abandon me again." Emily blocks the door.

"What? You gonna lock me in here? Force me to do your dirty work?" John stands straight to match Emily's height. He lifts his chin as if spoiling for a fight. "I told you I didn't want to mess with Carl's discoveries, but you insisted. And guess what? It backfired. Now you're out. Carl can't trust you. Nobody else in the field will either. You've become a pariah. Forget research. Stick to restaurants. You'd better call Orville right now and beg for your old job back." John puts his coat on.

"If you walk out that door, don't you bother coming back."

Chills grip Emily. The power of her threat surges through her body and sharpens her mind. It could alter her reality far more than losing her job has done. Her life swirls before her—a vortex into the unknown. The same self-destructive urges she caught terrorizing Ashley years ago now tempt her with the certainty she craves. She resolves to stand by her threat.

There's comfort in losing everything. At least I'll know what I've got. And I'll be free.

"I need some air. If you can't live with that, then I don't know…" John pauses. His next words could easily shatter their love, given its fragile state.

Emily's vortex engulfs them both. The remnants of their splintered bond swirl farther apart. She lunges out in a frantic attempt to collect them. Her venture evokes, within John, a vision of the power he now holds to usher in a new reality—one in which he and Emily are no longer a couple. Wicked words surge forth demanding to be released.

"Wait." Emily interrupts John's attempt to speak. "I need to tell you something."

"What?" snaps John. Infuriated by Emily's interruption, he is nonetheless grateful to be spared the risk of bringing his dangerous thoughts to life.

"Ashley's going to visit her dad in Honduras. She invited me to go with her. Thinks it'll be good for me."

"Of course she does. She loves Honduras but needs you to keep her dad from turning a relaxing vacation into a perilous escapade."

The last time John and Emily accompanied Ashley to Honduras, they returned emotionally and physically exhausted. For days on end, Ashley's father cajoled them into bushwhacking through the jungle in search of deadly snakes. At night, he took them to wild parties hosted by local gang leaders, proudly showing off his gorgeous daughter. Apparently, he finds fear intoxicating.

The college students, who had come seeking tranquility, felt like elderly vacationers when they pleaded for a single, languid day under the sun. Ashley added to the awkwardness by strutting through the entire week in a thong bikini, constantly drawing John's eye to her tan, wet, curvaceous body.

"It's only a week. Maybe a little time apart would be good for both of us," says Emily in her soft, tender voice—not her throaty whisper.

"Fine. I'll hack my way back into Carl's servers while you and Ashley go off and play in the sun. Just don't you two come back knocked up by a couple of gang bangers."

"Jesus, John!"

"I'm ordering pizza." John grabs his phone from his coat, calls to place an order, throws his coat on the couch, and stomps off to his computer.

Chapter Twenty-Three
The Letter

"THAT'S US," SAYS ASHLEY upon hearing the boarding call for their flight. She springs out of her seat.

"I really hope I'm doing the right thing," says Emily. She and Ashley get in line.

"You absolutely are, hon. You need this."

"I don't know. John doesn't seem happy with anything I do lately."

"I thought you said he was okay with you going."

"Well, he didn't vigorously object."

"You two are good then?"

"Or maybe he's just given up on me."

"He loves you, Emmy."

"What makes you so sure?"

"I see it in his eyes."

"Yeah, when he's looking at your nubile figure."

"That's the point, Emmy. He's never hit on me."

"Only in his dreams, then."

"Stop!" Ashley gives Emily a friendly slap on the shoulder. "He loves you. I'm sure of it."

Two men in dark suits and dark glasses approach.

"Emily MacMahon?" asks the shorter one.

"Yes?" replies Emily.

"Come with me, please."

"What?"

"Special Agent Brewer, FBI," says the taller one, flashing his badge. "This is agent Shipley. You need to come with us."

"Can't you see we're about to get on an airplane?"

"Not today, Ma'am," says Brewer.

"What's going on?" asks Ashley.

"You too, Ma'am," says Shipley.

"Don't call me Ma'am—I'm not the bloody Queen!" says Ashley with a wink, trying her best to affect an English accent. She whispers in Emily's ear, "I just love Helen Mirren and I've always wanted to say that. This seems like an opportune time."

"Ashley, I think these guys are serious," says Emily.

"Deadly serious, Ma'am," says Brewer.

"But we'll miss our flight," protests Ashley.

"Yes, Miss, you will," says Shipley in a monotone. He lifts his glasses to make eye contact with Ashley, "Now, please, come with us."

"Very funny," says Ashley, smiling at Shipley.

"This is no joke," says Brewer. "Let's not make a scene here."

"I was talking about the way he called me Miss, the pun, and, you know, how it sounded like Yoda. I mean, It's fu—"

"I get it," says Brewer. "He does that. Now let's go."

"Where are we going?" asks Emily, her voice cracking.

"We'll explain along the way," answers Shipley.

"On the way to where?" asks Ashley.

"That's enough!" replies Brewer, sternly but without shouting. "Do we need to cuff you?"

The agents escort Emily and Ashley to their black SUV parked at the Departures entrance. Shipley ushers Emily and Ashley into the back seat. Brewer drives. Emily texts John, explaining what has happened.

John responds, "U arrested?"

"Don't think so"

"Don't say ANYTHING until the lawyer gets there."

"Lawyer?"

"Yes, say nothing, where u going?"

"Where are we going, Agent Brewer?" asks Emily, looking at his face in the rearview mirror.

Brewer's eyes flash up to meet Emily's, "Our office in Chelsea."

Emily texts John, "FBI office Chelsea"

"Sit tight, say nothing, luv u"

"See? I told you," whispers Ashley, pointing to John's last text on Emily's phone. Ashley peeks at Shipley, who's sitting in the front passenger seat. "The short one's kinda cute, don't you think? And he's funny too."

"What's that miss?" asks Shipley.

"Nothing," insists Emily, shooting a stern glance at Ashley. Emily raises her phone to Ashley's face and scrolls up to John's earlier text, *Don't say ANYTHING until lawyer gets there.* Ashley feigns compliance through a sexy, sheepish look, pretending to button her lip with her fingers. Emily rolls her eyes. Brewer is looking at her in the rearview mirror. She glares at Brewer, pushing his eyes back onto the road as she sits up straight and summons a fierce resolve to protect herself and her best friend.

The agents sit across the table from Emily in the small, stark, but comfortable interview room. Images of all the people who might be staring through the one-way mirror flash through her head.

"Am I under arrest?" asks Emily.

"We just have some questions for you," replies Shipley.

"Questions that couldn't wait until next week?"

"Why were you fleeing the country?" asks Brewer.

"I wasn't fleeing anything. Ashley and I were just…" Emily stops. She folds her arms and looks down.

"Just…what?" asks Shipley.

"I'm not saying anything until my lawyer gets here!" asserts Emily.

"Guilty people wait for their lawyers," insists Brewer.

"That's bullshit and you know it," snaps Emily.

Brewer scowls as if offended by Emily's language.

"Do you want some coffee…or water?" offers Shipley.

"I want you to tell me what's going on."

"I thought you wanted to wait for your lawyer," says Brewer.

"Can't you at least tell me why I'm here?"

"We ask the questions."

"Fine. I'll wait."

There's a knock at the door. It opens. A young agent motions toward the tall, commanding presence behind him.

"Buzz Krechting, attorney for Ms. MacMahon." Buzz slips past the young agent with an easy air of authority. He is a lean, six feet three inches, with curly white hair flowing down past his collar and a white goatee consisting of a large mustache with a soul patch. The gentleman is impeccably dressed in a black suit, white cowboy hat, snakeskin boots, white silk shirt, braided leather bolo tie with silver tips, and a three-inch turquoise clasp. He hands a business card to each agent before tipping his hat to Emily, "Honored to be of service, Ma'am."

"Where's John?" demands Emily.

"We ask the questions," asserts Brewer.

"Oh, now, gentlemen. What could possibly be the harm in allowing me to tell the little lady, here, where her beloved is?" beseeches Buzz, in his genteel, Texas drawl.

Brewer rolls his eyes.

"Mr. Wells is at your apartment," says Buzz. "Agents are conducting a search."

"What?" exclaims Emily.

"It's all very routine, Ma'am," assures Buzz in his slow, steady, calm manner. "I'm sure they'll find nothing interesting."

"We'll decide what's interesting," insists Brewer.

"Yes, of course," concedes Buzz with a nod of respect. He waits for the agents to sit, then removes his hat and takes the chair next to Emily.

"And Ashley? Where's she?" asks Emily.

"Ashley's fine," says Shipley, "She's in the other room."

"Very talkative girl, your friend," says Brewer.

Emily's face pivots toward Buzz. He shakes his head ever-so-slightly, a signal that Brewer is probably lying.

Brewer opens a file folder the young agent had handed him. He slips out an 8x10 photo, closes the file folder, rotates the photo, and slides it toward Emily. "Do you know this man?"

Emily glances at Buzz, who nods his approval for her to answer.

"No, I don't. Who is he?"

Brewer produces another photo. "How about this man?"

Emily shakes her head. "Nope."

He shows Emily a third photo. "And him?"

"No. Who are these people?"

"You're absolutely sure you don't recognize any of these men?" Brewer adjusts the position of the photos until they're perfectly lined up. "Take your time. Have another look."

"No. I don't need another look. I've never seen any of them. Who are they?"

Emily gazes at Buzz. He raises one eyebrow and tilts his head, hinting that he will tell her who these men are after the interview.

"How about this guy?"

Emily is startled by this new photo of a man she does recognize. Her eyes dart over to Buzz. He nods.

"That's Ashley's Dad. Why do you have his photo?"

"Costas Papadopoulos?" asks Brewer.

"Yes, I'm pretty sure that's his first name. Ashley calls him Baba. I call him Mr. P."

"So, Mr. Papadopoulos was planning to hide you after you fled the country?"

"What? What are you talking about? We were going to visit. I was just trying to get away..." The corner of Emily's eye catches Buzz's disapproving glance. "Okay. Wrong choice of words. Ashley and I were going on a vacation."

"To hide out sheltered by a known associate of gang leaders in a country with no extradition to the United States."

"Gentlemen," says Buzz, "please allow me to point out that Honduras does, in fact, have an extradition treaty with us."

"Technically, yes. But it's nearly impossible to get fugitives out of there—especially when they're protected by those gangs."

"Fugitive? What fugitive?" asks Emily. She doesn't need John's hacking skills to work out the disturbing pattern in Brewer's questioning.

Another photo creeps toward Emily. Both agents are silent. They study her reaction.

"That's Carl. Carl Friedrich. Why? Did something happen? Is he Okay?"

"Why wouldn't he be?"

"I don't know."

"Have you always been against stem cell research? Or did your opposition harden when you saw how many babies Dr. Friedrich kills in his lab every day?"

"What? No. Carl doesn't kill babies. They're not babies. They're not even embryos. They're blastocysts."

"Did she say blast?" warns Shipley, scanning the room.

"What kind of blast are we talking about, here?" asks Brewer.

Brewer was making a joke, right? These guys aren't serious, are they?

Buzz places his hand gently on Emily's knee. Grasping his signal not to answer, she leans back in her chair, forcing herself to relax—or at least to look relaxed.

"I believe the young lady is referring to a tiny embryonic structure—a couple hundred cells—comprising an inner cell mass in some fluid that later forms an embryo, and an outer layer of cells that nourish and protect it. Is that correct, Ma'am?"

"Very good! I mean yes, that's it. And please call me Emily."

"Very well, Miss Emily."

"Jesus," says Emily under her breath, shaking her head. *Shit. My cheeks are probably bright pink.*

"Something you'd like to share with us?" asks Shipley.

Nobody speaks.

After a long pause, Brewer continues, "Was getting fired the tipping point? Is that what made you feel compelled to act against Dr. Friedrich?

To protect the unborn babies while you still had the chance?"

"Against Carl? No. I liked Carl. I don't understand—" Buzz touches her knee again. She stops talking.

"You said you liked him," says Brewer.

"Yes, very much."

"Past tense."

"Oh, no. Did something happen to Carl?"

"You tell me."

"What are you talking about? I haven't seen him in days. I can't even get hold of him."

"Did you mail the envelope to Carl, or did you have someone else do it?"

"Envelope? What envelope? I've never sent him anything by snail mail. We text and email each other."

"Are you saying you did not mail the letter laced with anthrax?"

"Wait, what? Anthrax? No! Is that what this is about?"

"Then who did?"

"I don't know! Oh, my God. Is Carl okay?"

"Dr. Friedrich is fine. But Roxanne Gordon is in the hospital fighting for her life."

"Rox? No. Oh, no. Oh, Rox!" Emily stops. She closes her eyes, pressing her thumb and two fingers against her forehead to hold back tears.

"Disappointed your weapon hit the wrong target?"

"What? No. I mean, Rox? Och. I mean…" Emily turns away to hide the tears she fears are imminent.

"I get the distinct impression that you fellas don't have enough to hold my client," contends Buzz.

"Well, let's look at what we do have, shall we?" insists Brewer.

Buzz is silent. Emily takes a breath, successfully holding back the tears, knowing she ought not to speak until Buzz speaks.

"Okay," says Brewer, "we've got your client here—a disgruntled employee who was fired after her boss discovers she and her boyfriend doctored his company's data, thereby putting the patent application for his new invention at risk. Further investigation uncovers that she and the boyfriend are members of some secret society hell-bent on stopping Dr. Friedrich and his machine from doing whatever it does. We notice an uptick in chatter among members of the Army of God—an underground terrorist organization with a history of murdering doctors. Now, they have plenty of members who believe stem cell research is tantamount to murder, just like abortion. In their twisted minds, murdering doctors is justified in the service of saving the lives of the unborn. And these fanatics are experts at hiding all evidence of their communication. With me so far?"

Emily summons enough will to quell her inner fire raging at these accusations. Knowing Brewer's question is designed to goad her into answering, she takes a modicum of satisfaction in thwarting him by staying silent and showing no emotion.

"Please, continue," says Buzz.

"As it turns out, your client's boyfriend is an expert at hiding the same sort of digital trail. And when our digital forensic investigators looked at Dr. Friedrich's data, they found evidence of hacking techniques identical to those used by terrorist organizations."

Brewer pauses, once again studying Emily's reaction. Emily successfully suppresses her simmering urge to refute every sentence he has uttered. She takes long, slow, deep—but quiet—breaths, attempting to prevent her cheeks from flushing more than they already have.

"But here's the kicker," continues Brewer. "When an anthrax laced envelope addressed to your client's boss arrives at his office, your client (who has access to a lab and the knowhow to make anthrax powder) is on her way to Honduras to hide out, protected by a known associate of gang leaders, who could scuttle any attempt at extradition."

"Fellas, that sounds like a big ol' heap o' coincidence to me," says Buzz. "Now, you heard my client deny she had anything to do with the envelope in question. And by her reaction, I'd say you could reasonably conclude she was genuinely alarmed to hear about it."

"There are just too many coincidences here," says Brewer. He asks Emily, "And where did you get the money to hire a high-priced lawyer from Ropes & Gray?"

Ropes & Gray? We can't afford this guy. What was John thinking?

Emily's breathing has worked. Her poker face has been perfected during this ordeal—and it comes in handy just now. She displays no surprise at all.

"Oh, c'mon fellas. You know perfectly well the details of my engagement are strictly confidential," says Buzz. He puts his hand on his heart. "Now I appreciate the pickle you're in—and I firmly believe you'll sort all this out when you catch the true perpetrator." Buzz stands. "But for now, if you do not plan to charge my client, we'll be on our way."

Emily stands.

The agents look at each other. Brewer eyes Buzz for a moment.

"You're free to go," says Brewer to Emily.

"Thank you, gentlemen" says Buzz. "Ashley will be coming with us."

"Fine," says Brewer. "Ms. MacMahon, I strongly urge you not to leave the country, or the state, or Cambridge, for that matter. Doing so could put you—and your friends and family—in jeopardy."

"Good day, gentlemen," says Buzz.

Buzz hurries Emily and Ashley into a limousine waiting in the parking lot, engine running, driver at the ready. He joins them. The driver speeds off the instant he hears the back door slam shut.

"Where are we going?" asks Emily.

"To Mr. Douglas' house. Mr. Wells will meet us there. It's not the tropical vacation you were planning, but he will make you perfectly comfortable. And we think it's safer than going home."

"Safer? Jesus. What about Ashley?" asks Emily.

"I'm with *you* Emmy," vows Ashley. "We're in this together now. Just like in our school days. It's Ashley and Emmy, backs against the wall, staying safe from the bullies and the popular kids."

Emily smiles, sighs, and hugs Ashley.

How are we going to keep Ashley safe without telling her about the Life Field?

Ashley tightens her grip. Emily permits herself a carefree moment to float in their embrace until a vision of Rox standing at her desk with downcast eyes thrusts her back in her seat as the limousine accelerates onto Storrow Drive.

"Oh, I really hope Rox is okay," mutters Emily. "I wasn't very nice to her the last time we spoke." She asks Buzz, "Who would do such a thing?"

"Well, those agents are pretty close, Miss Emily. It's the Army of God, alright. And those terrorists are trying to frame you—and Mr. Wells along with you. That first picture they showed you?"

"Yeah, who was that?"

"That was the Army of God's spokesman and most likely their leader, if they have one."

"Why would they want to frame me?"

"We'll talk about that when we get to Mr. Douglas' house."

"Who were those other guys?"

"Suspects in the 2001 Anthrax attacks. That's an ongoing investigation."

"They think I'm involved in that?"

"Probably not. I suspect they were just fishing. You see, the anthrax in the envelope addressed to Dr. Friedrich was identical to the stuff used in 2001, which also happens to be the same year the Army of God mailed hundreds of fake anthrax letters to abortion clinics."

"They didn't say anything about any of that. How do you know all this?"

"Well, Miss Emily, that's my job."

Chapter Twenty-Four
Allies and Adversaries

"Wow. Nice digs," says Ashley as the limousine pulls into Jimmy's driveway. "Who's this guy again?"

"We call him Jimmy D," replies Emily. "John works for him."

"Oh, that guy. This'll be interesting."

John and Jimmy are standing at the door. Emily peers out the window at John. Their eyes meet.

Is he still angry with her? Frustrated by her insistence on preventing Carl from discovering the Life Field? How could he possibly know how frightening the interview was? The torture of not knowing how much they know; the struggle to maintain composure; the intensity of her worry.

Does she know how much he regrets saying *there's no we here?* Of course, he loves her; wants her. He can't imagine life without her. The truth is, he'd do anything for her.

"John!" exclaims Emily. She runs to him. They embrace.

"Emily...my love," whispers John, "We're in this together. They've got no idea who they're messing with."

A warm glow radiates from John's heart. Emily's, too. John prevents his glow from expanding. So does Emily. Neither can allow their glow to touch the other. It's too dangerous.

"You must be Ashley," says Jimmy with an avuncular smile.

"Oh, I'm so sorry," says Emily, wiping the tears she had finally indulged. "Jimmy Douglass, please allow me to present Ashley Papadopoulos."

Jimmy extends his hand. Ashley shakes with gusto, locking eyes with Jimmy. Their instantly strong connection snatches Emily's attention away from her glow—and from John.

These two seem like they've known each other forever.

"Welcome to my home," says Jimmy, eyes still bound to Ashley's. He announces to everyone, "Please, come in."

Ashley whispers to Emily, "I like him already."

"Good, 'cause it looks like we may be here for a while."

"How you doin' Ashley?" asks John. "You look pretty good, considering all you guys have been through."

Ashley meets John's eyes with an alluring gaze. "Oh, John, today was hardly a teaser. Perhaps Emily has felt it necessary to shield you from the lowdown on all of our audacious exploits...hmmm?"

Emily flashes a stern glance at Ashley.

"Then perhaps you should rectify that," suggests John.

"Stop, you two!" whispers Emily with a scowl.

Ashley and John roll their eyes and smirk like schoolchildren misbehaving at the back of a classroom.

"I thought you might be hungry, so I took the liberty of ordering some luncheon," says Jimmy as he leads them to his kitchen. A large platter of roast beef, pastrami, and turkey sandwiches sits next to a tray of lobster rolls at the center of his long table, accompanied by assorted pickles, condiments, a bowl of fruit, three large bottles of sparkling water, and a plate of freshly cut lemon and lime wedges.

"Lobster rolls? Wow!" says Ashley. "I haven't had them in ages."

"Well then, please, be my guest," says Jimmy.

Ashley puts a lobster roll on a plate.

"Take two," offers Jimmy. "There are plenty to go around."

"Why, thank you, Jimmy!" replies Ashley with a charming smile. She takes another lobster roll and sits at the table.

Jimmy's convivial presence, along with the delectable luncheon, encourage Emily, Ashley, and John to loosen the tension they had been holding within their bodies. When Jimmy senses the three of them are sufficiently relaxed, he directs his attention to the reason why they—and Buzz—are in his home.

"Ashley, I saw that impressive profile of you in Communication Arts," says Jimmy.

"Oh, thank you. I was honored and surprised by it all. And here I am now, flattered you read it." Ashley looks longingly at Emily. "You know what the piece didn't say…my main reason for going to RISD was to be close to Emily." She winks.

Emily smiles nervously. *What's he up to?*

"I can see why that would be a prime motivator," says Jimmy, acknowledging Emily's smile with an impish glance. "Ashley, I wonder if you'd be interested in helping me with a project for one of my clients?"

"A design project?"

"This company is in need of a new website—and they keep bugging me to find someone to redesign it for them."

"In that case, they should talk to my boss at Hill Holliday."

"They're not going to hire Hill Holliday."

"Oh? Why not?"

"Too expensive, too much of a commitment, too—"

"Pretentious?" interrupts Ashley with a devilish grin.

"Let's just say my client would not make a good client for them."

"I get it. Really. Hmmm…the company pretends not to discourage moonlighting, but my boss would probably frown upon it."

"Doesn't your boss think you're on vacation?"

"Yes, she does."

"You can work on it while you're here—and they've got a decent budget. You'll be well compensated. I've got everything you need already installed on a brand-new, state-of-the-art workstation. Come, have a look." Jimmy stands.

"Ooh, this could be fun." Ashley catches Emily's eye as she stands. Emily offers a nod of encouragement.

Jimmy excuses himself. He leads Ashley to an office he'd set up for her.

Emily speaks to Buzz, "Sir, I truly appreciate you getting us out of there, today. Really, I do. But I fear we simply cannot afford you."

"My fee is being covered by Mr. Douglass. And please call me Buzz."

"He's one of us," says John.

"What does that mean…exactly?" probes Emily, her squint revealing suspicions she was not prepared to share.

"It means, Miss Emily, you can share any information you like with me—anything at all. Even Carl's proximity to discovering the Life Field. I am bound by the law to keep everything you say in confidence," answers Buzz. He puts his hand on his heart. "And I am bound by my duty as a Disciple to help you and Mr. Wells sort out your current predicament."

Emily gazes at John for a moment. John reaches his hand across the table. Emily clutches it. She closes her eyes, takes a breath, allows the glow to expand a little, opens her eyes, and stares at Buzz.

"You don't look like a typical Ropes & Gray attorney," says Emily, holding back tears. Or is it a giggle?

"No, Miss Emily. Truly, I take great pride in the fact that I do not."

"Don't let his smooth, genteel demeanor fool you," says John. "He's the most ruthless litigator they've got."

"I appreciate the compliment," says Buzz with a nod. "And I pray my litigation services will not be needed in this case."

"You said it would be safer for us to stay here," says Emily.

"Indeed, it is, Miss Emily."

"Safer from what?"

Jimmy returns.

"I'll let Mr. Douglass explain." Buzz sits back in his chair, grabs an apple, and takes a large, loud, slurpy bite.

"Your friend is quite the talent," says Jimmy.

"Very clever way to keep her occupied," says Emily.

"Yes, well it has the added benefit of solving a vexing problem I've been having with this client. And she'll be making good money, even as my client is saving money." Jimmy relaxes into his Windsor armchair. "John, why don't you fill Emily in on what we've learned."

"So…it turns out Van Owen *is* Andy's guy, and he *did* take Carl's machine to prevent Carl from conducting any more tests. Then things get strange."

"Strange?" asks Emily.

"Very strange," says John. "We think Van Owen told Andy that you and I told Carl about the Life Field. Andy's now acting as if he believes we showed Carl proof of its existence."

"What? But we did the exact opposite!"

"I know. It doesn't add up," says John. "But Andy seems convinced of it. So The Faithful got a few fanatics—members of the Army of God—to believe Carl's lab destroys hundreds of embryos every day, and you and I are helping the lab increase that number. The Army of God plans to kill Carl and frame us for his murder."

"So those fanatics sent the anthrax letter?"

"Looks that way. That's why we're not safe at home. Since their first attempt failed, we have no way of knowing what they'll do next."

"What the f—"

"That's how The Faithful operate," interrupts Jimmy. "They whip up fanatics to do their dirty work."

"Where's Carl?" asks Emily.

"We're not entirely sure," answers Buzz. "He does not appear to be home. He may be in a safe house…protected by the FBI."

"Speaking of the FBI, do they know about you guys?" Emily motions to the men at the table. "Are you the secret society they think I belong to?"

John and Jimmy begin to answer in unison, "We—"

"We don't think they know about us, Miss Emily," interrupts Buzz. "I believe Agent Brewer said that to get a rise out of you. And I feel I should compliment you on your cool head—not only your answer to that question—but during the entire interview."

"Okay, thank you. But how did they find out we doctored the data?"

"About that, Miss Emily, I am still perplexed," answers Buzz. "And I have my best people working on finding out how they knew or whether—once again—they were just fishing."

"Has anyone spoken with Andy?" asks Emily.

"He won't return my calls," says John.

"And Carl won't return mine. But if he thinks I tried to kill him, I kinda don't blame him."

"Tell her the strange bit," says Jimmy.

"The strange bit? Isn't being accused of doing the exact opposite of what we actually did strange enough?" sneers Emily.

"Yeah, here's the thing," says John. "Jimmy gave me all the info he has about every time he thinks The Faithful eliminated someone."

"So this is a regular occurrence? Murder?" asks Emily.

"I wouldn't characterize it as regular," replies Jimmy calmly. "Over the past 150 years, The Faithful have eliminated a few people who discovered the Life Field—or were on the verge of doing so—and were deemed, by their leaders, to be untrustworthy."

Emily aims her gaze directly at Jimmy. With a stern face and grave voice, she asks, "Is this the disagreement that caused the rift between you and The Faithful?"

"Yes, Emily. Indeed, it is," answers Jimmy with due gravitas while maintaining eye contact.

Nobody speaks for a couple of minutes. John allows his glow to expand.

"So," says John, "I found a pattern. And something about this situation doesn't fit that pattern."

"Oh?" says Emily. *Something tells me this might be a good thing. But I cannot fathom how that could possibly be.*

"In every other instance, The Faithful found a way to eliminate only the person they feared would reveal the Life Field—and they hurt nobody else."

"They're not evil," says Jimmy. "They're misguided, driven by fear."

"I don't know," counters Emily. "Murdering some of the smartest people on Earth seems pretty evil to me. I mean, maybe I'm a little biased now that I'm on their hit list."

"The point is," explains John, "eliminating Carl fits their pattern—assuming he somehow figured out he discovered the Life Field. Framing us does not."

"So, we're not some of the smartest people on Earth," says Emily.

Jimmy, John, and Buzz chuckle.

"It's not that, Emily," says Jimmy. "You and John have been helping Andy. I simply cannot imagine any scenario in which The Faithful would see you two as a threat."

"So, what are you saying? It's not Andy?" asks Emily.

"Tell her the other strange bit," says Jimmy.

"Oh Lord!" mutters Emily.

"When I first started working on Carl's data, I installed a backdoor onto his machine. If it gets turned on, it'll automatically find any available internet connection, and I can get in."

"Yeah, so?"

"It's on. And it's been on for a couple of days."

"What? But Carl—"

"Doesn't have the machine. The Machine tells me where it is. It's at Van Owen's estate."

"So, it's not at Sand Hill Road. I knew Frank was a lying sack-o-sh—"

"There's more."

"Oh, I don't like the sound of that."

John glances at Jimmy, then Buzz, back to Emily. "It's been modified."

"Modified? Modified to do what?"

"Hard to tell the full extent of the mods. The one thing I can tell is that it's measuring the Life Field again."

"This is exactly what I was afraid of and why we were right to keep Carl from realizing his machine discovered the Life Field." Emily pauses. Her eyes stare up toward the ceiling, drifting to the left. "Wait a minute." She raises both hands as if catching an idea out of thin air. "Van Owen's not a scientist or engineer, is he?"

"No," answers Jimmy. "He's a businessman. Smart, cunning, exceptionally well connected, and extraordinarily wealthy."

"And he knows about the Life Field because he's one of the Faithful? I mean, he knew even before he met Carl or saw any data from Carl's machine, right?"

"Yes, that's right," says Jimmy.

"And Andy told him to get the machine away from Carl?"

"Yup," says John.

"So, Van Owen must have turned against Andy," says Emily. "It's the only explanation that makes any sense. He wants the machine—and its power—all to himself. He probably told Carl his machine detected the Life Field and we doctored the data. He may have even told Carl we want him dead. He could easily have told the FBI the same thing. Maybe he told the FBI about The Faithful, too."

Buzz grabs his phone from his jacket and starts texting.

"Then why won't Andy return my calls?" asks John. "His pattern is to call me when he needs something. If Van Owen had turned on him, don't you think he'd call?"

"You say the machine has been modified, right?" asks Emily.

"Yes," answers John.

"Andy already believes Carl is a threat," says Emily, "or he wouldn't have gone to such lengths to get me to keep an eye on him. And he wouldn't have asked Van Owen to take the machine, right?"

"That's right," says Jimmy, intrigued.

"Now, you guys are always talking about how people see what they believe."

John and Jimmy look at each other. Eyebrows raise as they nod to Emily. Buzz is lost in texting.

"And, Jimmy, you've said more than once that The Faithful are ruled by fear."

"That I have." Jimmy's glow swells to encompass Emily and John, inspiring them to allow their glow to expand a little more.

"What if Van Owen found a way to modify the machine—a way to make it strengthen Andy's fear of Carl and expand his fear to include John and me?"

"That's a hell of a stretch," says John.

"Perhaps not," counters Jimmy. "From Van Owen's point of view…" he motions toward Emily, "assuming you're right about him… preying on Andy's pre-existing fear of Carl and expanding it to include you two has the added benefit of hiding his own betrayal. While Andy remains focused on threats fueled by his preexisting fear of Carl, he'll be blind to Van Owen's treachery. It's a brilliant sleight of hand."

"And if Carl refuses to go along with Van Owen's plan, he becomes a liability," says John.

"And so do we," says Emily.

"Okay," says John, "this all seems to make sense suddenly. But if the modified machine is affecting Andy, how do we know it isn't affecting us too?"

"More than likely," says Jimmy, "we are also being affected." He directs his gaze to everyone at the table. "All of us need to be diligent in checking our assumptions with one another before making decisions or taking any actions."

"And in that spirit," says Buzz, "I feel obliged to raise a certain complication." He puts his phone in his jacket pocket and leans over the table as if inviting a huddle. "If Carl doesn't have the machine, and Van Owen is not capable of making the modifications John detected, then we have ourselves another powerful adversary, about whom we know absolutely nothing—with one troubling exception." He pauses and sits straight up. "This individual possesses substantial technical prowess."

"True," says John. "We also have two potentially powerful allies."

All eyes are on John. Nobody speaks for a moment.

"Carl and Andy," says John. "The question is, how do we get them to talk to us?"

"I have some ideas on that," offers Jimmy.

Chapter Twenty-Five
Part 1: Contact

Two cymbal crashes startle Carl out of his hyperfocus. The brisk walking pace of "You Won't See Me" carries him back in time. He's beside his dad on their way home from Mario's.

The Beatles have invaded his computer—another in a long string of obstacles frustrating Carl's attempt to access his stolen machine.

Have I been hacked?

The music changes. 12 string acoustic guitar in F major with haunting, dreamy vocals.

Shivers shoot up Carl's spine. Simon & Garfunkel's "For Emily, Whenever I May Find Her" has snatched his focus away from his mission. The music stops.

Overcome by an obsession with finding the source of the music, he hits Alt-Tab and checks open windows. Nothing odd. He runs a virus scan. No malware. He invokes Ctrl-Alt-Del to open Task Manager. No unusual process running. He clicks App History…and gasps.

An app called "Truth from Your Little Genius" has the top spot. He clicks it. The app connects him to a cloud-based server. He scans for viruses. None found. What he does find is John's original analysis. It confirms the disturbances his machine detected are, in fact, evidence of the Life Field. Carl closes his eyes, breathes, rubs his head, and reads again. The evidence is surreal but conclusive. He's not dreaming.

There's more…a file named "notes" and an MP3 of each song. Carl needs to slow his breathing and his heartbeat before continuing. He clicks the MP3 of "For Emily." The song gives him goosebumps—as it always does and always has. Obeying his gut, he listens through to the end, knowing the music will lift him to a state of consciousness where he can read the *notes* from Emily and John with an open mind.

It works. Their claim of being framed has a ring of truth, and Van Owen has good reason to want him dead. He is relieved they admit doctoring his data and grateful for their apology. Saying they were pressured by Andy's obsession with keeping the Life Field Secret strikes Carl as out of character—especially for Emily, whose devotion to healing, he thought, was as strong as his own. Their full disclosure of the Life Field and its power matches Van Owen's description, giving him a little more reason to trust them. Even so, he's not sure what to make of their plea for help.

John fumbles with the heavy cast-iron pan he had pulled from Jimmy's oven. He plops the sizzling frittata onto the stove and grabs his beeping phone. *Server Access* is flashing on the screen.

"It's him!" shouts John.

"What? Carl? Really?" Emily looks up from her computer screen in the spare room Jimmy had converted into a temporary office for the two of them. She had been devouring research papers until John's voice snapped her out of a nice cozy world that, for a few hours, had replaced her uncertain, harried life with the comfort of research infused with the slowly cooking frittata's buttery, savory, nutty aroma.

John abandons the frittata. He races down the hall and drops into the chair at his computer next to Emily's.

"Carl found it," he says, shaking inside, mouth dry, body temperature rising, breathing hurried and shallow.

Emily jumps up to peer over John's shoulder. "Did he upload his answer to our request, like you asked for?"

"I'm looking. I'm looking." John's eyes scan the server's file list. The mouse jumps haphazardly around the screen.

Emily points. "There it is."

"Holy sh—"

"Open it."

"Hold on. I've gotta check for viruses."

"Jesus."

"What? You want us to let our guard down now? After all that's been going on?"

"No, no, no. You're right. Just—"

"I'm doing it as fast as I can."

No viruses found. John opens the file. It's a response from Carl.

John reads it aloud, "Meet me at the Larcom Theatre, 13 Wallis Street, Beverly, MA, at 10 am today." John glances at his watch.

Emily reads the rest aloud, "Text me when you get there for further instructions."

"A theatre?" says John. "Why does he want to meet there?"

"10 this morning?" says Emily. "How far is it?"

John launches MapQuest. "About an hour."

"That frittata looks and smells delectable," says Jimmy. "John, your cooking gets better every day."

"How long have you been standing there?" inquires Emily.

"Long enough," replies Jimmy. "You two better get going. Take my car."

John's eyes widen.

"The Mercedes, not the Cobra."

John breathes a sigh of relief.

"Don't go anywhere else, and please be extra careful. I'll be sure to save you some frittata."

"Garnish it with the roasted peppers I made yesterday, and a dollop of sour cream," instructs John as he clicks *Print*. "Oh, and don't forget the fresh herbs I chopped. They're still on the cutting board."

"John, let's go!" insists Emily.

"And make sure Ashley gets some," says John as he grabs the driving directions off the printer.

"C'mon, John. You're not their mother." Emily shakes her head. "What am I to do with you?"

Part 2: Trust

"That's it," says Emily. "There's a parking space right up ahead."
John parks while Emily texts Carl.

Carl replies, "Walk west, stop at last set of doors to brick building."

Their walk down the quiet, one-way street transports Emily and John to an earlier era. They come upon several large, vivid posters in the style of early twentieth century advertising, promoting "Le Grand David and his own Spectacular Magic Company." The posters hang inside antique glass cases on either side of glass doors to a lobby flanked by a pair of fifteen-foot-tall peacocks painted on brick. "LARCOM THEATRE" is carved in stone high above the lobby. Farther down the street, a black steel door opens with a loud crunch.

"Come in, quickly," whispers Carl. "Watch your step."

Emily and John scoot down the sidewalk and lurch up a couple of steps. Carl pulls the door closed behind them. It's pitch dark. Nobody moves. An elaborate hemp rope rigging system materializes out of the darkness. They are backstage, standing in the wing.

"Don't touch anything," instructs Carl. "Follow me."

They squeeze by ornately decorated giant set pieces with multiple doors, huge masks, golden mirrored balls, medieval scimitar swords.

"What is this place?" asks Emily.

"It's the longest running stage magic show in the world," answers Carl. "Did you see the posters?"

"Yup, we sure did," says John.

"Very old-fashioned looking," says Emily.

"Yeah, this show really takes you back to another time." Carl's anxiety lessens as he talks about the theatre. "Extravagant sets and costumes, lots of music, everything choreographed—and the illusions are top notch, very much admired in magic circles."

Emily and John follow Carl until a touch of stage fright stops them in their tracks. From center stage, they behold an elegant auditorium—walls covered in red silk, a spectacular horseshoe balcony faced in pressed tin with intricate gold relief and topped with a brass railing. They gaze in awe at the ornate ceiling forty feet above.

"How do they change the light bulbs up there?" asks John, hoping this tongue-in-cheek question will hide his own anxiety while keeping Carl's at bay.

"Not sure," replies Carl. "But that ceiling has seen plenty of bulbs since this place hosted Vaudeville shows in 1912. It opened with the slogan, *Lit Completely by Electricity!*"

Carl leads them up the red-carpeted aisle through tall, vibrantly painted doors into the bright, sun-filled lobby with giant peacocks painted on the walls.

"Stay away from the glass doors," warns Carl, his anxiety rising.

"When did the show open?" asks John.

"In the seventies at their theatre up the street." Carl points to life-sized paintings of the troupe. "These guys bought this place in 1984 and restored it—all by hand. It had been a porn theatre for over a decade."

"I sure hope they cleaned the seats," says Emily.

John and Carl chuckle. John winks at Emily.

"Nope. They reupholstered them," says Carl.

Carl grabs the carved wooden frame of an antique box office window. The entire structure is a heavy door. Opening it exposes a giant peacock painted on a substantial, steel, fire door. Carl slides the peacock door unveiling a mirror extending from the black marble floor up to the ceiling.

"This way," instructs Carl as he slides the mirror to one side and steps into an opulent function room with mirrored walls, a parquet floor, black marble trim, and a solid oak semi-circular bar.

"Will you look at this place!" exclaims Emily. She gazes upward.

"Those are Italian, hand-made, stained glass exit signs," says Carl while walking toward a Victorian iron spiral staircase with a brass railing. Peering up through the ceiling, he adds, "One of the magicians lives up there." He stops, grabs the railing, and faces Emily. "I'm hiding out down here." He heads down the spiral stairs.

"Why here?" asks Emily, frozen at the top of the stairs.

"I have a friend in the troupe who offered me sanctuary. These people are mysterious. Nobody bothers them. Their daily shows are at the other theatre. They're only here once a week. Few people know this room even exists, never mind the basement. It's a perfect place to disappear."

"We thought you might be in an FBI safe house." John cannot catch himself in time to prevent these words from escaping.

"Hell no!" exclaims Carl. "I can't trust those guys. Have you never heard of Whitey Bulger?"

Emily and John eye each other, dismayed that Carl's reduced anxiety was temporary. They peer down the spiral stairs at Carl without answering.

Carl stops to glare up at them. "Man, you kids need to wake up and smell the coffee." He continues down the stairs. "Hold the rail. Watch your step."

Emily and John descend the stairs, dispirited. Carl has lost the enormous respect he once had for them. They enter a long, well lit, basement room filled with vividly painted magic illusions.

"This is their museum of magic," explains Carl.

"It's open to the public?" asks John, revealing his alarm.

"No. You have to be invited. Hardly anyone is allowed down here."

"Then how can it be a museum?" asks Emily.

"I told you," says Carl, "they're mysterious."

They wind their way through brilliantly embroidered costumes, crystal balls, giant dragons, swords, brooms, and wands. Carl pushes against the serpentine stucco wall. Part of it pops back at him, opening into a cramped office lit only by a small desk lamp and two computer screens, one of which shows live footage of the street above, solving the riddle that had been nagging at John, *how did he know to tell us to walk west?* Several partially assembled machines clutter the room—wires, circuit boards, LCDs all hanging on with tape and zip ties. A soldering gun smolders next to the keyboard.

Carl points at two wooden bar stools rising from the clutter. "Pardon the mess. Have a seat."

John and Emily are forced to sit uncomfortably close to each other to avoid disturbing the blinking machines and dangling parts. John glances at Emily. She raises her eyebrows, tilts her head. John clears his throat and addresses Carl. "Emily and I are tremendously grateful you agreed to meet with us."

"Honestly, I'm not sure this was a good idea," replies Carl. "But something told me to give it a try. At the very least, maybe you can explain why you decided to come clean. What persuaded you to stop lying, to abandon your elaborate schemes to deceive me?"

Jimmy had predicted this question from Carl. Indeed, Jimmy had advised John and Emily to be wary of Carl if he didn't chastise them. Not expressing his anger would reveal he was hiding it from them—or worse, from himself, rendering him unpredictable and ultimately unreliable. Carl's obvious disappointment in them signals a promising opportunity, yet it does not lessen the sting of his scolding. All their lives, both have craved the respect of their elders. Now, they cringe like naughty children awaiting their punishment.

"Carl, we're terribly sorry," says Emily. "We realize we let you down, and we are prepared to make it up to you."

"Good. You can help me fake my death," replies Carl. "John, it looks like someone else may have access to my machine. Is that you?"

"Sort of, but—"

"Fake your death?" interrupts Emily.

"Well, I thought about killing Van Owen." Carl's voice is eerily matter-of-fact. "But he'd have to call off the hit on me first—and that's not gonna happen."

"Murder?" exclaims Emily. "You were really planning to commit murder?"

"Self-defense, Emily," says Carl.

"Carl, we don't think Van Owen ordered a hit on you," says John.

"Really? No, it makes perfect sense. I haven't heard a peep from him since I refused to sign his NDA. I told him I had no intention of revealing the Life Field on my own. And I was willing to wait until he thought the time was right. But I was not about to sign a document preventing me from ever discussing the machine I invented. He probably realized he'd be better off without me around. I'd already helped him secure millions in new investment. If I'm martyred in the cause of science, he can pay out the investors from a life insurance policy the company took out on me. Then, with all the publicity about my death—and my discovery—he can go back to the well for ten-fold the original investment. Plus, he can do whatever he wants with my machine without any interference from me, or you two, or anyone else. It's him alright."

John's training with Simon comes in handy. His ability to see someone's potential along with what blocks that potential has matured.

Carl's brilliant mind, enhanced intuition, and pure heart are clear. With a little training—and some smoothing of his rough, volatile edges—he could become a vigorous force for healing and a stalwart protector of the Life Field. But Carl expects a fight. He assumes people will instinctively take advantage of him…and eventually betray him.

This has been the defining pattern of Carl's life—a pattern so deeply ingrained that Carl believes it to be the natural order of things. His nature is to trust people, to devote himself to the service of others—his family, employees, colleagues, investors, healing. The instant someone takes advantage of him—or lies to him—Carl turns on himself. He hates himself for trusting, for missing the warning signs that appear glaringly obvious once he's been betrayed. The pattern is reinforced. Carl succumbs to bitterness, vowing never to trust again. But then, inevitably, he does… because it is his nature.

Carl is now in the throes of his bitter stage, vowing never to trust again. John knows this stage will pass, and when it does, he and Emily will have their only shot at regaining Carl's trust.

"Yes, Van Owen wants you out of the picture," says John. "But we don't think he ordered a hit. It's not like he hired Flemmi."

"Oh, so you do know something about Bulger," says Carl with a smirk. "I was beginning to think you two lived in some kind of bubble, insulated from the real world by that cult of yours."

"It's not a cult," insists Emily.

"Really?" says Carl.

"Look," says John, "Like we said in our note, we think Van Owen is planning to use your machine to control the Life Field and wield its power. But somehow, he's convinced Andy that you're the one who's doing this—and now Andy thinks we're helping you."

Carl draws a shallow breath, tilts his head, and scowls.

"Hear me out," continues John. "Assume you're right about why Van Owen wants you out of the way. From his point of view, Emily and I are also liabilities because we know your machine discovered the Life Field—and we know you invented it."

Carl leans in, palms up, and nods.

"So…Van Owen knows Andy was afraid your machine would detect the Life Field. He also knows Andy asked me to recruit Emily to deceive you. What better way to tie up all loose ends than to convince Andy that, instead of deceiving you, we told you about the Life Field. Now, Andy will see all three of us as major threats to The Faithful's mission.

"So, you're saying this Andy ordered the hit?"

"That's not exactly how these people work. No, they'll infiltrate some group of fanatics and convince members of that group to do their dirty work."

"You really think Andy convinced the Army of God that I'm a devil, so they'd try to kill me?"

"Yeah, that's about the size of it."

"All the more reason to fake my death. I checked these crazies out. If they were just hired guns, somebody might be able to call them off. But if they truly believe I'm evil, they won't stop until I'm dead. And they'll be hard to catch. They use hardly any tech. Nearly impossible to track. I'm not betting my life on the FBI getting these whackos before they get me."

"But Carl, your research," says Emily. "We were on the verge of a breakthrough. How will you continue your work if everybody thinks you're dead? Where will you go?"

"I'm working on that. I've got some cash in a Swiss bank account and friends in Geneva who can help me get set up there. I'm also working on a new machine—one that can reprogram fibroblasts into pluripotent stem cells." He points around the room. "That's what all this is."

"How are you going to fake your death without a body?" asks John.

"I thought you were a hacker," taunts Carl. "Creating the illusion of someone's death should be child's play for you."

John's eyes widen.

"Let me spell it out for you," continues Carl. "I'm going to the Cayman Islands in a week or so. There'll be a boating accident and I'll be lost at sea. You hack into wherever you need to get me a death certificate, a couple of news stories about my death, and a new identity with a U.S. passport, or a Swiss passport."

"Why the Cayman Islands?" asks Emily.

"They're not part of Interpol," answers John.

"And there's plenty of deep water to drown in," adds Carl.

"I'm an engineer," says John, "and I can hack when necessary. I can get you a Cayman death certificate and a couple of news stories. And I can build you a new identity. But I'm not a criminal. I can't forge a passport."

"Ask your friend Ashley's dad. Given what I've learned about his connections, I'm pretty sure he could get it done."

"We're not getting Ashley involved in any of this," insists Emily. "She doesn't know anything."

"She was picked up with you and interrogated by the FBI," retorts Carl. "Are you telling me she's an idiot?"

"Hold on," says John. "She does know about Carl. She wants to help. And she's smart—plenty smart enough to suspect we're keeping something from her. Giving her this job might be the perfect way to get her feeling helpful without divulging more than we'd like to."

"Maybe," concedes Emily. "But why wouldn't the FBI suspect John and I are responsible for your mysterious boating accident?"

"Geez, for a couple of geniuses, you two sound pretty stupid today." Carl shakes his head and rubs his eyes. "You know the FBI are keeping tabs on you, right? They'll see you're in Cambridge. You don't have any connections to the Cayman Islands, do you?"

"No," says John. He eyes Emily. She shakes her head.

"Didn't think so. Now, be sure to get Ashley a burner to use when she asks her dad for my passport." He hands Emily an envelope of cash. "Here's plenty of money to pay for it and the address of a bar in Grand Cayman where he should send it. He'll know how to get it there without it being traced."

John probes Emily's eyes. They take a breath together.

"Okay. We're in. We'll help you," says John. "Now we need your help with something."

"Of course, you do," says Carl. "I knew you wouldn't help me simply out of the goodness of your hearts."

"Carl, please…" says Emily.

"Am I wrong?" asks Carl.

John takes a breath, glances at Emily, back to Carl. "We need proof that Van Owen turned on Andy. If I can get the proof to Andy, he can get it to the Army of God and persuade them that you're not the problem—and neither are we."

"Well, I wouldn't bet on that" says Carl. "But you're right about Van Owen. He is definitely planning to discover," (air quotes) "the Life Field and control it using my machine. He's even set up a so-called educational foundation to manage a *scientific paradigm shift*, as he puts it. Self-important, son-of-a-bitch probably never even heard of Thomas Kuhn."

"Maybe not," says John. "But Kuhn would definitely consider exploration of the Life Field to be *revolutionary science*."

"We'll see about that. I'm not so sure the world is ready for this Life Field. That's why I've been trying to hack into the machine he stole from me. I'm looking for a way to shut it down."

"So, you have access to your machine?" asks John.

"No. I can't seem to get in. Something keeps blocking me. Is that you? Did you put a backdoor in when you were analyzing my data? Does it lock out all other attempts to get in?"

"For situations exactly like this."

"Fine, John. I get it. It's just…I would like to have known."

"I understand. And I'm sorry."

"When were you planning to tell me?"

"You never returned my calls, remember?" says Emily.

"Oh, yeah," says Carl. "Call the gal who's trying to kill you so her hacker boyfriend can trace your phone. That's a smart move."

"We're telling you now," says John. "Carl, we have the same goal. We want to disable your machine too."

"Tell him why, John," says Emily. "He deserves to know."

"Oh, brother," mutters Carl.

"We discovered something else about your Machine. It enhances intuition. That's what we were testing the day you called from California."

"Holy sh—"

"There's more," interrupts John. "Your machine has been modified, and I didn't do it."

"Well, I can't even get into my machine, so—"

"Then Buzz is right. Van Owen's got somebody modifying it. Somebody smart."

"Yeah, Van Owen certainly doesn't have the skills to do it himself. He mentioned some hacker guy when I was out there. Who's Buzz?"

"Our lawyer."

"Funny name for an attorney. Any good? I might need one."

"The best."

Emily takes her phone out of her purse. "I just texted you his info. Buzz already knows who you are."

Carl's phone beeps. "Thanks. But don't text me anymore—especially after I'm dead. So why do you think they're modifying my machine?"

"Well," says John, "we've already discovered the machine enhances intuition. It's not a stretch to imagine how it could be modified to enhance confirmation bias and fear. Andy already trusts Van Owen and believes you're dangerous. So, a modified machine could strengthen Andy's trust in Van Owen—and amplify his fear of you. And that might have helped Van Owen convince Andy to eliminate you. Also, Andy can likely sense someone has betrayed him. Van Owen knows this, so he's offered up Emily and me as the culprits. Andy would rather believe Emily and I betrayed him than believe his long-time partner, Van Owen, is a traitor. If your machine were modified to enhance confirmation bias, Van Owen could focus it on Andy. That would help Andy fit Van Owen's story of our betrayal into his own intuitive sense that he's been betrayed."

"Also, if Andy can convince the FBI that we're in cahoots with the Army of God, they'll never see Andy's connection with them. It's a brilliant sleight of hand." says Emily.

"Let me get this straight," says Carl, his hands in the air. He shakes his head as if he'd just emerged from underwater. "You think the Army of God are out to kill me because Andy exploited their pre-existing hatred of stem cell researchers; and Andy did so because Van Owen exploited his pre-existing fear of me. Not only that, Andy can sense he's being betrayed, but Van Owen is subverting that intuition to make Andy believe you are the traitors. And Van Owen is using my machine to enhance all of this fear, subversion, and confirmation bias?"

"Yes, Carl. That's what we think," says Emily.

"But if you can help me disable your machine—" says John.

"And give you the proof I have that Van Owen betrayed Andy," interrupts Carl, "you think Andy will turn the Army of God on Van Owen instead of you and me, don't you?"

"He might. He just might," says John.

"Well, I don't know if I want that on my conscience," says Carl.

"But a few minutes ago, you told us you considered killing Van Owen," protests Emily.

"I decided not to, remember?" says Carl. "But even if I had killed Van Owen, it would have been self-defense. Man to man. Honorable."

"You mean like a duel?" says Emily sarcastically.

"Look, kid, there was a time when men used to fight honorably. None of this manipulate-other-people-to-do-your-dirty-work bullshit."

"When was that? Back in the fifteenth century?"

"As a matter of fact, yes. But maybe even as recently as when this place was built."

"So, you don't think Henry V's speech at Agincourt was manipulative?"

"He fought right alongside his men. Honorably!" insists Carl. "And that speech you're referring to is Shakespeare's writing. Brilliant, beautiful language. 'Household words…' Rousing in every way. How can you not love that speech?"

"I do love that speech," says Emily. "That's my point. That speech (or whatever the real Henry said that day) manipulated his men into killing and dying for him. And what was in it for them? Glory?"

"Guys, can we postpone debating war, morality, and Shakespeare until…maybe…there's nobody trying to kill us?" asks John.

Emily is relieved to see Carl smile for the first time today. Returning the smile, she finds an opening in his heart. "Carl, I thought the reason you were trying to get into your machine is so you could disable it."

"Yes, that's right. And, on balance, it's probably the right thing to try—even if it is a long shot."

Carl, John, and Emily draw deep breaths together.

Carl exhales through his mouth with his lips rounded, making a faint whistling sound. "OK kids. Let's get to work. We few, we happy few, we band of brothers," Carl winks at Emily "…and sisters."

Chapter Twenty-Six
Camaraderie

VAN OWEN RISES from the wingback chair he had turned to face his Buddha. After only a few minutes of meditation, he had achieved a more powerful resonance with the Life Field than anything he had experienced before. Thirty years of arduous, daily practice had never produced such resonance. Finally, he could summon a state of flow in league with a typical member of The Faithful.

I know they recruited me for my money and connections. But now I am truly one of them. What a glorious day it will be when they witness the revelation I bestow upon the world in their honor.

Van Owen moves serenely to the cabinet he had custom-built into the wall near his desk. With due reverence, he unlocks the rosewood panel door and slides it open to unveil Carl's machine. He pushes the power button. The LCD screen lights up. Van Owen takes a breath while waiting for the machine to complete a quick self-test. *READY* appears on the LCD. The machine emits a double beep. He opens the machine's door. A single beep sounds. *READY* is replaced by *DOOR OPEN*—and it's blinking.

Van Owen opens his desk drawer, grabs the makeshift gadget he had crafted, and inserts it into the machine's door latch. *READY* reappears, accompanied by the double beep. He puts his left hand into the machine. His right fingers press 1-1-2-3-5-8 on the keypad. A soft humming sound comes and goes in half a second. His computer monitor comes to life displaying a graph. Van Owen smiles.

My personal best yet!

He calls Andy, as he does every morning, to perpetuate his lie.

John and Carl have lost track of time. John is at the keyboard, Carl on a bar stool next to him. They're stuck in an hours-long endless loop. Over and over again, Carl would suggest some way to disable his machine. John would write the code to trigger it. He'd upload the code to Carl's machine and the two would agree: *this one has to work*, only to be dejected when it fails.

Never imagining he'd want to disable his machine remotely, Carl hadn't thought to create a mechanism for doing so. Quite the contrary. All the machine's safety systems are mechanical—specifically designed to thwart any attempt at software hacking—remote hacking in particular.

John's phone beeps, jolting the two men out of the intense zone of camaraderie that had woven itself around their concentrated work together.

"Any luck?" is the text from Emily. She had driven back to Jimmy's to talk with Ashley in person about asking her father for Carl's passport. The plan is for Emily to pick John up at some point.

"No," replies John.

"OK, text me when ur ready."

Emily's interruption stirs John to alter his approach.

"Maybe the modifications Van Owen's guy made are telling your machine to ignore the code we're uploading," he says. "Do you have a copy of the original code you wrote for your machine? Comparing it to the code running on your machine now might lead to something."

"Yeah. I'll get it for you."

Carl and John switch seats. Carl brings up his original code on the screen in one window and the code currently running on his machine in another window. They switch seats again. John stares at the screen as he scrolls through both windows faster than Carl can read anything.

"Have at it. How about if I go get sandwiches."

"Sure. I haven't eaten all day." John pauses scrolling and faces Carl. "Wait, is it safe for you to go out?"

"Gotta eat, Kid. It's a nice walk and I need the air. What do you want?"

"I don't know. Roast beef, I guess." John returns to the screen.

Carl opens the secret door to his hideout. "On a sub roll? Mayo? Mustard? Oil? Hots?"

"Hold on!" exclaims John.

Carl shuts the door and sits on the bar stool.

"Look," says John. The code currently running on Carl's machine is changing before their eyes. "Your code is being rewritten. It's getting better, cleaner, faster, more efficient…No offense."

"None taken. You're the coder whiz kid, not me."

"Yeah, but this code is astounding. Better than mine."

Carl impersonates Groucho Marx, "Not only is he brilliant, he's modest too."

"Look at this!" exclaims John.

"Can you trace the connection so we can catch the son-of-a-bitch who's in there?"

"That's the thing. There is no other connection. It's happening spontaneously. It's as if…"

"What?"

John catches Carl's eye. "It's recoding itself, improving itself, evolving."

"Like an organism."

"Yeah… Like an organism."

"So, where's this *ultimate hacker guy* Van Owen said had detected your modifications to my data?"

"Probably another one of his fabrications," says John. "Remember, Andy didn't want you to know your machine had detected the Life Field. He asked us to doctor your data and hide the discovery from you. Since Van Owen was colluding with Andy, he would have known about my mods, but he had to tell you his hacker guy found them to convince you he wasn't in on it."

"You didn't trust me either. Otherwise, you wouldn't have bothered to create such an elaborate ruse. And now that I know my machine detected the Life Field, I'm doing exactly what Andy wanted—and what you seem to want. If you had trusted me in the first place, we wouldn't be in this mess."

"You're right. We were wrong. We should have trusted you. And we do trust you now."

"Only because you have no choice."

John refrains from arguing the point.

Carl gasps. He points to the graph that had been sitting dormant at the top-left of the screen. "Look!"

"Oh, the machine's testing something," says John.

"Look closer," says Carl. "It's not reacting with a cell culture in a petri dish. That's gotta be millions of cells. Maybe tens of millions."

"And whatever is in there has a strong resonance with the Life

Field—very strong!" John clicks on the graph to enlarge it. "Look at that."

"John…look at my code."

John minimizes the graph. Code fills the screen. Modifications are coming faster. An idea strikes. "I need to write a program to capture and analyze all the mods being made to your code in real time. It'll take me an hour."

"Nothing takes an hour," sneers Carl. "I'll go get those sandwiches. Let's see where you are when I get back."

"Okay. Bulkie roll. Mustard. No mayo. And definitely no hots."

John is hooked by Carl's one-hour challenge. He ups the ante, vowing to finish before sandwiches arrive. His gurgling gut agrees, offering hunger as further incentive.

"Done!" exclaims John when the door to Carl's hideout opens. Roast beef anticipation swirls him around to collect his lunch.

"Really?" says Carl. "Impressive. Hey, I got us a little side treat."

"Oh?"

"It's calzone day at Gloria's. I got a piece of their killer steak and cheese calzone for us to share."

"Never had steak in a calzone."

"You're in for a treat."

John devours the piled-high roast beef sandwich so quickly he tastes only his first bite. Carl, who had barely eaten half of his Italian sub, hands John the small, foil-wrapped piece of calzone. "Go ahead."

John unwraps one end and takes a bite. It's still warm. The melted cheese, warm meat, and rich—almost flaky—crust blend to create an altogether unique flavor, something John has never tasted before.

"Holy cow!" exclaims John with his mouth full.

"Told you it was killer. Have the whole thing. This is more than enough for me."

"You sure?"

"I'm sure, Kid. You need it more than I do."

Van Owen's new daily routine is exhilarating. After a brief meditation, Carl's machine confirms—and amplifies—his rapidly growing
resonance with the Life Field. He heightens his sway over Andy by calling
right after using the machine. Van Owen and Andy suspect the FBI might
be tapping their phones, so they speak in code.

Andy answers, "Good morning, sir."

"Good afternoon, Andy. Any developments?"

"Well, sir, Carl seems to have gone into hiding."

"You're cooperating fully with the FBI?"

"Absolutely, sir, but they say they don't know where he is."

"Then how can they keep him safe?"

"They're watching those two culprits. Nothing terribly unusual.
The culprits are laying low at the home of Mr. Douglass."

"Does the FBI have a theory as to why the culprits are avoiding
their own apartment?"

"No sir. In fact, one of the agents asked me about it."

"What did you tell him?"

"That terrorists are unpredictable."

"Does the FBI think Mr. Douglass is in any danger?"

"They don't seem to think so. But, sir, you know they're not very
forthcoming and I can only get hold of them every few days."

"Very well, then. Keep me informed."

"Will do, sir."

Perhaps because its crust strikes John as more like an empanada, three bites of the calzone spark an idea. John lays it next to the soldering gun, wipes his mouth on his sleeve, wipes his hands on his pants, and launches the program he wrote while Carl was getting sandwiches. He scrolls through several graphs.

"Interesting," says John.

"What?" asks Carl with his mouth full, holding the last third of his sub with both hands to prevent olive oil from dripping out.

"The backdoor I originally installed uses machine learning to detect intruders—and to figure out the best way to contact me using the fastest Internet connection it can find. The goal was for it to get continually smarter so it could perform these—and other tasks—faster and more efficiently. It looks like contact with the Life Field triggered your original code to adopt my machine learning algorithms. Now it has an even stronger connection with the Life Field."

"And it would explain why my code is being modified, getting more efficient. It's a virtuous cycle. Better code creates a stronger connection with the Life Field which generates better code."

"Exactly. But something else is also going on." John brings a graph to the screen with several colored lines on it. "Look. Interactions with the Life Field are changing. A new pattern is emerging."

Smudging the screen with his oily finger at a spot on the graph, Carl says, "Looks like the pattern is about to converge right there. Wonder why?"

"Hold on." John wipes the screen with his sleeve, opens a small window, and starts typing. "I got a notice this morning that your server use is increasing. Could be a clue there."

A long list of files appears in the small window. New files are being added at a furious pace. "What is all that stuff?" asks Carl.

John opens another window. "I'm checking."

"That looks like a database," says Carl.

John stops typing. He glances at Carl. "It is. Your machine built itself a new database, and it's saving all sorts of data it finds on the Internet."

"What kind of data?"

"Let me try something." John launches another program.

He and Carl shout in unison, "Holy shit!"

Hundreds of news stories flash before them—from Google, Yahoo!, BBC, PBS, and others.

"These stories are about stem cell research…and me!" exclaims Carl, "and Van Owen."

John pauses the stream of stories on a photo, "Is that him?"

"Yup."

John lets the news stories stream again.

"Stop!" says Carl.

John pauses the streaming.

"That looks like it's probably him 30 years ago," says Carl.

Upon closer inspection, they find they've landed on an article about Van Owen taking over his father's small venture capital firm in 1972.

"Listen to this," says John. Music begins playing. "Somebody wrote a song about you! This guy thinks you're a hero, standing up for science and all."

"That's Becky's husband."

"Becky? From your lab?"

"Yeah, that's her husband…there in the picture. He's a musician. Well, he works in a music store. But he'd like to be a musician."

"Yeah…that's not gonna happen, not if this song is any indication of his talent." John stops the music.

"What is this website?"

"It's called MySpace. It's a new social networking site. People upload their music, converse with other MySpace members, and build their fan base."

"Social networking?"

"Yeah. It's kind of like taking AOL and CompuServe to a new level. You create a 'Profile.' And you can communicate with anyone, anytime, anywhere in the world—as long as they're a member. A new one of these social networking sites launched a couple months ago. They call it 'The Facebook.' But it's really just for college kids. It's not flexible and it's not focused on music. I don't like it."

"Man, you kids keep finding new ways to sit at home and waste your time."

"Yup," says John. "And it's only gonna get worse. I've got a funny feeling these social networking sites are going to become very popular."

Posts from social networks and blogs along with thousands of web pages join the rapidly flashing news stories creating a hypnotic effect. John and Carl sit and watch, transfixed as it all streams by.

"Are you seeing what I'm seeing?" asks John.

"You mean the focus narrowing on fear, hate, brutality?"

"Exactly. I'm gonna check something." John moves the streaming window to one side of the screen so Carl can keep watching while he opens another smaller window and launches a new program. A graph appears with a single red line inching higher as it makes its way across the window. "Your machine is selecting the most popular content."

"Which is negative, violent, and fear based. Not surprising, really. You know the old journalism maxim, *If it bleeds, it leads.*"

John positions the graph with multicolored lines between the popularity graph (with the single red line) and the streaming window. "Look at that!"

Chills of fear engulf John and Carl.

"Interactions with the Life Field are converging almost to a single point," says Carl.

"As the most popular content becomes increasingly negative and fear-based," says John. "This is what your machine is learning about humanity. And it's altering interactions with the Life Field."

"If this Life Field of yours really is the source of life—the most powerful force in the Universe—wouldn't this fear and negativity be affecting everyone on Earth?"

"I don't know. My backdoor activated when Van Owen took your machine. And since then, it seems to have affected Andy the most."

"Evidence would suggest it's also affecting Van Owen. "It's been way too easy for him to convince Andy of two blatant lies—that I'm an existential threat, and you betrayed him. You thought Van Owen had someone modify my machine to do that. But we've just discovered the machine is modifying itself. It's building a new reality out of humanity's evil, our fears, our hate. And this new reality is feeding Van Owen's ambition."

"Van Owen had plenty of ambition before he had your machine, before my backdoor was activated, before the machine evolved."

"True. But he's more powerful now. He used to rely on money to build his power base. Now it's like he can cast a spell."

"You mean, on Andy?"

"Well, let's see. You say Andy is a smart guy. More importantly, he can resonate with the Life Field. You also say Andy's greatest fear is scientific discovery of the Life Field. More specifically, he's afraid I'll discover it.

"Since Van Owen took my machine, he's been able to enhance Andy's preexisting fear of me to the point where Andy wants me dead— even though, in reality, I'm as committed to keeping the Life Field secret as he is. Van Owen's also been able to hide his betrayal by convincing

Andy that you and Emily betrayed him. He didn't have to do anything or pay anybody. He didn't need a hacker guy. Concluding that the machine is helping Van Owen would be consistent with what we're seeing, wouldn't it?"

"Yes, it would. And for now, it may only be strong enough to affect people who are in direct contact with it—or with Van Owen."

"Well, you and I are in contact with it now. Why didn't it enhance my anger toward you? And why did you decide to trust me?" asks Carl.

"Good questions. I can think of only one plausible explanation."

"What's that?"

"Please don't think me immodest or presumptuous."

"Oh, Lord!" Carl rolls his eyes. "Go ahead."

"I've been training for months to resonate with the Life Field. I have a long way to go, but I have gotten pretty good at it. And since Emily got picked up by the FBI, I've been focused on winning your trust so we can work together."

"Ah, so it's all you, is it?"

"No. It's both of us. Somehow, you found it in your heart to trust me. And now our mutual trust is growing."

"Well, it couldn't have gotten any worse, could it?"

"That's the point. Our mutual trust grew today—just before we made contact with your machine. What if growth in our trust is an antidote to fear and negativity? If we can maintain the camaraderie we feel right now, we could remain immune."

"So, you believe your resonance with the Life Field, and your focus on winning my trust, along with my tentative trust in you, and today's growing trust between us is counteracting any negative effect the machine might be having on you and me?"

"That would be consistent with what we're seeing, wouldn't it?"

"It might. It just might," admits Carl.

"Now, we have to figure out how we can get Andy to look at your proof that Van Owen is the traitor."

"And we have to disable my machine before it gets even more negative...and more powerful."

John smiles at Carl. "Guess we've got our work cut out for us."

Carl smiles back. "Good thing we're finally in this together, isn't it?" Carl rummages through the overflowing pile of parts littering his desk. He pulls out a microcassette recorder and hands it to John. "Check this out."

Chapter Twenty-Seven
Divergent Realities

JOHN CLICKS PRINT on the computer in his temporary office at Jimmy's. He scans each page as it rises out of the printer. It's all there; Carl's NDA, foundation paperwork, life insurance policy, employment contract. He puts them in a manila envelope, adds the microcassette tape Carl had given him, and seals it.

Rather than whacking Van Owen's head off before the party, Carl hid a microcassette recorder in his jacket pocket the morning after the party.

When he and John listened to Van Owen describing his plan to reveal and control the Life Field, they agreed it might be enough to break the spell Van Owen has over Andy.

Emily is sitting at her computer. John approaches, "I'm off." He kisses her on the back of her head.

Emily's chair swivels. Clasping his cheeks in her hands, she implores him, "Please be careful" and seals it with a firm kiss on the lips.

"You two are just adorable," says Ashley, standing in the office doorway.

Emily rolls her eyes.

"Thank you, Ashley, for talking to your dad," says John. "I'm hoping I can talk Carl out of this plan. In the meantime, he's grateful that your dad's on board."

"Anything for you two love birds." Ashley winks at Emily as John heads for the front door.

"Aren't you behind schedule building that website for Jimmy's client?" asks Emily.

"Oh, c'mon Emmy. A girl needs a little entertainment when she's hiding out. Watching you two is better than that smutty novel I brought to read on the plane." She calls out to John, "Be careful Johnny Boy." Her voice turns sultry. "We need you back here tonight!"

"What am I to do with you?" says Emily, half to Ashley, half to herself. She swivels back to face her computer.

"What are you to do with me?" Ashley spins Emily's chair and clasps her face. "Love me the way you always have." She kisses Emily on the lips. "'Cause you're gonna live with my crazy love forever!"

The music club rotates into view as John rounds the corner a block away. The side door is unattended. He slows his walking pace and scans the street. Miriam is approaching from the other end of the block. At her swift pace, she'll reach the door before John does unless he runs.

Damn, I shouldn't have slowed down!

His attempt to run without being obvious results in an uncomfortable, ungainly stride attracting Miriam's attention. She picks up her pace.

John calls out, "Wait!"

Miriam walks past the door and stops in front of John.

"Follow me," she commands in a husky whisper. She darts across the street.

"Thank you," says John, out of breath as he follows.

"Do not speak again until I do."

John is struck by how much energy it takes to keep up with Miriam's brisk walking pace—and how effortless it is for her. She slips around a corner. John follows. She picks up her pace again. John matches it. She ducks into a narrow deli and nods to the busy owner behind the counter. He acknowledges her with his eyes while asking a short, older woman if there will be anything else.

John follows Miriam through whiffs of fried eggplant, tomato sauce, roast chicken, sausages, and brisket. They head toward the back of the deli, sliding behind customers who are shouting orders over the counter.

Miriam pushes through a door labeled "EMPLOYEES ONLY." John follows. The door shuts behind him with a hiss and a clank. They sprint past floor-to-ceiling shelves filled with supplies. Miriam takes a sudden left. She disappears behind bags of onions and garlic oozing their aromas. John catches up. Miriam hangs a sharp right, past the strong scent of bleach. With both hands, she presses the bar of a heavy metal door. Garbage odors rush in.

Miriam steps into an alley and dashes to the right. John slides past the door before it slams shut. They pass a dumpster next to empty boxes waiting to be broken down and a broken-down man huddled in a box waiting for a break in his life. The alley dead ends into a brick building with a rickety wooden staircase winding up the side.

"Do not touch the railing," warns Miriam. "You will get splinters." She trots up the stairs, stops at a rusty steel door, grabs keys from her purse, opens the door, and slides out of her shoes.

"Take off your shoes."

John unties his shoes, steps out of them, and follows Miriam into a lovely, tidy apartment filled with light. Tibetan thangkas adorn the exposed brick walls complementing the handmade antique rugs and embroidered pillows neatly arranged on the wide pine floor. A tall, white pillar candle sits at the center of the fireplace mantel flanked by a Tibetan singing bowl, small bronze statues of Siva and Shakti, and several tantric yoga ritual objects. The sweet scent of lingering incense helps John catch his breath.

"We can speak freely here," says Miriam.

"Where are we?" asks John, entranced by the surroundings.

"A friend lives here," answers Miriam with a polite but stern look. "Why were you following me?"

"I wasn't. I just want to talk." John offers her the manila envelope. "And give you this."

Miriam crosses her arms and looks down, refusing to accept the envelope. "Why did you betray us, John?"

"I didn't. Van Owen is the traitor." He holds up the envelope. "And this will prove it."

"Andy and his father fear you are dangerous."

"But you can sense that I'm not, can't you?"

Miriam takes a long, slow, deep breath. With her arms still crossed, she permits her eyes to meet his.

"Miriam, you know I speak the truth."

"John, you have a tremendous gift. And you are getting stronger every day. You could become a powerful healer and defender of the Life Field. But you are still so very young—and, I must say, a bit naïve. You have not yet developed the discipline required for the life you have chosen. Yes, you can maintain resonance with the Life Field for much longer now than when we first met. But I do not sense you are either willing or able to do what is necessary to protect our future. And *that* is what makes you dangerous."

"Maybe I don't agree with everything you believe is necessary."

"So, you think Carl should patent his machine and sell it to everyone who wants to manipulate the Life Field, regardless of their intentions?"

"Absolutely not!"

"Then why were you and Emily helping him get his patent? Why did you give the machine to Mr. Cummings—the patent master?"

"Frank? He took the machine. Emily tried to stop him."

"She cannot possibly have tried very hard, now, can she? Was she being held at gunpoint?"

"She thought Carl had agreed to let Frank take it."

"My point exactly. You and Emily were doing everything in your power to help Carl get his patent."

"No. We doctored Carl's data to get his focus off the Life Field and onto something else."

"Then why did Mr. Cummings say the data you gave him was everything he needed to file the revised patent application? If Mr. Van Owen had not stepped in to rescue the machine and halt the patent process, Carl's application would have already been filed—and, as you know, filings are public."

"Rescue? No! Van Owen took Carl's machine because he's planning to reveal the Life Field—and use the machine to control it."

"Oh, John. Please do not insult my intelligence. We know the artificial intelligence software you installed onto Carl's machine is modifying it to your specifications. And it prevents anyone else from accessing it. Even our best people are locked out. You certainly have proven yourself to be skilled at hacking. It is a shame your motives are not aligned with ours."

"But they are! I've been trying to disable the machine for days."

"You expect me to believe the best hacker in the business—and the only person with access to the machine—cannot disable it? Do you take me for a fool?"

"No…It's complicated."

"Ah, so you think I am a simpleton."

John takes a breath to avoid being utterly consumed by frustration. He drops his mounting defensiveness into the flow arising from his breath. Miriam's reality appears before him—a distant image gradually coming into focus.

"Miriam, you are one of the most remarkable people I have ever met. I have great respect for you."

"Then perhaps you would like to show your respect by explaining what is happening with the machine."

"Look, the backdoor I installed uses machine learning. Now, it appears that exposure to the Life Field triggered it to modify Carl's original code. But not to my specifications. The machine is creating its own specifications based on all the data it gathers from the Internet. And one of those specifications is not to allow anyone—not even me—to shut it down."

Miriam unfolds her arms. "Well, John. That is the first thing you have said I feel I can trust. I sense you have shared something you honestly believe to be the truth."

"Everything I have told you is the truth."

"Then why do I feel you hiding from me?"

"Because I don't feel safe! Andy is trying to frame Emily and me for attempted murder."

"Oh, John. That is an FBI fantasy. Andy had nothing to do with it."

"Really? Then who got the Army of God to try to kill Carl? I'm sure they didn't think of that on their own."

"That was an unfortunate mistake. But it was not Andy's. It became urgent to prevent Carl from revealing the Life Field and Mr. Van Owen offered to help."

"Wait, what? You mean Van Owen has contacts within the Army of God?"

"It appears he does. In any event, he has recognized his error in judgment. And Andy is doing everything he can to help the FBI catch the perpetrators, being careful, of course, to avoid implicating Mr. Van Owen."

"So, you no longer want Carl dead?"

"We never did. We just wanted to prevent him from filing the patent."

John finds an opening in Miriam's heart. He offers the envelope once again. "Miriam, please. Take this. Read it. Listen to the tape. Give it to Andy and his dad."

Miriam tentatively accepts the envelope.

"Carl will not sign the patent application," says John. "And without his signature, I don't think it can be submitted. He and I will not rest until we find a way to disable the machine."

"You are still working with Carl?" asks Miriam warily.

"You, Andy, Carl, and I are all on the same side here. I promise."

"Very well, then." Miriam lifts the envelope. "I will have a look."

"Thank you. Please ask Andy to call me after he's seen it."

"We must leave now."

Miriam opens the door, holds it for John, and locks it after they have exited. She slips on her shoes, descends the stairs, and vanishes into the alley—all before John has finished tying his shoes.

Chapter Twenty-Eight
The Plan

SOPHIA SCANS THE CAFÉ. John stands, catches her eye, and sits right back down, lost behind the crowd. Sophia heads for the last booth in the back. Normally, John would stand again to greet her, but today, he needs to remain as invisible as possible. He merely extends his hand.

"Sit," says John, motioning to the opposite bench.

"And good morning to you, too!" says Sophia with exaggerated cheerfulness. She grabs his hand, pulls him toward her, and leans down to kiss him. Her free hand reaches behind John's head to pin his lips tightly against hers.

Sophia's lips interrupt John's obsession with his mission. He waits patiently to be released, allowing himself to enjoy the moment.

"Sit, please."

Sophia keeps her eyes trained on John as she sits. A teenage server drops off two raisin scones and two cups of coffee before racing off without saying a word.

"You look terrible," says Sophia. "You okay?"

"Just a little stressed."

"I would have responded to your text sooner if I had recognized the phone number."

"It's a burner."

"Why the cloak and dagger?"

"Emily and I are in trouble. And we have a huge favor to ask of you. I'll completely understand if you say no. It might even be—"

"John, you're the best friend I have in the world." Sophia slides her hand across the table. John takes her hand cautiously. She lays her other hand on top of his and squeezes. "I would do anything for you, or for Emily. I love you both."

Unexpected warmth emanates from Sophia's grip. Although they haven't seen each other since they were last in this café, their bond has been nurtured as if they had been living together all along. Their love is stronger now than it had been when they were a couple. This newly potent love rushes from Sophia's hands through John's, racing up his arm to his chest, where it expands in all directions until it engulfs them both and triggers a powerful flow within John. A clear vision of Sophia working with him alongside Emily, Carl, and even Andy materializes behind his eyes.

In the shortest version he can muster, John fills Sophia in on all that has happened since Emily and Ashley were picked up by the FBI. Sophia listens intently. She affirms everything he says as if they are reminiscing—reliving an old adventure for the hundredth time.

"So, what did Andy say?" asks Sophia.

"Well...he said the evidence I offered convinced him Van Owen has betrayed The Faithful. But I'm still a little wary of Andy."

"Why?"

"Because he knows that's what I want to hear."

"So, you're afraid he's just saying that to win your trust and soften you to his schemes?"

"Possibly."

"Did he offer to help you disable the machine?"

"Sort of."

"Sort of, how?"

"I told Andy the only way to disable the machine is for me to write a virus and put it on this new thing called a USB flash drive. Then, someone has to insert that USB drive into the machine. I figured he could find an excuse to visit Van Owen, find the machine—we think it's in his office—and insert the USB drive. My virus will do the rest."

"And?"

"Andy thinks Van Owen would be suspicious; he might sense Andy's true motives."

"Could he be right?"

"Maybe."

"So, you have someone else in mind for this gambit with the USB thingy."

"Yeah."

"Someone you can trust."

"Yup."

"Someone Van Owen won't suspect."

John nods. He looks down.

"Of course, I'll do it, my love. But I can't just call up Van Owen and ask to come visit, can I?"

"That's where Andy comes in. Van Owen is throwing another one of his famous parties. Andy can get you hired as the entertainment. You've made quite a splash in the music scene, you know—especially since your new album charted."

"Why thank you, my dear!"

"So, what do you think?"

"I think it's brilliant. When's the party?"

"It could be dangerous. Van Owen is ruthless. If he finds out what you're up to—"

Sophia stands, grabs John's shoulders with both hands, yanks him toward her, and growls, "When's the party?"

"Don't you at least want to talk this over with Craig?"

Sophia throws John's shoulders away so powerfully it thrusts them both back into their seats. "Och."

"Wait, what happened?"

"Craig doesn't have a clue what it means to be a musician."

"Uh-oh."

"He seems to think that as soon as I took the job at Berklee, I'd settle down, wear a tweed jacket, and live the life of a college professor."

The image of Sophia clad tweed and giving a lecture induces a chuckle.

"It's not funny, John."

Sophia's eyes fill with water. John cradles her face in his hands. He wipes her cheek. She blinks the water away.

"I'm sorry," says John.

Sophia sniffles. "He says he loves me, but he doesn't love *me*. He loves *his idea* of me. I told him before he moved here that he was shacking up with a musician. That's who I am. That's who I'll always be. Music is my life. I made it abundantly clear. Musicians don't settle down, work a nine-to-five job, raise kids in the suburbs, barbecue on weekends, and take two-week vacations to go hiking at Yosemite!"

"Is that really what he wants?"

"It's not what he says he wants, but everything he does shouts it from the rooftops. He took a job at Ropes & fucking Gray!"

"Jimmy's lawyer is from Ropes & Gray, and he's not your typical—"

"Craig is in asset management!"

"Oh." John pauses. Sophia's wide eyes won't let go. "I thought you said he was thinking of joining the Innocence Project!"

"Kind of a big switcheroo, isn't it?"

"I'm so sorry, Sophie."

"I'm not. I should have known. All the warning signs were there. He's terrified of the unknown. What hurts me the most, though, is when he scoffs at my dreams. And now I see how he's been doing it since we first got together."

"Scoffs at your dreams?" John's outrage is obvious.

"It used to be subtle. Maybe he didn't even know he was doing it—you know, snide remarks about my being in the studio for 16 hours straight, or how time on stage is less than ten percent of the time spent on tour. That kinda stuff."

"And now?"

"He poo-poos every musical choice I make," she imitates Craig, "Nobody listens to that anymore," she continues in her own voice, "and mocks every guest appearance I get offered," imitating Craig again, "Oh, so you're gonna waste a year on tour with that loser?"

"Oh, boy."

"And he complains about the money I spent mixing and mastering. My money! Not his. And this record is up for a Grammy, but he could care less. He's got a plan for his life, and I guess I just don't fit into it anymore."

John takes a long, slow, deep breath. He wishes Sophia had someone to support her dreams the way Emily supports his.

I could have been that person if I hadn't put my own career first.

"So," says Sophia. She puts her hands on the table and leans forward, "when's the *friggin' pahty*—as they say, here in Mass?"

John chuckles and shakes his head. "If you're sure you want to do this, keep the 15th and 16th open. Andy will have Van Owen's event planner book you through your agent to avoid any suspicion."

He removes a small, black, leather case from his pocket and hands it to Sophia. "Take this. It has a layout of Van Owen's house showing his office, a drawing of the machine, and a little USB flash drive the size of a stick of gum. Somehow, you'll have to make your way to Van Owen's office, find the machine, and stick that USB drive into the spot I've indicated on the drawing. The rest will happen automatically." John looks at the ceiling for a second. "Now that I say it out loud, I don't know how you're gonna…" He unzips the case. "Here…let me show you—"

Sophia puts her hand on John's. "I got this." She zips the case shut, shoves it into her purse, gets up, and slides onto the bench next to him. Clasping his neck, she whispers into his ear, "Thank you, John. This little caper of yours will save me from having to kick that small-minded, cowardly, company man out of my apartment."

"What?"

"Well, I can't tell Craig what I'm doing and why."

"You did promise to keep my secret."

"Exactly. And when I tell him that I can't tell him…let's just say that'll be the last straw. He won't be there when I get back."

"Oh, Sophie."

"No, it's good. I'm done—over him already." Sophie kisses John on the lips.

"Are you sure about this?" asks John.

With a single, sizzling dance move, Sophia slides out of the bench, pops up, grabs her purse, twirls around, and smiles at John. "Give my love to that enchanting bride of yours."

"She's not my bride."

"Not yet, she's not. But you could fix that."

John rolls his eyes.

"Bye sweetie," says Sophia in a sing-song voice, dancing her way toward the café exit.

Chapter Twenty-Nine
Part 1: Catering

"SO, WHAT DO YOU THINK, JIMMY?" Emily grabs a slice of pizza from the pie at the center of Jimmy's kitchen table. She drops it onto her plate and douses it with hot red peppers.

Jimmy considers his answer, pausing until Emily has taken a bite. He and John stare at her in silence.

"What?" asks Emily with her mouth full.

"I felt I should be poised to call 911 after your giant mouthful of hots," answers Jimmy.

"She likes it hot," says John.

"Indubitably," says Jimmy.

"Stop, you two!" Emily swallows. "Seriously, Jimmy, what do you think?"

"Well…on the one hand, you make a good point. What Sophia has so heroically volunteered to do is dangerous—and there is no assurance of success. She could certainly use the help."

Emily shoves the slice into her mouth and bites off another piece like a lioness tearing into her prey. "Mm-hmm?"

"But Andy could very well be right. Even if he could convince Van Owen's event planner to add you to the catering team, Van Owen can resonate with the Life Field and he's likely to sense your presence."

"Or at least sense something is amiss," says John, "And that might put him on guard. Sophia needs Van Owen to have his guard down."

Emily swallows. "That seems like a risk we should be willing to take."

"Don't forget, the FBI told us not to leave Cambridge," says John.

"Oh, Buzz should be able to handle them." Emily shakes more hots onto the remains of her slice. "Right, Jimmy?"

"Probably," replies Jimmy.

"At the very least," says Emily, "don't you think we should ask Sophia whether she thinks the risk is worth the help?"

"What do you say, John?" asks Jimmy.

"I'll call her now." John grabs the burner phone from his pocket and calls Sophia.

She answers, "What's up Doc?"

"I'm here with Emily and Jimmy."

John puts the phone on speaker. Emily and Jimmy greet her in unison, "Hi Sophia."

"Hi guys. It might be a little noisy, I'm walking to the studio."

"No problem," says John, "We'd like to run something by—"

"John and I think we should be at Van Owen's party," interrupts Emily, "The event planner can put us on the catering team."

"Hold on," says John.

"We just want to be there for you, Sophie," insists Emily, "in case you run into any trouble."

Traffic is the only sound coming from the phone.

"Sophie?" says Emily. "You there?"

"I'm here," says Sophia. "Yeah, I get the impression you two don't agree on this."

"Here's the thing," says John, "Van Owen might be able to sense that we're there, which could make him generally wary. And that might—"

"I get it," interrupts Sophia. "Guys, you're gonna have to sort this one out between yourselves. I agreed to the plan, not expecting either of you to be there. Obviously, I'd welcome any help I can get, but you can divine the risks better than I can. I'll be fine with whatever you decide. Just let me know. Gotta go now." The call ends.

"Well, that was enlightening," says Jimmy.

"You're kidding, right?" says Emily, frustrated.

"Not at all," replies Jimmy. "She's smart, resolute, and frightened. Everything you want in a reliable hero."

"So, do we go or not?" asks Emily.

"That, my dear friends, is for you two to sort out, as Sophia has advised."

"And how do you suggest we do that?" asks Emily.

"Ask yourselves. Your inner selves." Jimmy slides a slice of pizza onto his plate and stands. "You'll find the answer there. I promise you." He leaves the kitchen.

John and Emily stare at each other in shock for a moment. John draws a breath. Emily matches it. They exhale. Both know intuitively what to do.

"I'll go see Andy," says John, "and convince him to get us on the catering team."

Maureen Banks, the catering manager, is at her wit's end. "Look, I don't know what your game is here—"

Emily tries to look and sound reassuring, "All we—"

Maureen raises her stubby, calloused, wrinkled hands. "I don't wanna know. I don't want you here. But here you are, anyhow. So, listen to me good: If you cause even a teensy-weensy bit of trouble or interfere in any way with this event, I'll have you thrown outa here so fast your head will spin right off that skinny little neck of yours. Got it?"

John, chest out, steps in front of Emily. "Ma'am, you don't have to—"

"Got it, Ma'am," interrupts Emily. She grabs John's arm. "You'll get no trouble from us." Emily drags John into a hallway.

Maureen grumbles to herself in her exasperated, raspy voice, "I'll be so glad when this cluster fuck is over and done with."

Once they're out of Maureen's sight, Emily kisses John on the cheek. "I appreciate your chivalry, my love, but let's try not to antagonize the staff, hmm?"

"Fine. You'll get no trouble from me."

Emily slaps John on the shoulder. "You've got another flash drive in your pocket, right?"

"Yes, but we agreed to stay out of sight and away from Van Owen's office. We can't risk him seeing us. Remember, he's seen our photos. He might recognize us."

"Carl says Van Owen is so focused on money and so full of himself he wouldn't even recognize his own children if he had any."

"Yeah, well, let's just keep a low profile and make sure one of us can see Sophie at all times like we agreed, okay?"

"You'll get no trouble from me."

Part 2: Music

"He's dying to meet you," says Mark.

"Now?" complains Sophia, "I thought a tour manager was supposed to protect me from this sort of unwanted attention."

"Yeah, but this guy's paying your fee."

"Fine. I'll be right out."

Mark winks. "You can't even keep up the bitch act for 30 seconds. How am I supposed to prepare for a *real* tour?"

"Oh, so I'm not a *real* artist?"

"Whoa! Baby! You cut me to the quick." Mark clutches his chest feigning a heart attack. "You know you're my favorite artist. There's nobody else for me. But you're not touring, remember?"

"What if that were to change?"

Mark kneels before Sophia. He bows his head as if preparing to be knighted by the Queen. "At your service, Your Majesty."

Sophia cradles Mark's chin in her hand, lifts his head gently and smiles down at him. "Get up, silly."

Mark jumps up. "Really? You've reconsidered? You might take that European tour?"

"Bobby seriously wants me to. He keeps begging me to let him start booking. He says we'd do very well."

"I would be honored to be your TM for Europe—or any other tour."

"Good." Sophia puts her arm through his. "Now let's go meet our host."

Arm in arm, Sophia and Mark walk from the dressing room, through the wing, onto the stage in the grand ballroom.

"Look at this place..." says Sophia, "the dressing room, the stage, the lights, the PA. This guy's private ballroom is nicer than most theatres I've played."

Mark points to the mic stand at center stage, "See what I got for you?"

"Oh, thank you, Mark." Sophia smiles up at him like a little girl whose mother had let her lick the icing off a spatula. "You know me too well."

"For some reason—I'll never comprehend—when you get up from the piano and sing downstage, I have to admit your performance is better if you have that stupid straight stand with the heavy-ass, round base."

"Because I can dance with it, silly. You can't dance with those flimsy tripod stands."

Sophia dances with her hands up around Mark's neck. Mark straightens, stiffens, puts his arms at his side, and imitates the mic stand tilting whichever way she pulls. They lose their balance and barely recover before falling.

"Oh, I see Luke has another new pedal?" says Sophia, laughing.

"Yeah, it just showed up there." Mark's sarcasm is obvious. "He must be experimenting with the thing before he incorporates it into that massive pedal board of his."

"Don't say anything, Mark. You know how testy Luke gets when you inquire about his new toys."

"That's him," whispers Mark into Sophia's ear. He loses himself in the sweet scent and tickle of her curls. Van Owen's rapid approach obliterates Mark's temporary intoxication. He ushers Sophia down the steps from the stage into the ballroom.

"Mr. Van Owen, please allow me to present Grammy Nominee Sophia Bella." Mark bows, extending his arm toward Sophia.

"Enchantée," says Van Owen. He lands a wet kiss on Sophia's

hand while his eyes consume her entire body.

"Very pleased to meet you, Sir," says Sophia, tracking his eyes.

"You know, I've become quite a fan of yours."

"Why, thank you."

"You may find that having a fan, such as I, is most advantageous for your career, young lady."

"Oh, I'm sure it will be. Why, it already is. This evening is proof, isn't it?"

"Well, I should hope so. I'll have you know that Steinway you'll be playing tonight cost me a fortune."

"It is a gorgeous instrument, Sir. I only hope I can do it justice."

"I'm sure you will, my dear. Perhaps we can have a chat after my little soirée winds down a bit."

"That would be delightful. I look forward to it."

"Good. Well, then, I'd better let you get on with sound check, hadn't I?"

"Thank you. We want to make sure everything is perfect for you and your guests tonight."

Van Owen nods and turns to follow the butler who is walking by. "Ah, Sanders. Whatever happened to my instructions? I mean, just look at these…"

"Dear God, you laid that on thick," exclaims Mark, "and after he practically raped you with his eyes!"

Sophia wipes the back of her hand on her pants. "That presumptuous little lech can imagine anything he likes behind those beady eyes of his. I've got him right where I want him."

"You think he might bankroll a tour for you? Or your next album?"

"We've only just begun, Mark." She kisses him softly on the cheek.

Mark stares at Sophia, mouth agape.

Luke's appearance on stage snaps Mark out of his shell shock. "Looks like the guys are done with load-in. I'll get sound check going."

"Thanks, Mark." Sophia smiles at him, knowing she successfully sent him down a path entirely divergent from hers. He is guaranteed to remain perfectly safe from the chaos Sophia expects will ensue tonight. "I'll join you in a minute."

She heads to the dressing room while texting John, "I'm in."

Sophia delivers the most stellar performance of her life. The magnificent piano dares her to take chances during her solos, inspiring extraordinary creativity and spontaneous applause. When singing from center stage, she breathes life into the mic stand, dancing with her buoyant lover to cheers from the crowd. Sophia's charisma sparks a contact high in her band, stirring them into a tight, perfectly blended unit. A couple of winks at Mark arouse the clearest live mix he's ever mastered.

After her set, Sophia offers the mic to Van Owen, followed by a beguiling smile and a polite hug. Van Owen pulls her in tight, squashing her breasts into his soft torso. She shimmies out of his grip. The guests notice nothing. Everyone in the grand ballroom is on their feet in applause. Shouts of "Bravo!" pepper the room.

"Wow!" says Van Owen into the mic as he takes center stage. "What a performance!" He touches his lips to the mic causing a squeal of feedback. "Sophia Bella, everybody!"

Mark scrambles at the soundboard to kill the feedback made even worse by Van Owen's shouting, but little can be done to attenuate the distortion. He catches the wink Sophia throws him from the wing.

Van Owen continues, his lips slobbering all over the mic, his voice shrieking, "Wow! Amazing! Thank you, Sophia. And your amazing band, too." Another roaring round of applause. Van Owen winks at Sophia. She waves shyly. Mark's console magic has removed all feedback and most of the distortion.

"I could say goodnight right now and you'd be glad you came if only for the music and the food and the wines," continues Van Owen, "but I'll bet you're eager to hear about my latest invention and my new foundation dedicated to educating people about my new discovery."

Polite applause greets Van Owen's message. Some guests spot Sophia standing in the wing. They wave at her, trying to coax her back on stage.

"And after my announcement, the lovely Sophia Bella will play another set!"

Roaring applause erupts. Van Owen winks at Sophia again. She offers a faint smile.

As the applause dies down, conversations brew among the guests.

Van Owen shouts to overcome the crowd, "Okay, okay, settle down, everybody." He motions to Mark to turn him up. Mark obliges.

Part 3: The Voice of Truth

A faint voice arises from the back of the ballroom. "Tell the truth!"

The crowd quiets a bit. People near the back look behind them.

"Tell the truth, Van Owen!" says the voice.

"What? Who's that?" Van Owen's piercing query rages from the speakers, startling everyone—even him.

The ballroom is silent.

"I invented the machine," says the voice, louder now as it approaches the stage, "I made the discovery. You stole it all from me!"

"Carl?" shouts John from his post near the ballroom's rear exit, "What are you doing here?"

Carl ignores John and continues toward the stage. The crowd congeals around him. John tries to push through. The crowd closes in behind Carl, edging John out.

A strong hand yanks John from behind.

"Get back there," orders Agent Brewer. "It's not safe for you up front."

"What?" asks John. "Brewer? What are you doing here?"

"We tracked Army of God terrorists here. They're after Dr. Friedrich—and maybe you too."

"Oh, so you don't think Emily tried to kill—"

"Not now, kid. Where's your Emily?"

"Here somewhere."

"Find her—and the both o' you stay outa sight."

"I thought all the guests had to pass through a metal detector."

"It's not a gun that worries me."

"What the—"

"Go!"

John obeys his instinct to heed Brewer's advice. With Van Owen on stage and distracted by Carl, this may be the best chance to find and disable the machine. But first, he must make sure Emily is safe.

"Is that you Carl?" says Van Owen, "I thought you were in hiding."

Carl jumps on stage.

Van Owen recovers from the shock of seeing Carl and shouts into the mic, "Carl Friedrich, everybody!"

The bewildered audience responds with polite applause. Guests chatter among themselves.

"Biotech genius," continues Van Owen, "founder of MGH," he reaches up to put his arm around Carl's shoulders, "Some of you remember him from my last party."

Brewer spies a skinny, sullen man shuffling away from the crowd toward the rear exit. Touching his earpiece, he says, "Shipley, do you see that guy?" He fiddles with his earpiece, waiting for Shipley's reply.

"Affirmative. He's heading my way," says Shipley.

"You're sure the explosive is disarmed?"

"Watson's sure, and he's still alive after 10 years on the bomb squad."

"Come again?"

"Watson's never wrong."

"Do you think the AOG knows?"

"No, sir. Watson left it right where it was—on stage next to all the other pedals. He assures me it will appear to the AOG as armed and ready."

"Don't touch that guy until you see him with a cellphone or some other device he could use as a detonator."

"Roger that."

A giant, bear of a man, dressed in a tuxedo, has stood motionless all evening watching the stage from his post near the ballroom's side exit. John finds Emily hiding behind him. It's the perfect spot to see across the stage and keep an eye on Sophia in the wing.

John kisses Emily on the cheek. Emily grabs his head, rotates it to face the stage and points. Sophia is leaving the wing. John heads for Van Owen's office, leaving Emily to watch the stage so she can text him the minute Van Owen exits.

Sophia had lifted Van Owen's keys from his jacket pocket during her awkward, on-stage hug. They had been her quarry all evening.

Shortly after arriving at the estate, Sophia had charmed members of the staff into disclosing that Van Owen had recently commissioned a new locking cabinet to be built for "something revolutionary" that must be kept secure in his office.

Carl yanks the mic from Van Owen, "You put on a show of friendship for your flunkeys, but your deeds betray you. You claim my machine as your invention, my discovery as your own. You fund my work, then you order me killed!" Gasps flair up from the crowd. Carl continues, "You live in splendor, but you're nothing more than a common hood. And the only reason you weren't locked up long ago is because you've duped us all into letting you get away with murder. But tonight, the truth comes out!"

Van Owen frantically signals to Mark to cut the sound. Mark complies. The crowd is silent. All eyes are on the stage.

Carl continues his rant, shouting at the audience, "And you, you brood of vipers, why are you here, huh?" Like a swordsman, he points the mic at Van Owen, who is standing center stage, stunned. "You think you've made it 'cause you're on his guest list? Get a rush being so close to this much wealth? This much power? Well, I got news for you, people: none of this is real! The only real thing here tonight was that glorious music!" he stares into the wing, looking for Sophia.

Van Owen grabs the mic from Carl. He motions toward the soundboard to turn it back on. Mark is gone.

Carl continues shouting, "He only has power because you give it to him. He only has money because you allow him to rape the collective wealth we've all worked for centuries to build. You believe he's better than you because that's what you've been conditioned to believe. You admire his powerful friends, but you are those friends. It's all a ruse."

Shipley grabs the skinny, sullen man's phone the instant it appears out of his jacket pocket. He covers the man's mouth, drags him into the hallway, and cuffs him to a radiator—all quietly enough to avoid detection by anyone in the crowd.

"Got him," says Shipley. "He was attempting to detonate."

"Roger that," says Brewer.

"Pause your frenzied lives and look around for a moment," continues Carl in a softer voice, having captured the crowd's undivided attention. "The truth is simple. It's been right here all this time." With both hands, he points to his heart. "Look in here. Can you feel it?" Carl raises his voice and extends his hands, "Do it now! All of you!"

Guests touch their hands to their hearts. They glance around at each other. Pockets of nervous chatter erupt.

Part 4: The Giant

The giant tuxedoed man lurches toward the stage. He brutally shoves everyone in his path, trampling over those who fall.

"Brewer!" shouts Emily, realizing the giant began his charge upon seeing Shipley grab the skinny man near the rear exit.

The giant steps on the pot belly of a fallen guest and leaps onto the stage. A wave of screams erupts through the crowd. The giant grabs the straight mic stand at the top, lifts it upside down with both hands, swings the heavy round base in a wide circle over his head like a lasso, and shouts, "No more dead babies!"

He swings at Carl. The heavy base bashes into Carl's head, opening a gash in his skull. Blood gushes from Carl's head and shoots out his eye. His head crashes onto the stage as he falls.

"Carl!" screams Emily. She runs to the stage.

"Everybody down!" shouts Brewer, his gun aimed at the stage.

Emily disregards Brewer's command and continues running. Guests drop to the floor. The wave of screams fades into whimpers.

"Burn in hell, you traitor!" shouts the giant. He whacks Van Owen in the upper chest. Van Owen clutches his neck, gasps, and falls. The giant twirls the mic stand. Stradling Van Owen, he raises it over his head like an axe preparing to strike. Van Owen covers his face with his hands, screaming, "No! No!"

One shot rings out from Brewer's pistol. His bullet pierces the giant's thigh and cracks a bone. The giant falls. The mic stand follows. Its heavy base lands on the giant's chest, knocking the wind out of him. Brewer storms the stage and subdues the wounded attacker.

Shipley calls for three ambulances. He abandons his prisoner, draws his gun, and races down the hall to search the rest of the house.

"What was that?" says John, startled.

"Gunshot," says Mark. "Who are you?"

"That's John!" says Sophia.

"Oh, you're John?" says Mark. "I thought you'd be—"

"Boys!" snaps Sophia, "We've gotta find the office. We'll have time for introductions later."

"If we're still alive," says Mark.

John studies the map. He points to a door at the end of the hallway. "That's it."

John, Mark, and Sophia race down the hallway. Sophia tries the door. It's locked. She fumbles with the keys, distracted by shouting and crying coming from the ballroom. Mark grabs the keys from Sophia and deftly unlocks the door with the first key he tries.

"Go," commands Mark.

Sophia and John race in. Mark follows, shuts the door, and locks it.

"There!" says Sophia pointing to the locked cabinet. Mark unlocks the cabinet door and slides it open.

"I got this!" says John.

"Get back, Ma'am," orders Brewer.

"Oh, Carl!" cries Emily, ignoring Brewer's command. She cradles Carl's bleeding head in her lap.

"This man is injured," insists Brewer. "Step away."

"This man is my friend!" shrieks Emily through tears.

Carl agonizingly lifts his arm to touch Emily's hand, covering it in blood. "I had hoped we could become friends." He coughs, spraying blood into Emily's face and hair.

"Of course, we're friends," whispers Emily. She wipes her face. "I feared our friendship was doomed after we lied to you. I am so, so sorry, Carl." She dissolves into tears.

Carl struggles to lift his head, sending blood shooting from his eye.

"Don't!" cries Emily. "Save your strength." She shouts at Brewer, "Did you even call an ambulance, you knucklehead."

"They're on the way, Ma'am."

Carl raises his shaking arm. Gazing into Emily's eyes, he touches her cheek, smearing it in blood. "It's all yours now, my little genius. Use it wisely."

He raises his arm higher, making a fist as if grabbing something out of the air above him. With sudden strength, he lifts his head and shoulders to stare at a point right above his fist.

Emily glances up to catch a glimpse of Carl's mysterious, airborne prize. Carl's arm falls, pounding the stage as it lands. Brewer obeys his instinct to reach for his gun. His hand relaxes upon watching Carl's body go limp. Emily peers through Carl's eyes, tightening her grip on his head. Life escapes his eyes, casting them aside, relegating them now to mere body parts. Emily buries her head in his chest and weeps.

Part 5: The Job

"Somebody's in there, sir," says Sanders as he unlocks Van Owen's office door.

"FBI! Freeze!" shouts Shipley. His gun moves back and forth, aiming, in turn, at John, Sophia, and Mark.

Ignoring Shipley's command, John continues his struggle to yank the machine out of the cabinet far enough to expose the USB port. Mark raises his hands. Sophia steps between John and Shipley before raising her hands.

"I said Freeze!" shouts Shipley. "Back away from the machine."

John runs his finger along the side of the machine, stopping when he feels the USB port. He dips his other hand into his pocket to grab the flash drive.

"Back away and get your hands where I can see them now!" orders Shipley.

John pulls the flash drive out of his pocket. "I'm unarmed." He raises both hands above his head showing the flash drive to Shipley.

"Drop that thing, whatever it is, and put your hands on your head!" orders Shipley.

"Can't do that, sir," insists John.

"Don't make me shoot you, son," says Shipley.

"You'll have to shoot me first," says Sophia.

"Sophia!" yells Mark. "What the fu—"

"Don't shoot her!" says John. He pushes Sophia aside, out of the line of fire.

Sophia steadies herself, lurches toward John, and slaps his face.

John jams the flash drive into the machine, puts his hands on his head, and smirks at Sophia. "Hey, that hurt."

Sophia winks at John with one eye and Mark with the other eye.

Mark shakes his head. "Jesus."

"What is it with you kids?" says Shipley. "Now, back away from the machine…slowly…all of you. And no more games. That machine is evidence."

A tender hand touches Emily's shoulder from behind, "He's gone, Ma'am," says a sweet, southern, voice of an angel, "We'll take him from here."

Emily lowers Carl's head to rest serenely on the stage. She musters the will to stand, braced by the stunning woman with smooth, dark black skin and deep brown eyes wearing a bright blue EMT uniform. Emily hugs her and bursts into tears.

"It'll be okay, Honey," says the EMT. "Now, you need to get checked out."

"It's not my blood."

"That's fine, Honey. We still need to check you out." She snaps her fingers at a young EMT. "Matthew, this girl needs a full assessment!"

"Yes, Ma'am," says Matthew as he approaches Emily. He takes her arm, "This way."

"This man is under arrest," says Brewer.

"I get it, but he doesn't have a lot of time," says the med flight crew leader. "We need to go now, and we can't take anybody else in the chopper."

"Where are you taking him?"

"Sonoma Valley Hospital." The leader points to Van Owen on the gurney. "Look, he's got a broken clavicle, broken ribs, head injury, possible organ damage. He's not going anywhere."

"Fine. I'll have a detail meet him there."

"You got it." The leader shouts to the crew, "Let's go."

The crew rush Van Owen into the helicopter. Brewer pauses while it takes off from Van Owen's lawn.

Something doesn't feel right, but I can't quite put my finger on it.

He touches his earpiece. "Shipley, did you secure the machine?"

"We've got a problem," replies Shipley. "You need to see this."

"On my way."

Brewer stops at the ambulance on his way to Van Owen's office. The giant tuxedoed man glares at him from the gurney. Brewer motions to a uniformed police sergeant. "Send somebody good with this prisoner. Consider him large and dangerous."

"Yes sir," says the sergeant.

"And order a detail to secure Van Owen at Sonoma Valley Hospital."

"Who?"

Brewer points at the helicopter, its red and green flashing lights vanishing into the night sky. "That guy. He's under arrest too."

"Mr. Van Owen? The host of this party?"

"Yes, him. Is that a problem, Sergeant?"

"No sir."

Sitting compliantly with the others under threat of Shipley's gun, John does his best to hide how puzzled he is by the machine's reaction to the flash drive. He expected his virus to infect the machine, corrupt the startup sequence, and turn it off. He did not expect the recent flurry of activity. Gibberish flashing on the LCD. A cacophony of whirs, beeps, and clicks resonating from within. As befuddled by Carl's presence and behavior as he is with the machine, he is nonetheless glad Carl is here and hopes he'll join them soon.

Carl might be able to make sense of all this.

John glances, once more, at the computer monitor on Van Owen's desk, hoping to see something—anything but Van Owen's photo staring back at him.

How self-absorbed do you have to be to set your own photo as your desktop background image?

"Why do you keep looking at that computer?" asks Shipley.

"To see if it can explain what's happening with the machine," answers John. He stands.

"Sit your skinny ass back down," orders Shipley, "nobody moves until my partner gets here."

"I'm worried it's getting hot," says John, heading toward the machine, "We don't want it to start a fire, do we?"

"This guy probably didn't plug it into a GFI," says Mark.

"That could be a problem," says John.

Shipley points his gun directly at John. "I said sit down!"

John sits.

Brewer enters the room. "What's going on here?"

"These three were messing with the machine," says Shipley. Pointing to Mark, he adds, "Looks like he stole Van Owen's keys."

"Van Owen gave me his keys," says Sophia. "He asked me to wait for him in here after my set."

"I'll bet he did," says Shipley, raising his eyebrows.

"Never mind that," says Brewer, "What did you do to Van Owen's machine?"

"It's Carl's machine," says John, "and he gave me a flash drive to install in it. Ask Carl if you don't believe me."

"Can't do that," says Brewer.

"Look, you guys know you were wrong to be suspicious of Emily and me before. You're wrong again now. Ask Carl. He needs to see this anyhow. Maybe he can explain what's going on with it."

A loud bang startles everyone. Brewer draws his gun. John looks at the machine. Sophia looks at John. Mark shoots his hands in the air. The machine exudes a burning smell.

"Guys, c'mon," says John. "Like I told you before, that machine needs to be unplugged. It could start a fire. Where's Carl?"

"Fine. Unplug it. Then come with me," orders Brewer. He says to Shipley, "Go take a statement from Miss MacMahon."

"What?" exclaims John. "Emily? She OK? What happened?"

"Just unplug the machine and follow me," says Brewer. "We'll need statements from all of you."

The machine bursts into flames, setting off the smoke detector.

Mark eyes the bookshelves on either side of the fireplace. Nothing. He scans the room, then jumps behind the bar, frantically looking under the shelves. He opens the cabinets and mutters to himself, "What kind of idiot has a fireplace in a wood paneled room full of books and no fire extinguisher?"

"Go. Get out of here!" shouts Brewer, barely audible over the deafening squeal of the smoke detector.

Sanders appears with a large fire extinguisher. He douses the machine, putting out the fire. Some foam spills onto Van Owen's desk. Sanders removes his jacket and uses it to wipe off the foam.

"Hit it again!" Brewer strains to be heard over the still squealing smoke detector.

"Oh, dear Lord," mutters Sanders. He empties the fire extinguisher into the cabinet. The lights go out. Battery powered emergency lights throw a harsh glare onto the melted, smoldering, twisted metal, plastic, and wire that was once the machine.

"Was that you?" yells Brewer.

"Yes. I had maintenance kill the power to this office."

"Good!" The smoke detector goes silent. "Good job," wheezes Brewer, hoarse from shouting.

"Why, thank you, sir." Sanders stares forlornly at his jacket and Van Owen's desk, both covered in foam.

Chapter Thirty
The Gift

John Wells is grateful to be alive. In his dreamy state, emotions are free to come and go as they please. They waft through like alluring aromas meandering out of a bakery to tease passersby.

Blended patterns unfold. Colors emerge. The torn, yellowed, paper window shade—Emily calls it atrocious—diffuses the bright sunlight. A golden glow spills onto her angelic, sleeping face cradled in her auburn hair. Soft blankets undulate like distant rolling hills sculpted by her perfect body. The shade's circular pull swings back and forth on its frayed cord, propelled by hot air rising from the radiator. This hypnotic pendulum summons a deep sense of gratitude for his first night back in his own bed. He draws a breath. Aching muscles, tight from days on end of adrenaline-fueled readiness in the face of danger, release their tension.

Memories call. He waves them by. What-if scenarios vie for attention. His steady breathing bids them adieu.

Emily's Love seeps from his heart into his consciousness. What mysterious force had inspired him to recognize it, name it, cherish it, nurture it? The Life Field perhaps?

Gratitude returns. For Sophia—his first love and best friend. For Jimmy and Simon and Dr. Z—and his choice to study with them. For Miriam and Andy and Andy's father—and his own determination to heed his gut when it told him to pursue an alliance.

Emily moans and writhes in her sleep. Her stirring had jarred John awake every couple of hours all night long. Laying his hand on her arm for a few minutes would calm her fitful twitches. When her noises ceased, John would drift back to sleep.

Now that he's awake, Emily's velvet skin evokes new emotions. Compassion for the love of his life, who is still haunted by the trauma of Carl dying in her arms. Despair over his defeated attempts to console her in the hotel shower while she scrubbed and raged, and scrubbed and cried, and scrubbed and whimpered, and scrubbed some more, desperate to get Carl's blood out of her hair and the stench of death out of her nose—a lingering sense that torments her still. Fury at the bureaucrats who prevented Emily from visiting Rox in the hospital on the way home from the airport. Frustration at his failure to take away Emily's pain.

You cannot heal anyone by taking their pain. Simon's admonition interrupts John's wallowing. *You heal them by loving them. And with love, you guide them through their struggle to surrender their reality of pain and embrace a new, pain-free reality—just as Miriam did with you. Taking someone's pain robs them of the gift of growth offered by the pain.*

John's trust in Simon's wisdom does not lessen the pain induced by witnessing Emily suffer. He knows he must surrender his own reality of pain if he is to help Emily surrender hers.

Emily is quiet once again, fast asleep. John's phone beeps. Emily rolls over without waking. John slinks out of bed, grabs his phone and clothes, sneaks out of the bedroom, and silently closes the door. He throws on his shirt and pants, then peeks at his phone. It reports new access to the server. He skates across the floor in his socks, sliding into the chair at his computer.

There's a new file on the server—a video. His heart races through the virus scan. He starts the video. Carl is speaking directly at him. John gasps while hitting STOP. Eyes close. Hands raise. He turns away.

Who put up that video? It couldn't have been Carl!

He traces recent server access to an IP address from Geneva, Switzerland. Using his tools for finding the owner of an IP address turns up nothing.

This guy doesn't want to be found.

John checks the server logs. One file has been modified—the file Carl had uploaded requesting the meeting at his hideout. Now it's encrypted.

Maybe the password is in the video.

He slips on headphones to listen without waking Emily. His heart pounds, reverberating through the headphones. Steadying his shaking hand on the mouse, he clicks the video again. The frame contains a tight headshot of Carl, harshly lit against a background that looks like it could be his hideout. John clicks *PLAY*.

Carl speaks through the computer, "Emily and John, if you are watching this video, then my concerns were warranted, and the FBI was unable to protect me from Van Owen and the Army of God. I know the risk I take is enormous, and the odds of success are low. But my heart rules this day, for it knows what must be done. As Pascal said, 'Le coeur a ses raisons que la raison ne connaît pas.'

"By my invention, I have been invited to dwell within the aura of two power centers: your Life Field, and Van Owen's worldly throne. How can I ever again live on the periphery, anonymously, haunted by the truth that I shirked my duty to prevent calamity and advance healing?

"As it turns out, the mystery I have spent my entire life investigating was solved long ago. But this revelation has been kept secret. Why? For fear that people like Van Owen would exploit it?

"Fear? Really? How could we have fallen so far? Are we now ruled entirely by our fears? Have we forgotten our obligation to face our fears and leave this world a better place than we found it?

"Yes, Van Owen is evil. And he must be stopped. But Emily…you, of all people, should understand. We cannot abide the fear of knowledge. We must embrace all knowledge, all discoveries—even those we fear are dangerous. We cannot allow anything to thwart our healing mission!

"I admire you and John. Your courage. Your ingenuity. Your dedication. But you are still so very young. Despite all your extraordinary talents, you lack the wisdom to do what is truly needed in this case…ask for help. So, I have decided to help you. Without your knowledge at first, but once you see me, you're smart enough to detect my plan. I'll be giving you plenty of cover so you can disable the machine while I disable Van Owen and clear your names.

"I got word to the Army of God that I'll be at Van Owen's party. They'll be coming for me. The FBI will follow them or you or me. They will see that you and John are not a threat. Hopefully, they'll also be able to apprehend those whack jobs who want me dead before it's too late. Then you won't have to watch this video, in which case I'll tell you all of this in person.

"But if you are watching, I implore you, do not mourn for me. Choose instead to honor me by continuing my work—our work.

"Emily, I have given you everything you need to do so. I know you share my passion for discovery and healing. I felt it the moment we met. Open the file I sent in response to John's invitation to meet. The password is *little genius*—one word, all lowercase except for an uppercase G. Everything is explained in that file.

"Be well, my little genius!"

The doorbell startles John. He throws off his headphones and skates across the apartment, racing to answer before it rings again. Nobody is at the door. A large metal case is sitting on the stoop with FOR EMILY written in deep purple marker on top. He scans the sidewalk. Nobody close enough to have just delivered anything. A door slams shut on a black SUV with tinted windows parked near his building. He memorizes the license plate as it speeds away. The case is heavier than it looks. He hefts it inside, marshaling extra strength to set it quietly on the floor.

Carl's voice drifts through the apartment. John shudders. Emily is in his chair. He approaches. Her eyes are filled with water. Much to John's relief, she is not sobbing. He lays his hand on her shoulder. Emily touches it. When Carl is finished, Emily squeezes John's hand and smiles at him. Her silent greeting exudes a warm, clear energy.

She moves her hand to touch his face. "Open the file, My Love."

John leans over her, takes the mouse, closes the video, and clicks on the file Carl had modified. Emily wipes her eyes, types the password, *littleGenius*, sniffles, and wipes her nose.

Emily and John are stunned by what they see—instructions for accessing Carl's Swiss bank account, complete schematics for a new design of the machine, a new patent application, and a note: *I cobbled it together the best I could in the time I had. It may need a bit of tweaking. You should have it soon.*

"I think it's here," says John tenderly. He leads Emily to the case near the door. "Open it. It's got your name on it."

Emily stares at it for a moment. Nobody speaks. She opens the case with reverence as if opening the lid of a coffin. Inside, they find a machine.

It looks remarkably like Carl's original, with one major enhancement.

"Look at that," says John, pointing to what appears to be a flat-screen monitor covering the machine's top. Emily touches an indent at the top-center of a shiny silver frame. The screen springs elegantly upright with a soft hiss and locks into place with a firm click.

"This should be interesting," says John.

"Not now, my love," says Emily. "Did you see what time it is? We've slept most of the day. Buzz will be here in an hour and a half. We should get ready."

John hugs Emily. Carl's video should have triggered her trauma and deepened her grief. He is as delighted as he is surprised when her glow expands to meet his and fill them both. She tightens her grip, offering a silent invitation to escort her to a new level of consciousness.

Is this really her wish? Is she ready for this? Am I ready? Or is it just wishful thinking on my part?

"Are you okay, Babe?" asks John.

"I'm fine. I love you. Let's take a shower...hmmm?" Emily takes his hand and leads him down the hall.

Chapter Thirty-One
Destiny

"Out front" is the text from Buzz.

Emily lays her cup of coffee on the kitchen table to type her response, "Be right out." She calls out to John, "He's here."

"Coming," yells John. He steals one last glimpse of himself in the bedroom mirror, wearing Grandma's final sweater over the Khaki pants his mother had sent him off to college with.

This outfit seems appropriate for tonight.

"You're gonna eat Jimmy's famous spaghetti and meatballs wearing that?" asks Emily. "You know I love you," she pokes him in the chest and belly, "and you also know how messy you are."

John tugs the collar of Grandma's sweater, "I'll wear a napkin in here," then tugs his belt, "and another here." He kisses her, squeezes her butt, grabs her hand, and heads for the door. She bites his ear, smiling to herself.

Buzz is standing next to his limousine. "Welcome back, my intrepid friends." He extends his hand as John and Emily descend the steps. "And please allow me to congratulate you both on a job well done."

John shakes, probing Buzz's eyes for a glimpse of the world he hides behind his gallant façade. Nothing visible.

Emily shakes, then lowers her eyes. "I don't know. You might have been able to call it a good job if Carl were still alive."

Buzz cocks his head, catching Emily's eye. "Now, Miss Emily, you must not blame yourself for the evil perpetrated by others. You did everything within your power to put things right."

Emily maintains eye contact. "Yeah, but it wasn't enough, was it?"

"Well, I might be inclined to agree if you were an FBI agent. But you are a scientist, Miss Emily. Protecting Carl was their responsibility, not yours."

Hearing Buzz refer to her as a scientist expands the glow in Emily's heart. Carl smiles at her from within the glow, provoking her to smile at Buzz. Buzz returns the smile. The glow continues to expand. Buzz opens the limousine door and ushers Emily and John inside. He joins them and gently closes the door. The driver pulls away, accelerating much more gradually than the last time Emily had ridden with him.

"At least the FBI got Van Owen," says John. "Has he been charged with murder?"

"Well, it appears they've hit a snag," says Buzz.

Emily and John exclaim in unison, "What?"

"That med flight chopper was a sham. The crew were medics, alright, but they were Van Owen's people. He never showed up at the hospital they said he was going to."

"So, he's vanished?" asks Emily.

"I'm afraid so, Miss Emily."

"Does the FBI know where he might be?" asks John.

"My sources tell me the FBI claims to be hunting for him, but the hunt may be as big a sham as that med flight."

John and Emily stare at each other for a moment, the wind having been knocked out of them. Their heads fall back against the headrests.

"At least, the two of you are off the hook," says Buzz, sensing their frustration, "Turns out the FBI eliminated you as suspects right before Van Owen's party."

"But they didn't yet know about Van Owen's connection with the Army of God, did they?" asks John.

"No. They thought the Army of God was acting on their own. Now, the problem is…that still makes a perfectly believable story. And Van Owen's influence reaches far and wide…and extraordinarily high!"

"Are you telling us Van Owen might just get away? Scot-free?" asks Emily.

"Not necessarily, Miss Emily. And I would deem any conjecture, with respect to Van Owen's future, to be lacking any factual basis, at this point in time. Suffice it to say, you and Mr. Wells courageously challenged one of the most powerful men on Earth, accomplished your mission, and returned unscathed. You should be proud of yourselves."

John lays his hand on Emily's knee. Emily grabs it. They breathe together, knowing Buzz is technically correct. They did return physically unscathed. Yet, surely, they have been profoundly changed.

Ashley is waiting outside Jimmy's door when the limousine arrives. Unable to hold back tears, she races toward Emily. "You scared the bejezus out of me!"

John and Buzz stand by patiently, entranced by witnessing Emily and Ashley in their sustained embrace. Emily cradles Ashley's face in her hands, tenderly drying Ashley's tears with her long, elegant thumbs.

"You are a sight for sore eyes," whispers Emily.

"Oh, Emmy!" cries Ashley. She buries her head in Emily's chest.

Emily tightens her grip on Ashley's head. The sensation of Ashley's moist tears against her chest sends Emily back in time to the car ride with Ashley that unveiled her intuition. She allows herself to savor this moment, sensing a touch of nostalgia with a wholly different flavor. Rather than pining for her younger days, she is grateful for her heightened psychic power and self-awareness.

Ashley and I always find the ideal way to support each other no matter what they throw at us.

Jimmy opens the door, "Well, hello there. Come on in. Dinner is nearly ready."

The alluring aroma of olive oil, onions, garlic, herbs, simmering tomatoes, and meatballs coaxes everyone to follow Jimmy into his kitchen. The long table is set for six, a giant wooden bowl filled with salad at its center. A large pot of water is coming to a boil.

Jimmy grabs two fistfuls of his handmade spaghetti.

"Sophia is coming, isn't she?" he asks.

"Yeah," replies John. "She probably ran into traffic on the way back from her dad's. He needed to see her."

"Good." Jimmy plunges his spaghetti through the olive oil dancing atop the boiling salted water. "John, decant the wine for me, will you? It's in the pantry." He stirs the spaghetti.

"Gladly."

John revels in the blessing sung by the wine as it flows into the decanter.

The doorbell rings. John (from the pantry) and Emily (from the kitchen) yell in unison, "I'll get it." They race each other to the door.

Jimmy shoots Buzz a cheeky smile. "Those kids sure do have a lot of energy!"

Buzz nods. "Indeed, they do."

"Now, Miss Ashley," says Buzz, "perhaps you'd be kind enough to show me the revolutionary design you created for our mutual client. Mr. Douglass simply cannot stop raving about it."

"Oh, goodness," says Ashley. "Well, of course. I'd be delighted." She winks at Jimmy. He winks back while stirring the pot, basking in the comfort arising from the warm steam and warmer company. Ashley escorts Buzz to her workstation.

John and Emily reach the front door at the same instant. John hesitates long enough for Emily's hand to touch the doorknob before he does. She opens. Sophia stands straight as a statue on the marble landing. She says nothing. Her stern face gradually morphs into a radiant smile. The three embrace, encircled by a loving glow. Their individual spirits meld into one powerful force resonating with the Life Field. A cold wind launches Sophia's long black curls up around Emily's thick auburn mane onto John's neck. They relax their hands, breathe together, and gaze at each other for a moment.

Sophia reaches up, clasps Emily's face between her hands, and kisses her on the lips, holding Emily long enough to obliterate her shock and replace it with ardent devotion. She does the same with John.

"Thank you two for having my back," says Sophia.

"Thank you for being our hero," says John.

"Oh, stop." Sophia pretends to slap John's face. John reacts as if he's been slapped. He lightly punches her arm like a schoolboy.

"How's Mark?" asks Emily.

"Still in shock. He'll never leave his apartment again."

"Oh, no!" says John. "So, he won't be your TM?"

"Just kidding," says Sophia with an impish grin, "He's already advanced most of my European shows—in eight languages, no less. Keeps his mind off the trauma."

"And what about Craig?" asks Emily.

"He moved out."

"Oh—" says Emily mournfully.

"No," interrupts Sophia. "It's for the best. He's a very decent guy, but all wrong for me. And I'm even worse for him."

"One day, Sophia," says John, "one day you'll find the man who's right for you."

Sophia grabs both of John's hands. Her deep brown eyes engulf his field of view. Their gaze whisks them back in time to relive the journey of their young life together. A glimpse of the new world they are about to enter—also together—materializes before them.

"Our love, my sweet, set an exceptionally high bar." Sophia moves one hand onto John's cheek and the other onto Emily's. "And now you have found your true love." Her eyebrows flash at Emily. "This is the perfect woman for you. So, don't screw it up!"

"Oh, Sophie!" says Emily in tears.

"I love you, girl," says Sophia, holding back tears. "Take care of my boy, will you?

John's eyes fill with water.

"Hey, is that meatballs I smell?" asks Sophia before any tears fall.

"With Jimmy's famous handmade spaghetti," says John, wiping his eyes.

"Then why are we standing out here in the cold?" says Sophia. She grabs Emily with one hand, John with the other, and leads them through the door.

Jimmy, Buzz, and Ashley greet Sophia with three cheers and a hero's welcome.

"Let's eat," says Jimmy.

There's a natural place at the table for each of them. After a few quiet moments, they are all drawn to find it and sit comfortably. Jimmy extends his hands. The circle of clasped hands breathes in silence. Energy flows.

Ashley smirks at Emily, *I wonder when they'll trust me enough to tell me.*

She knows! Emily nods to Ashley, chuckles to herself, and winks.

Jimmy raises his glass, "To Jesus, the Christ, who shows us the way to live, the way to love, the way to heal."

All raise their glasses, pause, then drink in silence. After the wine has carried his words deep into their being, Jimmy asks John to decant another bottle. John is grateful to oblige. He'll take his time in the pantry. He deserves to enjoy the experience.

The cool, stainless-steel corkscrew steadies his hand. His attention is focused. He slices through the bottle's capsule. The silky feel and swishing sound of steel against glass and foil clear his mind. He takes a breath. Exhales. Energy flows down his front and up his back. Each turn of the corkscrew deepens the flow. As the cork slides up, resonance with the Life Field arises in John. He tips the bottle preparing to welcome the wine's private blessing. His eyes close, hands pause. A chorus of cheerful voices drifts in from the kitchen. Voices of his best friend, his teacher, his lover—all sharing the simple joy of a meal together.

The first few glugs dive out of the bottle where they had spent years maturing in preparation for this moment. Their blessing carries John out of his body. His spirit soars with the wine through the air where it breathes. He rides the flow as the wine plunges into the decanter, ready to fulfill its destiny.

Aroma rises from the decanter, lifting John up toward the ceiling.

He stares lovingly down at himself from *The Escoffier Cookbook*. Recalling the night of his initiation, he's grateful to Jimmy for insisting his greatest dreams were limiting his visions. How agonizing it was to hear that truth at that time. Where would he be now had he not summoned the resolve to comprehend Jimmy's riddle? Clearly, his current calling outshines any dream job he could have imagined when he enrolled at MIT. He permits himself a touch of pride.

I've done it. I've kept all three promises I made to myself…

He stops pouring.

…so far, that is.

He tilts the bottle. A steady rhythm of glugs resumes.

All those people, with all their power, failed to groom me for a meaningless life, an obedient worker, a slave to consumption.

The glugs skip a beat.

Why can't I explain how I held my own against them? Or how I rose to higher levels of consciousness? Are they really higher levels? Or is it just my imagination? Could it all be just pretend? Has Jimmy got me fooled? Am I fooling myself?

His hand quivers. Wine sloshes.

What if this isn't my true destiny? Even if it is, I have no idea what comes next. Even if I did know, I can't possibly be ready.

John stares at the deep, ruby-red wine swirling in the decanter. All at once, he is transported to the plane of consciousness, where he had encountered the mysterious entity while singing with Sophia in the Café. Just as before, this "vision" transcends visuals, language, thought. John's body is irrelevant. There is no sense of space or time. He is swirling amid all his prior experiences with the entity—including everything he had forgotten.

He floats into the kitchen. From the ceiling, he watches himself fill everyone's glass with wine, take his seat at the table, twirl spaghetti around his fork, and stab it into a piece of meatball.

The heat, aroma, tang, and texture of the food in his mouth sucks John back into his body. He remembers only the link and the answer:

Yes. This is your destiny. You are ready.

Everyone at the table is smiling at him as if he had just said something kind to them. His phone beeps. He swallows.

"Excuse me," says John. He takes his phone from his pocket.

Shielding the phone so nobody else can see, he ponders the text message from an unknown number, "Hello, John."

Afterward

For more information about the author—and the music, food, science, technology, history, and spirituality referenced in the book, please visit GoodJobPublishing.com.

You can also get a sneak preview of the sequel and other fun tidbits.